DARK HUNTER'S QUERY

THE CHILDREN OF THE GODS BOOK 56

I. T. LUCAS

Published by Evening Star Press

EveningStarPress.com

Print version: ISBN: 9781957139067

Ebook version: ISBN: 9781957139005

CONTENTS

1

ALENA

Alena, eldest daughter of the goddess Annani, a mother of thirteen, a grandmother of seventeen, a great-grandmother of twenty-three, and a great many times over grandmother of nearly every member of her clan, gazed at her phone's screen and sighed like a besotted schoolgirl.

In her over two millennia of existence, Alena had never reacted so strongly to a male, let alone to a mere depiction of one. The portrait had been created by a talented illustrator, but it hadn't been embellished in any way. The forensic artist had merely given life to a verbal description taken from a human's memory, and Annani had attested to its accuracy.

Annani had hung the framed original in her receiving room, a fond reminder of the male's father—the god Toven, whom she'd greatly admired in her youth. According to her mother, father and son looked so much alike that they were nearly indistinguishable.

Taken by the immortal's striking looks, Alena had captured Orion's image with her phone so she could gaze at it whenever she pleased, which was often. By now, she had every detail of the drawing committed to memory—the intelligent eyes, the chiseled cheekbones, the full sensuous lips, the aristocratic nose, the shoulder-length dark hair, the strong column of his neck—and yet she still felt compelled to pull out her phone and gaze at it.

Despite being an artistic construct, the drawing looked so lifelike, Orion's face so expressive, that it made her feel as if he were looking straight into her soul.

But it was all an illusion, and getting excited over a pretty face was as shallow as it got. She was too old to be blindsided by skin-deep beauty and wise enough to know that the only beauty that mattered was the kind found on the inside.

The male was gorgeous, perfect in the way all gods and the first generation of their offspring with humans were. It didn't mean that he was a good man, or that he could carry on an intelligent conversation, or that he was the truelove mate she'd been secretly hoping for.

Alena was the eldest, and yet the Fates had bestowed the blessing of a truelove mate on her younger siblings first. She wasn't jealous of their happiness and wished them the best their eternal lives had to offer, but she wanted her own happily ever after, and she was tired of waiting.

Except, Orion couldn't be the one for her, and if he was, the Fates had a really sick sense of humor. He was a compeller, and Alena could never be with a male who could take away her will at his whim. Just imagining being so helpless and at the mercy of another made her shiver. So even though his beautiful face evoked a powerful longing and caused a stirring—the kind Alena had never experienced before—and even though she pulled up his damn picture and stared at it numerous times a day, he could never be her truelove mate.

Her one and only probably had not been born yet, or he

was making his way toward her while she was letting herself get enchanted by the pretty face of another.

Alena sighed.

Hopefully, the one the Fates chose for her would have longish black hair, piercing blue eyes, and a face that looked like it was lovingly carved from granite by a talented sculptor—precisely like Orion, just not Orion himself.

Could her fated one be Orion's father? Except, Orion hadn't inherited his compulsion ability from his human mother, and Toven was probably a compeller as well.

Maybe Orion had a brother? One who hadn't inherited the ability?

After all, Geraldine was also Toven's daughter, and she wasn't a compeller.

Hope surging in her heart, Alena closed her phone and put it back in her skirt pocket.

She was running out of patience.

Supposedly the Fates rewarded those who selflessly sacrificed for others or suffered greatly with the gift of a truelove mate. Had she sacrificed or suffered less than her siblings? Was that why she was the last one left even though she was the eldest?

Kian had dedicated his life to the clan, so she could understand why he'd been granted a mate first. Amanda had lost a child, which was the worst suffering Alena could imagine, so it was only fair that she'd been the next one in line to find her fated mate. Sari had worked almost as hard as Kian to better the lives of those clan members who'd chosen to remain in Scotland, so it was also fair that she'd gotten her happily ever after.

Alena deserved hers as well.

She wasn't a natural leader like Kian or Sari, and she hadn't suffered a terrible loss like Amanda, but she was the de facto mother of the clan, and she also sacrificed a lot to keep her own mother out of trouble.

Not that any of it had been a great sacrifice or had caused her any suffering.

Motherhood was the best possible reward in itself, and traveling the world with Annani wasn't exactly a hardship either.

As Annani's companion, Alena had been an unwilling participant in her mother's crazy shenanigans, but she had to admit that most of them had been fun and not overly dangerous. She also enjoyed the babies and toddlers who arrived at the sanctuary to be kept safe until it was time for them to transition.

Life had been good to her, but she'd been doing the same thing for two thousand years, and it was time for a change.

Her only solo adventure had been impersonating a Slovenian supermodel in the hopes of luring Kalugal out of hiding.

After the fun time she'd spent with the team who'd accompanied her to New York, it had been difficult to go back to the routine. For a few precious days, she'd enjoyed being different, being her own person and not her mother's shadow.

It seemed like such a distant memory, like it had taken place in another lifetime.

The face she saw in the mirror was the same one she'd been looking at for two millennia.

Gone was the sophisticated hairstyle she'd adopted for the New York trip, replaced by her habitual loose braid, her face was free of makeup, and she wore one of her long, comfortable dresses instead of the fashionable clothes Amanda had gotten her for that trip.

Those had been given away to charity soon after she'd returned from New York.

There was no reason to dress up in the sanctuary, where everyone expected her to look the part of Annani's devoted daughter—the goddess's companion and advisor —a part she'd been playing for so long that no one could envision her doing anything else, including herself.

Not that there was anything wrong with it.

Her position at Annani's side was a duty and an honor that Alena had proudly and lovingly performed for centuries—a position that could not be filled by anyone but her.

2

ORION

Orion regarded the leader of his captors, noting the hard lines of Kian's face, the stiffness of his shoulders, and the sheer size of him. The guy was big, he was gruff, but he wasn't cold, and that gave Orion hope.

So far, other than the damn tranquilizer they'd knocked him out with, these immortals hadn't treated him too badly. Nevertheless, they were holding him against his will, and even though the apartment he'd woken up in was as fancy as any high-end hotel suite, it was still a prison cell.

Other than having been born immortal, he hadn't done anything to them, and they had no reason to hold him, but he was at their mercy, his compulsion ability nullified by the earpieces they were all wearing.

Without it, he was as helpless as any human, and the only way out of the situation was to cooperate with his captors and give them what they wanted, which was information about his jerk of a father.

No skin off his nose.

If they could find the god, Orion didn't care what they did with him.

Kian put his paper cup down on the table and crossed

his arms over his chest. "Now that you've eaten breakfast and gotten caffeinated, I want to hear the story of how you found your father and got him to admit that he was a god."

It was clear that the guy's patience was wearing thin, but Orion needed a little more time to think. The coffee break he'd practically begged Kian for had helped ease the pounding headache he'd woken up with, but his mind was still foggy.

He didn't mind telling them about his father, but there were other things he'd learned from the god that he wasn't sure he should share with them.

Did it matter if they knew that he was hunting for the god's other potential children?

They already knew about his sister and niece and had accepted Geraldine and Cassandra into their clan, but had their motives been pure?

They needed new blood for their community—more genetic diversity. They might try to get to his other siblings first and draft them into their clan.

Was that so bad, though?

Perhaps they could help him with his quest.

Orion had exhausted all of the information he had, but they might have access to resources that he didn't.

Damn, if only his head would clear so he could follow one thought to its logical conclusion instead of all his thoughts jumping around in his head like bunnies on speed.

Were these people trustworthy?

Were they a force for good or the opposite of that?

Was he lucky that they had found his sister and him?

The effects of the tranquilizer were beginning to wane, but he was still having a hard time reconciling what he'd learned from his captors with what he'd been told by his father. Some of it confirmed the god's story, but there was so much more that his father hadn't shared with him.

For nearly five centuries, Orion had been convinced that he was the only immortal, an anomaly, and then he'd met his father who'd claimed to be a god—not a deity, but a lone survivor of a superior race of people who'd been annihilated by one of their own.

Herman, aka Toven, had claimed that the gods from various mythologies had been real people. At the time, Orion had doubted his father's story, had suspected that the guy was either delusional or being deliberately deceitful, but his captors had confirmed everything Herman had told him. The gods hadn't been the constructs of human imagination, and what's more, his father wasn't the only survivor.

Had his father known about the two goddesses who'd escaped the attack and chosen not to tell him?

Had he known that some humans carried the dormant godly gene and withheld the information on purpose?

"Whenever you're ready," Kian prompted.

"Can I bother you for another cup?" Orion cast the guy a pleading look. "My head feels like it's stuffed with cotton. Usually, I don't suffer from such maladies, but the tranquilizer your guy injected me with must have been incredibly potent."

Kian grimaced. "It had to be to knock out an immortal."

"I'll brew a fresh pot," Onegus said. The male mated to his niece was the head of the clan's security forces, and yet he got up to reload the coffeemaker. "It will take a couple of minutes."

Apparently, these people didn't follow strict hierarchy. The guy could have asked one of the guards to brew the coffee but had chosen to do so himself. They acted more like a family or a group of friends than a military organization, which Orion took to be a good sign as to the kind of people he was dealing with.

Next to him, his sister winced. "I'm so sorry."

He patted her knee. "My head already feels much better."

"I didn't mean the headache." Geraldine smiled apologetically. "Well, that too, but what I'm really sorry about is entrapping you. You wouldn't be in this situation if I hadn't dug into my murky past."

"Why did you?"

"Do you mean why did I want to find out about my past or why did I help the clan trap you?"

"The first one."

"As long as I was oblivious about having had another life, I was content with the one I had. But after I discovered that I had a daughter who I couldn't remember, I had to find out how it happened. But I should have just moved on." She sighed. "In part, it's your fault that I didn't. You compelled me not to leave the house for more than a day, so I couldn't start my new life with Shai in his village."

Orion nodded. "Indeed, and that means that my capture is on me, and you have nothing to apologize for." He cast a sidelong glance at Kian. "I've been careful not to get noticed by humans, but I never anticipated other immortals. Although with the advent of the modern era and the proliferation of imaging devices, avoiding discovery by humans is getting more difficult. I can rely on my compulsion ability to get out of tight spots, but I can't compel inanimate objects, and nowadays, there are surveillance cameras everywhere and everyone has smartphones they can use to snap photos with. I had to develop new tactics to avoid getting my image recorded on electronic devices."

Ironically, though, his capture hadn't been the result of technology or even his negligence. Orion had followed the best protocols he could devise. What had gotten him in trouble was precisely the thing his father had warned him against—family, people he cared about, people who could lead others to him.

His sister and her daughters were his Achilles heel.

Next to him, Geraldine shifted her knees sideways and put her hands in her lap. "I have to admit, though, that your compulsion wasn't the only reason I didn't leave the house. As much as I hated the idea of trapping you, I wanted to talk to you and not forget the conversation as soon as you left. We pieced together most of what had happened to me, but there were still so many holes in the puzzle, and I wanted answers. I needed closure."

He put a hand on her knee. "I understand. You don't need to keep apologizing."

Geraldine lifted her big blue eyes to him, so much like his own that it was like looking in the mirror. "You're my brother, but I didn't know that, and I thought that you were my inducer. Do you know how awkward it feels now that I know the truth?" She shook her head. "It gets worse. When I finally recalled our interactions over the years, I was offended that you didn't find me attractive." She chuckled. "Although, I should have known something was up because I wasn't attracted to you either." She waved a hand over his face. "If you were ugly, that would have been understandable, but you are so gorgeous that I can't take my eyes off you."

Orion had never felt comfortable with the looks he'd gotten throughout his life, either covetous from those interested in him sexually or envious and outright hostile from others, but Geraldine was his sister, and her complimenting him on his good looks didn't feel as awkward. It reminded him of his mother and the way she used to regard him with love and adoration in her eyes.

"Thank you." Absentmindedly, he reached for Geraldine's hand and gave it a gentle squeeze. "I'm curious. How did you suddenly recover your memories of me? Did your mate have anything to do with that?"

"The goddess released them." Geraldine shifted her eyes to Kian. "Is it okay for me to reveal that?"

"It's fine."

So that was how she remembered him. Orion had wondered about that, thinking that maybe her boyfriend or one of the other immortals was powerful enough to unlock her submerged memories. But it had taken a goddess to release them, which meant that the others were not as powerful as he was.

He tucked away that bit of information for later use. "Is the goddess here?" He looked at Kian. "Can I meet her?"

Kian chuckled. "The Clan Mother is very curious about you, and I have no doubt that she will want to meet you as soon as possible. She's very fond of your father and speaks highly of him."

Orion grimaced. "He must've changed a lot since she last interacted with him."

"Here you go." Onegus handed him a mug of freshly brewed coffee.

"Thank you." Taking the mug with him, Orion leaned back against the couch cushions and crossed his legs at the ankles. "Perhaps I should start my story at the beginning, many years before I met my father." He took several sips from his coffee before putting the cup on the table.

"Please do," Geraldine said. "I want to know everything about you, or at least the highlights of your life."

Now that Orion's head was clearer and his thought process faster, deciding which information to share and which to withhold became easier.

The coffee break had been a test, and it had allowed him to observe his captors interacting with each other, and more importantly, with his sister and niece.

There was no faking the loving glances between Onegus and Cassandra and between Geraldine and Shai.

His sister and niece were indeed happily mated to these clansmen, which made the men his family as well.

Besides, the clan had little to gain from what he could tell them, and he didn't have much to lose.

So far, Orion's query had yielded only one result—Geraldine—and he'd been unsuccessful in locating any of Toven's other children. Perhaps he and Geraldine were the only ones, or maybe he needed help locating the others.

3

KIAN

"As I mentioned before," Orion began, "I was fourteen when I discovered that I was immortal."

"Hold on." Geraldine lifted her hand. "That's not the beginning. I want to know where you were born, who your mother was, and how you ended up on the battlefield at such a young age."

Kian stifled a groan. At this rate, it would be nighttime before Orion reached the part about his father, and Kian had no intentions of staying in the keep for so long.

He called his mother when Orion had been captured, but because the guy had been knocked out cold, he'd had nothing else to report. His mother was no doubt anxiously awaiting an update and getting more aggravated with every passing moment.

Besides, as fascinating as hearing about Orion's life was, he was more interested in Toven's, and even that was not as important or as fun as spending time with his daughter.

Just thinking about Allegra's cute smiles and the adorable sounds she made eased the tension in his shoulders and lightened his heart.

Orion sighed and leaned forward to pick up his coffee

mug. "The man who I thought was my father was a merchant in a small town near Milan. I was born nine months after he was killed in what is known as the Great Wars of Italy or the Habsburg-Valois wars. Because of the opportune timing, no one ever suspected that the grieving widow gave birth to a child that wasn't her deceased husband's, and neither did I." He chuckled. "Although even as a small boy, I knew that I looked nothing like that fat, ruddy-cheeked man in the portrait hanging in our home's entryway. What little hair he had was light brown, and my mother was a blond." He lifted his hand and smoothed it over his chin-length raven hair. "As you can see, my hair color is nearly black."

"You have beautiful hair," Cassandra said. "Did no one wonder about the little boy who looked nothing like his deceased father?"

He shrugged. "My mother was smart. She told everyone that I was the spitting image of her cousin, and she repeated it enough times for the fib to become truth. I think that after a while, she started believing it herself."

"Did you believe the lie?" Cassandra asked.

"Why wouldn't I? I adored my mother, and I had no reason to doubt her."

Kian huffed out a breath. "You must have realized the truth after surviving the injury that should have killed you."

Hopefully, jumping ahead to that would shorten the story time.

"Not right away." Orion's lips lifted in a crooked smile. "I came up with several possible explanations, starting with a guardian angel and ending with a good witch."

"What about being bitten by a vampire?" Geraldine asked.

"That came later, after my fangs started growing. I panicked, afraid that I would become crazed with blood lust, so I packed up my things and was about to leave in the middle of the night. My mother intercepted me, and when I admitted my fears, she said that vampires didn't exist but that I might have inherited strange things from my father, who wasn't the man she'd been married to. She told me that I was old enough to learn the truth, and that if I wanted to live, I needed to keep it a secret."

"How did she manage an affair?" Cassandra asked. "I mean, war was raging, and her husband was gone. And how did Toven find her? Did he just stroll into town and seduce her?"

"I don't know. She didn't divulge any details, only that he'd been a stunningly good-looking man and very smart. I'm not sure that she remembered much more than that. When I started discovering my own powers, I realized that he must have tampered with her memories."

Geraldine tilted her head. "Do you think that Toven compelled her to be with him?"

Orion shook his head. "My father is a jaded bastard, but he's not a rapist. My mother accepted him with open arms. I know that it makes her look bad, but she'd been practically sold to her husband by her family, and the arranged marriage was a disaster. He was a terrible man, or at least that was what she claimed, and when he died, she rejoiced at finally being free and celebrated with a very handsome stranger."

"How did she remember her affair with Toven?" Onegus asked. "Did he leave at least some of her memories of him intact?"

"My mother was an artist." Orion looked at Geraldine. "Our father had a thing for creative women. Your mother was an artist as well."

Her eyes widened. "Did you meet my real mother?"

He nodded. "I did, but I'll tell you about that later. I don't want to jump all over the timeline."

Kian was still trying to understand Orion's answer to Onegus's question. "What does your mother being an artist have to do with remembering Toven?"

"Indeed." Orion smiled. "She told me that she'd drunk a lot of wine after her husband's death, and she didn't remember much about the man she'd celebrated her freedom with, but her artist's eye remembered enough of him to draw a portrait." Orion waved a hand over his face. "When I reached adulthood, I realized that I looked just like him, but that's getting ahead of the story as well. You wanted to know how I found myself on the battlefield at the age of fourteen."

Geraldine nodded.

"Quite simply, I was the only male in the household, and they demanded one from each family. My mother wasn't very wealthy, but she wasn't destitute either, and she tried to bribe the recruiters. They took her gold and drafted me anyway. Back then, a woman alone was powerless. There was nothing she could've done to prevent them from taking me."

Geraldine put her hand on his arm. "I can't imagine how terrified you were."

"I was. I just knew that I was going to die. I'd never trained with any kinds of weapons. Heck, I didn't know how to hold a pike or a crossbow."

As Geraldine's chin started to wobble and tears slid down her cheeks, Kian cast her an amused glance. "But he didn't die. That's not a ghost sitting next to you."

The redheaded guard snorted. "I disagree. We have with us the ghost of Orion's past."

4

ORION

As everyone laughed, Orion closed his eyes. The horror of that day nearly five centuries ago was still fresh in his mind as if it had happened a week ago.

He didn't remember much of the battle or how he had been gutted. It had all been a blur of terror, and dying hadn't been the worst part of it. He'd been glad that it was over.

Except, he hadn't died.

Sometime later, he woke up with dirt filling his nostrils, his mouth, his throat. He'd been buried with the rest of the fallen. Choking, starved for breath, he'd clawed at the loosely compacted earth, had dug up against the flesh of the dead he'd been buried with, and had blindly inched toward the surface.

When he'd finally broken free, Orion had coughed and spat and vomited, and then lost consciousness again. The next time he opened his eyes, he had patted his stomach, searching for the injury, but other than caked-on blood, no trace of it had remained.

That had terrified him almost as much as regaining consciousness in the mass grave had. He'd thought that he was in hell, and in a way he was. Living was purgatory, and unlike the rest of humanity, his would last forever. He was stuck on this horrid plane of existence with no chance for parole.

"Orion?" Geraldine's soft voice pierced the darkness of his memories. "Are you okay?"

Fighting against the phantom choking sensation, he forced himself to suck in a breath. "Yeah, I'm fine. Nearly five centuries to the day, and I can still taste the dirt in my mouth."

"They buried you alive," Kian guessed. "They thought that you were dead."

Orion nodded. "I think that I was actually dead and was resurrected somehow."

The redhead leaned forward. "Was there water in the mass grave? Did it rain?"

"I don't think so." Orion wiped a hand over his mouth. "I remember that the dirt was dry. Why do you ask?"

"You might have entered stasis, but you could have appeared dead to humans even without going into that deep state."

"What year was that?" Shai asked.

"1525."

"So you were born in 1511," Kian calculated. "Was Orion your given name?"

He shook his head. "My mother named me Orlando. I've used many different names over the centuries, but I chose Orion after meeting my real father."

"When did you find him and how?" Kian asked for the fifth or sixth time.

But unlike before, this time he'd get an answer. It was a relief to jump ahead in the timeline, bypassing hundreds of terrible experiences, large and small, that had each left a scar on Orion's soul.

His body was a perfect machine that healed all injuries

without leaving a single mark, but his soul was a different story. It was wounded, scarred, and aching, with no hope of ever recovering.

"Thirty-eight years ago, on Rue de la Jussienne in Paris, a chance encounter brought me face to face with my father. I was heading toward my favorite café when I saw him walking toward me. We both stopped at the same time and stared at each other. It was like looking in the mirror. And yet, it didn't occur to me that he might be my father. Everyone is supposed to have a doppelgänger, right?"

Cassandra snorted. "Not someone who looks like you." She turned to Kian. "Or you. Your godly heritage is unmistakable. No human is that perfect."

Kian arched a brow. "Did Toven also think that you were his doppelgänger?"

"No, he knew who I was, but he pretended that he didn't. He gave me a tight-lipped smile and kept walking. I hesitated for a split second before rushing after him.

"*Excuse me,* I said as I fell in step with him. *I wonder if we are related. Looking at you is like looking at the mirror.*"

"*We are not,* he said. *You don't know me, and you've never seen me. Go away.*"

"That's when I knew he was either the one who sired me or a half-brother of mine. He tried to use compulsion, but it didn't work because I had the same power. I told him the same thing Onegus said to me when I tried to use it on him. *Your tricks don't work on me. I'm just like you.*"

Cassandra grinned. "I would have paid good money to see the bastard's face when you told him that."

"He wasn't happy, and he was even less so when he realized that he couldn't get rid of me. I followed him to the townhouse he was renting at the time, and he had no choice but to let me in."

Kian leaned forward, bracing his elbows on his knees.

"How long did it take you to force him to admit that he was your father?"

"Not long. I told him that I wasn't going anywhere until he told me everything I wanted to know."

"Did he?" Geraldine asked.

"He told me a lot, but apparently, not nearly enough."

5

VROG

Still baffled by the sudden early morning evacuation from his cell and transport to the village, Vrog sat on a barstool in Stella's kitchen and sipped on a cup of herbal tea that tasted like dishwater.

"I'm sorry that we don't have coffee," Stella said. "I was supposed to go grocery shopping this morning, but then Kian called with the good news—"

"And you got stuck with me," Vrog finished for her.

Vlad and Wendy were both at work, so Stella had kindly agreed to welcome him to the village and entertain him until Vlad returned from his shift at the bakery.

To say that it was awkward to be alone with her at her home was to put it mildly. Vrog sat on the stool stiff as a plank of wood, and Stella wasn't doing much better.

Like him, she probably expected Richard to walk in at any moment and kick him out. The guy hadn't been happy about the uninvited guest when she'd called him earlier.

"Would you like a tour of the village?" She pushed to her feet. "I can show you the construction site Richard works on."

"A tour would be lovely, but I don't think it's wise to

antagonize your mate further. Hopefully, I'll be gone before he goes on break."

"Don't mind him." She rolled her eyes. "Richard is all bark and no bite. He just needs to get used to you being here. And as soon as you find a lady, he'll relax." She smiled conspiratorially. "Perhaps our tour of the village should start at the café. You'll get to say hi to Wendy and enjoy a decent cup of coffee."

He was on his feet in an instant. "Lead on."

"I knew you'd like the idea." Stella lifted a shawl off the couch, wrapped it around her shoulders, and threaded her arm through his.

He stopped and gently removed her arm. "We shouldn't act too familiar with each other. Richard still thinks like a territorial human, and if he smells me on you, he might jump to conclusions."

"He won't," she said but didn't touch him again. "Richard and I have bonded, which means that cheating is impossible. He knows that." She walked to the front door and pulled it open.

As Vrog followed her out, he made sure that there were at least three feet between them. "How come?"

"It's an immortal thing. It doesn't happen to everyone, but those who bond are physically incapable of feeling attraction towards anyone other than their mate."

"What happens if a mate dies?"

She winced. "It's bad. To lose a truelove mate is devastating, and it takes a long time for the addiction to wear off. Luckily for us, deaths are rare."

"I don't understand. Before, you referred to it as a bond, and now you're talking about addiction. Are the two one and the same?"

"Yes and no." Stella tightened the shawl against the morning chill. "The venom is addictive, but only if an immortal couple is sexually exclusive for a significant length of time. Historically, those who wanted to avoid the addiction played around, but that was during the gods' era, and since it wasn't relevant to the clan's situation, it was forgotten."

"Why wasn't it relevant?"

"Because none of us had long-term relationships, and we only hooked up with humans. Up until a few years ago, all clan members were Annani's descendants, too closely related to mate with each other, and there were no known immortals outside of our clan, other than the Doomers that is, but they didn't count."

"Your enemies. I remember you asking me if I was a Doomer. I didn't know what you were talking about."

She cast him a sidelong glance. "You still remember that?"

He nodded. "Over the years, I thought of you quite often."

She chuckled. "No doubt contemplating how to choke the life out of me to avenge your people, since you were convinced that I was responsible for their demise."

"Not always. Sometimes, I wondered about our son and what kind of man he turned out to be." He smiled. "Vlad has exceeded all my expectations. You've done a great job with him."

"Thank you." She let out a breath. "I'm very proud of Vlad."

Vrog had a feeling that he was making her uncomfortable. It was safer to talk about the clan and the problems it faced than about their shared history.

"So, back to the bond and addiction issues. How did the clan become aware of the venom's addictive properties?"

She seemed relieved. "No one remembered that until Kian and Syssi became a couple and bonded within days. When the addiction followed within less than a week, Kian was reminded of what Annani had told him about it many years ago."

"So, Kian's mate was the first Dormant your clan found?"

Stella nodded. "There have been more since, but the vast majority of clan members are still waiting for the Fates to bless them with a truelove mate."

"What about these newcomers you've told me about? Your former enemies. Can't they mate with clan females?"

She chuckled. "There is plenty of partying going on and hookups galore, but so far, only one couple has bonded." She sidled up to him. "There are many available females for you to choose from."

Vrog took a step sideways to put more distance between them. "I don't know how to act with an immortal female. Are there dos and don'ts that I need to know about?"

"You did fine with me."

"That's because I thought you were human."

"You were charming and sexy back then. Just act the same now, and you'll be fine."

That had been a long time ago before his entire family had been slaughtered and his world had fallen apart. He'd been carefree back then, or as carefree as a Kra-ell male living among humans could be. He'd been young and hopeful, but he was no longer that guy. In fact, Vrog could barely remember him.

6

ORION

Paris, France, thirty-eight years ago.

As he followed the immortal through the door, Orlando half expected the male to slam it shut in his face, but he didn't. Instead, he took off his coat and scarf, hung both on a coat rack, and walked over to a bar cart.

Orlando remained standing at the doorway even though he had no intentions of leaving. If the guy didn't invite him in, he would stay anyway, but he wanted to see what he would do.

Lifting a bottle of Glen Grant 1953, the man poured the golden liquid into two glasses and then turned to look at Orlando. "Are you going to just stand there?" he asked in perfect Italian. "Come in, take off your coat, and close the door behind you. You're letting the draft in."

"How did you know that I was Italian?" Orlando hung his coat on the rack, walked over to the man, and took the glass from his hand.

"You have an accent."

"I do not." Orlando had an uncanny talent for languages. He could speak

all of the Western European languages fluently with no trace of a foreign accent. He could also converse in twenty-some others.

"It's very slight, but I have a good ear." The guy sat down in one of the two overstuffed armchairs facing the fireplace. "Take a seat."

"Thank you." Orlando looked around the living room, taking in the stacks of books and newspapers.

The place was clean but cluttered, and it was quite obvious that no woman lived in the townhouse. It was a bachelor's pad—an old bachelor who was more interested in the company of books than females.

The immortal took a sip from his whiskey. "How did you find me?"

"I wasn't looking for you if that's what you're asking. Our encounter was fated." Orlando lifted his glass. "Should we toast it?"

The guy shrugged. "I guess I should be intrigued, perhaps even happy to see you, but regrettably, I have lost the ability to get excited over anything." He took another sip from his drink. "When you've lived as long as I have, you'll understand." He grimaced. "It's all quite pointless."

Orlando knew precisely what the immortal was talking about. Life was worthless without people to love, and as a lone immortal, he was condemned to walking the earth alone.

"I've lived for nearly five centuries," he said. "I've lost people I loved, so I get it."

It seemed that this had been the right thing to say because the guy's expression softened a fraction. "What's your name?"

"Orlando Farnese."

A genuine smile brightened the male's face, a stark transformation from the deadened expression he wore like a dark cloak. "Oh, yes. I remember your mother." He pushed to his feet and walked over to a table that was laden with leather-bound books. "I have her portrait somewhere."

Well, that answered the question of how they were related. "You are my father." A statement, not a question.

The guy shifted his gaze from the books and leveled it at Orlando. "I thought that was obvious. You are the spitting image of me." He picked up one of the books, looked at the spine, put it down and picked another, and then another, until he found the one that he was looking for.

Clearly, the man hadn't lied about being emotionally dead. If Orlando had discovered that he had a son, he would have been over the moon. Perhaps the guy had spread his seed far and wide and had sired thousands of children over his long life. One more was of no consequence to him.

"You could have been my brother or my grandfather or an uncle."

"Not likely." The guy grimaced. "All of my relatives were long dead before you were born, and I'd given up on siring a child even before that, which was many thousands of years ago. You're most likely the only one." He brought the journal with him to the armchair, sat down, and flipped through the pages. "Here she is." He handed it to Orlando, opened on a sketch. "That's how I remember Gilia."

It was a portrait of his mother the way she looked in her youth—radiant, happy, sensual. It was a lover's sketch.

Even if the guy hadn't fathered a horde of children, he still must have dallied with thousands of women. To remember his mother's name, she must have left quite an impression on him.

It was a small consolation, but it was better than nothing.

Orlando scanned the writing underneath the sketch, but it wasn't in any language he knew. He kept flipping through several written pages until he reached the next portrait of a lovely young woman.

It seemed that his father kept track of his lovers, either as sentimental mementos or for some other reason.

"My mother must have left an impression on you."

"Gilia was a remarkable artist."

"She was. She drew a portrait of you and hung it in her bedroom. Even if I didn't grow up looking just like you, I would have recognized you from that painting." Orlando handed the journal back. "By the way, what should I call you? Other than Father, that is."

The guy cradled the journal in his lap. "I go by many different names, but these days, I call myself Herman." He looked at Orlando from under lowered lashes. "I hope that you are careful and hide your immortality. You should also change your name every couple of decades or so."

"I do." Orlando's lips contorted in a grimace. "I wish you had been around when I was figuring out all of this on my own. Your advice would have been helpful."

Not a shred of guilt passed through Herman's cold eyes. "Do you ever check on your past lovers to find out if any of them has conceived?"

"I did at first, but I stopped when it became evident that I was infertile."

Herman smiled, but the smile didn't reach his eyes. "I thought the same thing, and yet here you are." He turned to the journal in his lap and started flipping through the pages. "Who knows? Maybe I have sired more than one offspring over the years."

Orlando glanced at the leather-bound book and then shifted his gaze to the many others stacked on top of the table and on the floor. "Do all of these contain portraits of your past lovers and their descriptions?"

Herman's eyes followed his to the stack on the table. "Many of them do. I can't share my life with a woman or even stay around for longer than a few days. There have been so many that my memories of them started to blur and became interchangeable. It upset me, so I decided to prolong my relationship with those who were special to me by immortalizing them in these journals and making them the heroines of the stories I write. Naturally, I'm the hero of each of my novels, albeit in disguise." He waved his hand at the stacks piled on the floor. "The other journals contain my stories."

"Is that how you support yourself? You write books?"

Herman laughed, but his laugh was mirthless. "I have more gold than I could ever spend. Writing just helps pass the time."

Given that Herman could live forever, he must have stockpiles of gold hidden somewhere. Hell, he probably had an entire goldmine that no one knew about.

The question was why he'd told him about it. Didn't he fear his treasure's discovery?

Orlando tucked the information away, and instead of commenting on the gold, he asked, "Do you publish your books?"

"Some, not all. Naturally, I use a different pseudonym for each book, and I vary the style. I don't want anyone tracking me by my stories."

Pushing to his feet, Orlando walked over to the bar cart. "May I?" He lifted the whiskey bottle.

Herman waved a hand. "Help yourself."

"Someone might recognize the style and figure out that these books were written by the same person." Orlando filled his glass to the brim and returned to the armchair.

"I'm not worried." Herman put his still half-full glass on

the side table between the armchairs. "Back in the day, I was known as the god of knowledge and writing. I can write in many different styles."

For a moment, Orlando just gaped. "You are a god?"

Given Herman's pinched expression, he hadn't meant to disclose that. "A very minor one. Nothing to get excited about. It's not like I'm a deity and can perform miracles. Humans regarded my people as gods because we could manipulate their minds to think that we were divine. But we were just a more advanced species."

"Am I a god?"

Herman shook his head.

"Your mother was human, so you are only an immortal."

"I can also manipulate human minds. Doesn't that make me a god? What's the difference between a god and an immortal?"

Letting out a long-suffering sigh, Herman rose to his feet and walked over to the bar cart. "It's a long story, and what you can learn from it is not going to help you in any way." He refilled his glass even though it hadn't been empty. "It's getting late. You should leave."

Orlando had no intention of leaving without learning all that he could from his father. He had a feeling that tomorrow Herman would no longer be in the townhouse, and he would never find him again.

"Nevertheless, I would like to know what kind of blood flows in my veins."

7

ORION

"What do you know about mythology?" Herman put the glass of whiskey on the side table and walked over to the fireplace.

"Which one?" Orlando asked.

"Any of them." The god added a new log to the fire.

"I know the Greek and the Roman and some of the Norse."

"Good enough." Herman sat back on the armchair, stretched his legs in front of him, and crossed them at the ankles—a pose nearly identical to Orlando's. "They are all based on the more ancient myths of the Sumerian. The pantheon of twelve major gods remained pretty much the same, just with different names, but the Sumerian pantheon was the first, and it was based on real people."

"Are you an alien?"

"My parents and my older half-brother were born on a different planet, but I was born on Earth. Does that make me an alien?"

"If both of your parents were gods, then I guess it does."

"I guess." Herman took a small sip from his whiskey. "For a long time, I thought of myself as an honorary human. My father was what nowadays would be called a humanist. He championed human causes, and I followed in his footsteps. But I got disillusioned. No matter what I did, even pretending to be a real deity to make them fear me, they remained bloodthirsty savages. Whatever I tried to teach them, they managed to distort into something horrific—killing and maiming and torturing in my name." He emptied the rest of the whiskey down his throat and got up to refill his glass. "I decided that humanity was a lost cause, stopped playing God, and disappeared."

Orlando felt compelled to defend humanity. "Humans have made big strides. It's not as bad as it used to be."

"In some ways, they have." Herman sat back down. "It only took them five thousand years to become as civilized as they were back then. Without the powerful gods to guide and control them, they were no better than chimps."

"What happened to the gods?"

"Gone. My brother killed them all and died along with them." He shifted his deadened gaze to look at Orlando. "We can die, you know. Even I can't survive a decapitation or injuries that are too massive for my body to repair. Don't take your immortality for granted, and don't do stupid things. If you fall out of a plane, you'll die."

Was Herman trying to impart fatherly advice?

It was too little too late, but at least he was making an effort.

"I figured as much. I'm resilient, and I can compel and put humans under my thrall, but I don't have magic."

"Smart boy."

Orlando chuckled. "I'm nearly five centuries old. I had a long time to test my limits, and I'm not stupid. I'm also not a boy."

"I know. I just wanted to test how it felt to give fatherly advice."

So he'd been right. Couldn't fault the guy for trying,

though, and what Herman was telling him about the history of the gods was not something Orlando could have found in books.

"Why did your brother kill the other gods?"

Herman shrugged. "He murdered another god, which was punishable by entombment. When the council found him guilty and passed sentence, he decided to get rid of them all, including our father and me. I knew that he was power-hungry and unstable, but I never thought that he would go so far. He must have lost his mind completely."

"How did you survive?"

"I got tired of listening to the endless and pointless discussions and snuck out. I was never interested in politics and voting to entomb my own brother depressed me. I flew to a faraway land I was researching at the time, and when I returned many months later, I found the entire region devastated. I flew to the north and searched for my brother in his stronghold. After I learned from his servants that he'd never returned, I compelled them to forget that they'd ever seen me, flew back to where I came from, and stayed there for a very long time."

"Until you got tired of humanity."

Herman nodded, emptied his third glass of whiskey, and got to his feet. "I'm tired, and I've told you enough. Please see yourself out."

"Wait." Orlando followed him. "Can I come back tomorrow, and we can talk some more?"

The guy's lips lifted in a mockery of a smile. "I won't be here tomorrow, and we are never going to see each other again. I wish you the best, but I don't wish to have a relationship with you."

Orlando had suspected as much, but he still asked, "Why not?"

"Because we look too much alike and it's dangerous for both of us."

"We can talk on the phone, and we can send each other letters. I don't expect you to be a father to me, but I could use a friend."

Herman shook his head. "I'm glad that we ran into each other and that I know that you exist. If I want to see you again, I will find you. Please, see yourself out." And with that, he turned around and climbed the stairs to the second floor, leaving Orlando standing in the middle of the living room alone with the coat rack by the door.

It seemed surreal that the guy didn't want to have anything to do with him, and Orlando wasn't going to beg the bastard to change his mind. Besides, even that wouldn't have touched the guy's dead heart.

Other than asking for his name, Herman hadn't asked him a single question. He was completely uninterested in learning anything about his only son, or rather, the only one he knew of.

His eyes darting to the journals, Orlando walked over to the table and lifted one. There were dates on the spines, and as he took each and examined a date, a plan started forming in his head.

Herman was a lost cause, but if he had sired more children, Orlando could locate them and do for them what he wished someone had done for him—befriend them and show them how to hide who they were while living among humans.

His best chance was to find the women his father had immortalized in his journals who were still alive. If he could track them down, he could find out whether they had children and then find them as well.

It was a long shot, but Orlando was eager to hunt for the brothers or sisters he might have. If he found even one, it would be worth the effort.

Without feeling an iota of remorse, he took the most recent journal—the one that was marked with a starting date of 1929 and no end date—and tucked it under his arm.

At the door he took his coat, shrugged it on, and zipped it over the journal.

Casting one last look up the stairs, he shook his head and saw himself out.

8

WENDY

As Wendy prepared cappuccinos for Vrog and Stella, she watched the two talking at their table, and it was quite obvious that they weren't comfortable with each other, more so on Vrog's part than Stella's. He was leaning away from her as if her breath was stinky or her perfume overpowering, but Wendy was sure that neither was the cause.

Did he still think that Stella had been somehow responsible for his people's demise?

Except, even from where she was standing, Wendy could see that there was no hostility in Vrog's eyes, only wariness.

What was he afraid of?

She still remembered being in his situation. After a lifetime of bad experiences, it had been difficult to believe that Vlad and his clan were good people. Wendy hadn't had faith in anyone, and she'd treated Vlad deplorably.

And yet, he'd not only forgiven her but had fought his way into her heart, barreling through all of her prickly defenses and convincing her that she wasn't the evil bitch she'd believed herself to be.

Vrog needed almost as much help as she had back then, but unlike her, he didn't have anyone willing to fight for him.

She needed to find him a good female, someone aggressive who would appeal to his Kra-ell side, or maybe someone soft and loving who would appeal to his human half.

Working at the café, Wendy was uniquely positioned to do so, and as soon as she figured out which kind of female was best suited for him, she could start sending out feelers to see who was interested.

It shouldn't be too difficult to find him a suitable match. Vrog was a handsome fellow, and he seemed like a nice guy.

Hopefully, not many knew about his attack on Stella.

When the cappuccinos were ready, she loaded them on a tray, added a few pastries and sandwiches, and carried everything over to Vrog and Stella's table. "So, what do you think about the village so far?" She set the tray down.

"It's beautiful and so peaceful." Vrog reached for one of the paper cups and removed the lid. "A true paradise." He took a sip from the cappuccino and let out a sigh. "Divine."

"We ran out of coffee," Stella said. "Poor Vrog couldn't stomach the herbal tea, but it was the only thing I had."

Wendy frowned. "Do you have dietary restrictions like Emmett? Do you need blood?"

He shook his head. "I can exist on a human diet as long as it's mostly lightly cooked meat. I don't eat bread or pasta or rice, but I can tolerate some vegetables and fruits. And I love coffee." He took another sip, the froth painting him a milk mustache.

Wendy's eyes widened. "What about cows' milk? Can you tolerate it?"

"Cappuccinos are a weakness of mine, but I don't

tolerate the milk well," Vrog admitted. "It upsets my stomach."

Wendy stifled a chuckle.

Contrary to what she'd thought before turning immortal, farting wasn't exclusive to humans and other mammals. She could just imagine how bad those produced by a lactose intolerant half Kra-ell male would be.

"I can make you a cappuccino from alternative milk. We have soy, almond, and coconut."

"Perhaps I'll try some next time." He took another grateful sip. "When is your shift over?"

"We close the café at six, but Vlad will be back much sooner. In any case, Stella can walk you over to our house, and you can make yourself comfortable there. Your room is ready."

"Thank you." He smiled. "It's so kind of you to invite me to stay with you and Vlad. It will give me an opportunity to get to know my son. I just wish there was something for me to do in the village. I don't like being idle."

"You can help out in the café if you want. Wonder and I can always use another pair of hands in here."

It would also put him on display for the ladies, which would make it much easier to find him a match.

"I would love to," Vrog said. "I can also assist in the construction project. The Guardian who transported me here said that Kian employs Chinese crews. I can translate if needed."

Wendy chuckled. "Do you really want to work so closely with Richard?"

He grimaced. "Good point."

Stella cast Wendy a reproachful look. "Don't make Richard into a monster. If he needs help translating from English to Chinese or vice versa, I'm sure that he would appreciate Vrog's offer."

9

GERALDINE

"That's one hell of a story." Kian pushed to his feet, walked over to the suite's bar that doubled as a kitchenette, and refilled his coffee cup. "So you got the journal, but you couldn't read it. If it was written in the gods' language, no one in the human world could have translated it for you."

"Fortunately, it was written in Aramaic," Orion said. "The first linguist I took the journal to recognized the language and referred me to another who was proficient in Aramaic. I had him translate the journal for me, and then I erased his memories of the work he had done."

"Was that how you found my mother?" Geraldine asked.

Orion nodded. "By the time I tracked her down, she was a grandmother of eight. Fortunately for me, she still lived in the same town and even used her maiden name in addition to her married one. I had to thrall her to admit that she'd had a daughter out of wedlock who she'd given up for adoption."

"Did she tell you why?"

As Orion took her hand in a show of support, Geraldine braced for the worst, but his tone was soft when he explained, "You have to understand that things were different back then. It wasn't easy to be a single mother, and very few ladies dared. They had special places for unwed pregnant women where they waited until their babies were delivered and then they were immediately taken to their adoptive parents. Your mother said it was difficult to give you up, but she never regretted her decision. She'd gotten married, had three kids, and lived a good life. She assumed that you did as well because she'd been told that the couple who adopted you were nice people."

"Maybe they were, but not to me. I was told that my adoptive parents sent me to work on a farm, and my aunt and uncle treated me like a slave." She rubbed her temple, trying to remember who she'd learned from. Had it been Darlene or Rudolf who'd told her about that?

His eyes were full of compassion as he gave her hand a gentle squeeze. "You were born an immortal, Geraldine. You could hear conversations that you shouldn't have been able to, you were too strong, too fast, and you never got sick. When you fell down and scraped your knees, they couldn't understand why you were crying because your knees looked perfectly fine. Your adoptive parents were terrified of you."

She snorted. "What did they think, that I was possessed by a demon?"

Orion nodded. "What else could they think? By the time they shipped you off to their relatives in Oklahoma, you'd already learned to stifle your abilities, but they were still scared of you. When you married Rudolf, and he didn't seem to notice anything strange about you, they were overjoyed. They thought that you were cured."

"I see." She pulled her hand out of his and folded her arms over her chest. "How did you find them, though? Did my birth mother know who adopted me?"

"She didn't, but she remembered the name of the lady who arranged the adoption, and I tracked her down. She remembered your case well."

"Why?"

He cringed. "They tried to give you back."

"How awful." Cassandra turned to Geraldine. "I'm so glad that you don't remember any of it."

"Right." Orion frowned. "It just occurred to me that you knew about Rudolf and Darlene, but the goddess couldn't have retrieved your memories from before the accident because they were lost forever. How did you find out about them?"

"It's a long story." Geraldine turned to Kian. "Is it okay if I tell Orion?"

"Go ahead." Kian waved a hand. "In the meantime, I'm going to step outside to make a few phone calls." He motioned for Onegus and Andrew to follow him out.

"Thank you." She shifted her eyes to Kian's guards, but neither one made a move to follow their boss.

Evidently, they deemed him safe with just Onegus and Andrew by his side.

She waited until the door closed behind them before turning back to Orion. "It all started with Cassandra meeting Onegus at a charity gala. Her boss needed a stand-in for his wife, who had a concert that night, so he invited Cassy. She and Onegus took one look at each other and immediately felt the connection."

"Oh, Mother." Cassandra rolled her eyes. "You don't need to embellish the story." She smiled. "I thought that Onegus was a stuck-up billionaire, but oh so handsome." She batted her eyelashes.

"Anyway," Geraldine continued. "They started dating, and when things kept blowing up around Cassy, Onegus figured out that she was the cause. Paranormal abilities are a strong indicator that a person might be carrying the godly genes, and that made him suspect that Cassy was a Dormant. Since the godly genes pass through the mother, he suspected that I was as well. But then, as he got to know me a little, he picked up on clues that led him to suspect that I was already an immortal. To test the hypothesis, he took my picture and gave it to Roni to run through clan-developed facial recognition software."

"Hold on a moment." Orion lifted a hand. "Our Roni? Your grandson?"

"The same." Geraldine smiled. "That's a story for another time, but I'll let Roni tell it to you when you meet him. He's an immortal now."

"What about Darlene? Did she turn immortal as well?"

Geraldine's smile wilted. "Not yet, and I hope she will attempt transition as well, but it's more complicated with her. Leo is one problem, and her age is another…"

"What about Leo?" Orion asked. "What does he have to do with it?"

"That's another long story. We have so many that it will take days to fill you in on everything. Let's get back to how I found out about my past. Roni recognized me right away from the pictures his mother had shown him. As it turns out, he already knew that I was immortal and had been searching for me for several years." She smirked. "You taught me to hide so well that even my genius hacker grandson couldn't find me. Anyway, Onegus and Cassandra decided to test how fast I healed to make sure, and Onegus's mother scratched me. When I healed almost instantly, they got the confirmation they needed that I was indeed immortal."

"Not just any immortal," Cassandra said. "Her healing was so rapid that we knew she must be close to the source, but no one could have imagined that she was the daughter of a freaking god."

"What does it mean, being close to the source?"

"Just what it sounds like," Shai said. "It means first- or second-generation immortal."

10

ORION

"I see." Orion ran his hand over his hair. "I still have so much to learn about immortals and gods and the history of our people. My father was very stingy with what he told me."

His prick of a father had told him just enough to get rid of him, but the joke was on him. Thanks to the journal Orion had swiped, he'd found his sister, and thanks to her, he'd found the descendants of a goddess who'd actually shared with them what she knew.

Geraldine patted his knee. "That's okay. Cassandra and I are learning new things every day. You don't have to figure out everything in one go. It's a lot to take in." She chuckled. "Isn't it ironic that I'm the one who knows more than you now?"

"It is. So, I guess Roni heard from Darlene about your relationship with your parents?"

"Not quite. He didn't know much. Cassandra and I devised a plan to meet Darlene. We pretended to be the daughters of her mother's twin sister."

"You don't have a twin."

"I know that." She scrunched her nose. "Though to be

honest, I wanted to believe it, and I even convinced myself that having a twin was the only explanation that made sense. I couldn't fathom not remembering my own child, so having had a twin sister who was Darlene's mother and drowned was tragic but convenient."

"I'm sorry." He took her hand again. "I really thought that it was for the best. You didn't remember anything from before the accident, and I figured it was better to spare you from what you would anyway be forced to do in the near future. Imagine how difficult it would have been for you to fake your own death when you could no longer hide the fact that you were not aging."

"She could have dragged it on for a few more years," Shai said. "She could have waited until Darlene went to college instead of orphaning her at twelve."

"I know." Orion winced. "And if not for the accident, I would have helped her do just that." He turned to Geraldine. "Given the memory issues you had after recovering from the accident, it was too risky to send you back to them. I did what I believed was best for everyone, and I looked out for Darlene. I arranged for her to get a full-ride scholarship at an excellent university, and later, I got her worthless husband a well-paying job, which he lost when Roni was caught hacking. I had to wait for things to calm down before getting him a new one."

"We suspected that you were behind Leo's cushy new job," Cassandra said. "Thank you for that. I just wish that you had helped Roni to get out when he was caught."

Orion sighed. "I'm an antiques dealer, not an undercover operative. He was being watched twenty-four-seven by agents and by electronic devices. I could have handled the humans, but even that was too dangerous. I was afraid to tangle with the government."

"You were smart to stay out of it," the redheaded guard said. "It was one hell of an operation to get Roni out of there, and it took months of planning. There is no way you could've pulled it off on your own."

"I can't wait to hear that story, but let's finish this one first." He turned to Geraldine. "How did you approach Darlene?"

"Do you know about those genetic tests that you can mail order nowadays?"

"I've heard of them."

"Roni knew that his mother had done one, so he planted fake results for Cassandra and me at the same place. Cassy called Darlene and told her that we were such a close match that we must be cousins. We set up a meeting and got her to tell us about her father. Cassy suspected that Rudolf had something to do with my accident. That perhaps he wanted to kill me for the insurance money."

Orion shook his head. "Rudolf wasn't a bad man, and he loved you."

"I know that now." Geraldine heaved a sigh. "Anyway, long story short, we went to visit Rudolf, pretending to be Sabina's twin sister's daughters. We found out that you were not as careful as you thought you'd been. He'd seen you with me, and you'd left quite an impression on him. He was convinced that we were having an affair."

"Impossible."

"What? That he saw you or that he thought we were having an affair?"

"That he saw me without me seeing him. He was such a simple guy."

"Never underestimate the resourcefulness of a jealous husband," Cassandra said. "We got an incredibly talented forensic artist to draw your portrait from Rudolf's memory." She pulled out her phone, scrolled for a moment, and handed it to him. "See for yourself."

Orion glanced at the sketch, which was so incredibly accurate it could have been his photograph. "I'll be damned. That's incredible." He handed her the phone back. "The artist must have a paranormal ability to do that from Rudolf's forty-year-old recollection of me."

Geraldine snorted. "Tim is something else, and he charges accordingly. Poor Shai had to part with a big chunk of money for the service."

"I'll pay you back," Orion immediately offered.

"No need." Shai lifted his hand to stop Orion from pressing the point. "I did it for Geraldine."

He decided to let it go for now and repay the guy in some other way in the future. A priceless antique or a rare painting would do great as a wedding present.

When Orion nodded, Geraldine continued, "We told Rudolf that you were mine and Sabina's third sibling who had also been given up for adoption." She put a hand over her heart. "You should have seen the relief on his face. It was like a huge weight had been lifted off his shoulders." She lifted a finger to wipe a tear away. "Up until then, I didn't feel anything toward him, but that touched my heart."

"So you'd already known that I was your brother?"

She laughed. "I didn't. It was just a story we made up to ease Rudolf's tortured soul. He agonized about my supposed infidelity for four decades."

"Damn." Orion shook his head. "Talk about good intentions paving a road straight to hell. If I had known that he had seen me and was tormenting himself over an imagined affair, I would have thralled him to forget me."

"Didn't I tell you about it? Because Rudolf said that he'd confronted me about my alleged affair several times. According to him, I told him that I didn't know what he was talking about, and I don't think that I lied. You probably erased yourself from my memory after each visit."

"I did, and you never mentioned Rudolf's suspicions. Perhaps I made a mess in your head with thralling you to forget me and then releasing the memories when I returned for another visit."

"Did you thrall Rudolf not to notice my peculiarities?"

"I didn't need to. You'd been suppressing your abilities for so long that it was like you didn't have them, and he had no reason to suspect anything. Naturally, you didn't know why you had those abilities, but just to be safe, I compelled you not to show your hand."

She narrowed her eyes at him. "Why did you make me forget you? Did you even tell me who you were?"

"You asked me to do that, so you wouldn't miss me and also so you wouldn't accidentally blurt out anything about me. The way we set it up was for you to remember me as soon as you saw me and forget me once we parted, but after your injury, I had to be more careful. You really didn't remember who I was, and I decided not to tell you that you were immortal. I wasn't sure how long my compulsion would hold, and I figured that the less you knew, the better." He turned to look at Cassandra. "Even your own daughter didn't notice anything unusual other than your memory issues, right?"

Cassandra nodded. "She couldn't use her immortal strength even after we both knew that she was immortal." She grimaced. "You did a good job on her."

"I truly couldn't lift that planter," Geraldine said. "I gave it all I had, and it wouldn't budge."

"That's the power of suggestion," the redhead said. "I once saw a show where a hypnotist told a subject to forget the number four, and then he told him to count from one to ten. The guy counted three times, and each time, he skipped over the number four. He didn't even know that he was doing it."

11

KIAN

"So, what do you think?" Kian asked Onegus and Andrew as the door closed behind them.

"I didn't detect any lies," Andrew said. "He seems like a decent guy."

Onegus nodded. "I didn't smell deceit on him, only anxiety and then excitement when Geraldine and Cassandra arrived."

That had been Kian's impression as well, but he wanted a second and third opinion before allowing the guy into the village. Hell, he still wasn't convinced and planned to ask Edna to probe him.

Kian had to remind himself, though, that Orion's case was very different than Lokan's or even Kalugal's.

Orion was an unaffiliated immortal, who was pretty clueless about his heritage but still dangerously powerful. On the other hand, he cared deeply about Geraldine and Cassandra, and he wasn't the clan's enemy. Besides, Annani was probably already packing and getting ready to head over to the village.

She would demand that Kian invite Orion right away.

Andrew pulled out his phone and checked the time. "If you no longer need me, I should go."

"I'm sorry for keeping you for so long. I didn't expect Orion and Geraldine to go down memory lane." Kian chuckled. "But I should have." He clapped Andrew on the back. "Thank you for coming."

"Any time." Andrew returned Kian's clap.

When his brother-in-law headed toward the elevators, Kian pulled out his phone and called Edna.

She was in her city office today, which was only a few minutes' drive away from the keep. Hopefully, she wouldn't mind swinging by and probing their guest on such short notice.

"Hello, Kian," she answered.

"Good morning. Are you busy?"

"What do you need, Kian?"

"I need you to probe our latest guest at your earliest convenience. I have him in the keep. How soon can you get here?"

"Who's your guest?"

"Orion, son of Toven."

For a long moment, a loaded silence stretched over their connection. "So you've finally caught him."

"We did. The guy slipped by our surveillance and watched Geraldine and Shai from her neighbor's house. His mistake was to follow Shai, who lured him into a trap that we set up for him on Red Canyon Road."

"Why did he follow Shai?"

Kian chuckled. "I asked Orion many questions, but it didn't occur to me to ask that. I arranged for Andrew to be there when Geraldine, Cassandra, Shai, and Onegus came. He listened to Orion's story and then to Geraldine and Orion reminiscing about the past and comparing notes, and he didn't detect any lies. But I want to be absolutely sure about Orion's motives before I bring him to the village, which is why I need you to probe him."

He heard Edna getting up and walking. "What's your impression of him?"

"Andrew, Onegus, and I agree that he seems like a decent guy who was looking after his sister. The way he found her is a fascinating story, but even more so is how he met his father. That encounter had the Fates' fingerprints all over it."

"Interesting." He heard Edna unlock her car and open the door. "Where and when did he meet Toven?" She turned the engine on.

"It was a chance encounter thirty-some years ago on a street in Paris. Toven tried to get rid of Orion by using either thralling or compulsion, but neither would work on Orion because he's immune. He's a compeller himself, and apparently a powerful one. He followed Toven to his place of residence and demanded answers, but Toven brushed him off with the bare minimum of details and sent him away."

"Why? From what Annani told me about Toven, he sounded like a good guy. He didn't sound like the kind of male who discovers that he has a son and wants nothing to do with him."

"Quoting Orion, 'Toven is a jaded bastard who cares about nothing.'"

"Toven lost his wife in the bombing. Perhaps losing his mate broke him."

Using his fingers, Kian brushed his hair back. "I think my mother said that they weren't truelove mates, but that doesn't mean that he didn't love her. He'd been loyal to her." Kian chuckled. "In that respect, Toven was nothing like his father and brother."

"As I said, Annani's descriptions of Toven were favorable. Then again, given who his brother was and who his nephew is, it's possible that he flipped. Insanity runs in families."

Kian snorted. "And yet we allied with Lokan and Kalugal, who carry the same genes."

Edna let out a breath. "I really like Kalugal, and I like Lokan too, but I'm keeping my eyes on Kalugal, and so is Rufsur. If he starts acting insane and making plans to annihilate half the world, Rufsur is ready to stop him."

"Good to know that I'm not the only one who is wary of Kalugal's heritage." Kian glanced at Onegus, who was nodding his agreement. "When you get to the keep, head straight to the dungeon level. I'll probably still be outside in the hallway making phone calls."

"Very well. By the way, why are you not in there with Orion and the others?" Edna asked.

"I thought it would be a better utilization of my time while Orion and Geraldine are reminiscing."

"I would have found that conversation interesting," Edna said with amusement in her voice, "but I understand your need to wrap things up quickly and go home. Send my regards to Syssi when you call her."

"I will." Kian terminated the call.

Onegus arched a brow. "How did she know that you were going to call your wife?"

"If you're worried that Edna can probe us over the phone, she can't. She's just smart enough to deduce it."

"Yeah, but how did she know that you didn't call her already?" Onegus leaned against the wall and crossed his arms over his chest.

"I have no clue. Perhaps Edna had spoken with Syssi earlier, and Syssi told her that I haven't called her yet with updates about Orion." He sighed. "I need to call Annani, but I want Edna to probe Orion first. If he's hiding malevolent intentions, I'd rather know that beforehand."

"How come you didn't have her probe Vrog?" Onegus pushed off the wall.

"Because there was no point. Vrog is pretty transparent, and the only thing we have to worry about is his loyalty to Jade and what he might do if she orders him to go against us. But then we know the answer to that. Having Edna confirm that he's loyal to his former mistress would have served no purpose."

12

ORION

When Orion's cell door opened again, Kian returned with Onegus and a stern-looking woman. Andrew, the not-so-subtle lie detector, wasn't with them.

"This is Edna," Kian introduced the female. "She's the clan's judge and a member of the council."

Orion rose to his feet and offered her his hand. "Am I on trial?"

She gifted him with a smile that was just a tiny upturn of her lips. "In a way, but you are not on trial for past transgressions." She took his offered hand. "I'm here to assess your intentions, your aspirations, and the makeup of your soul."

She wasn't joking.

From the corner of his eye, Orion saw the redhead wince, and even the stoic blond let a shadow of emotion cross his eyes, but whether it was out of respect or fear, Orion wasn't sure. The guy was hard to read.

"That sounds ominous." He smiled down at her.

Despite her modest stature, she seemed like a force to

be reckoned with, and given the respect on everyone's faces, it wasn't just his impression.

"If you have nothing to hide, this should go easy." She cast a quick glance around the room and nodded her hellos. "It's too crowded in here for what I need to do. Is there anywhere else you could all wait until I'm done?"

When Geraldine darted a panicked glance at Kian, the judge added, "I'll call you back in when I'm ready to share what I've learned."

"Of course." Kian turned to Geraldine and Cassandra. "You can wait in my old office. Onegus will show you where it is." He turned to Geraldine's mate. "I'll stay here with Anandur and Brundar. You can go with them." He turned to Edna. "If that's okay with you."

When the judge didn't object, Geraldine rose to her feet and put her hand on Orion's arm. "Good luck." She stretched up on her toes and kissed his cheek.

Cassandra cast him an encouraging smile before following her mother and the chief of security out.

As the door closed behind them, Edna sat on the couch and motioned for him to sit beside her. "Give me your hands, look into my eyes, and don't say a thing. If you do, Kian will suspect that you compelled me, and we don't want that."

Orion wanted to ask her what he should expect, but heeding her warning, he just nodded.

"What I do is similar to thralling, but I go much deeper. On my way down into the depths of your soul, I might see scenes from events that shaped who you are today, but I'm not going to reveal any of it. I'll only give my opinion about the kind of male you are."

Stifling a witty remark, he nodded again.

"I mean you no harm," Edna said. "If you resist my intrusion, I will have to push harder past your barriers, which will make the experience more difficult for both of us. If you relax and let me in, this will be over much faster."

He nodded again.

As he looked into her ancient eyes, the room faded away, and as her ghostly fingers gently sifted through his memories, he let her dive as deep as she wished.

Orion had nothing to hide, no crimes he felt guilty about or injustices he might have committed. There had been many sorrows in his life, but only a few regrets. He thought of himself as a good man. He was no saint, that was for sure, but he always tried to be the best version of himself.

When one lived forever, accumulating even small regrets could become a crushing weight over time. He was better off avoiding them as best he could.

Just as Edna had promised, her probe didn't take long, and once she was done, she gave him a genuine smile and let go of his hands. "Congratulations, you passed the test."

"Thank you." He inclined his head.

"What's your opinion, Edna?" Kian asked. "I need more than a pass or fail grade."

She turned to look at her leader. "Orion harbors no malevolent plans, not for the clan and not for anyone else. Family is important to him, and he is very protective of the one sister he has found so far and her family."

"Are you still searching for other siblings?" Kian asked.

Orion grimaced. "I've exhausted all the information contained in Toven's journal, and I've only found Geraldine. I was unable to track some of the women described in the journal, though, so perhaps there is still hope. Maybe with your clan's resources, you might succeed where I've failed."

"If there are any out there, it's imperative that we find them," Kian said. "I'll provide you with all the help I can." He shook his head. "I cringe thinking about unaffiliated immortals who have no idea who they are, why they are not aging, and where their special abilities come from. Some might use those abilities in unsavory ways, risking exposure and causing harm." He smiled at Orion. "I'm impressed that you didn't use your powers to take unfair advantage, especially since you had no mentor to teach you the proper rules of conduct for an immortal and instill in you the right values."

Orion cast a sidelong glance at Edna, who shrugged. "As I said, I'm not here to judge you on past misdemeanors. If you want to confess, it's up to you."

The way she phrased it made it evident that Edna didn't judge him harshly for what he had done. Hopefully, Kian wouldn't either.

"I used my powers when I needed to. I thralled women to forget my fangs, I compelled business associates to tell me the truth, and I forced those who tried to cheat me to give me a much better deal than I would have accepted if they were dealing fairly with me."

"I see no problem with any of that. I would have done the same thing."

Edna cleared her throat. "Strictly speaking, thralling and compulsion are only allowed to hide who we are and protect clan members from danger or discovery. That's why thralling the memory of a venom bite is sanctioned, while thralling a reluctant partner into your bed is definitely not."

Orion put a hand on his chest. "I would never do that. It's no different than rape, probably worse."

13

KIAN

After thanking Edna, Kian called Shai to let him know that it was okay to return and asked him to order lunch for everyone.

Several hours had passed since they'd had breakfast, and he didn't want to bring Orion to the village hungry and then worry about feeding him. He also needed to call Ingrid and have her prepare a house for the guy.

Thankfully, Kalugal's men had moved into their part of the village, so there was no shortage of available houses.

Perhaps he could fob off Orion on his cousin?

Kalugal had a cook, so the problem of feeding Orion would be solved.

Nah, he was overcomplicating things. Geraldine and Cassandra could take care of Orion's needs.

When the two couples returned, Kian rose to his feet. "I need to make a few more phone calls." He turned to Anandur. "Let me know when lunch is here."

"No problem, boss."

Stepping outside, Kian left the door open and headed to his old office to call his mother.

"Hello, my son. What news do you have for me of Orion? Is he okay?"

"We treat him as an honored guest, and I intend to invite him to the village, with proper security, that is."

"No cuffs," Annani commanded.

"None. I just don't want him to know where the village is, but that's not treating him any differently than the majority of clan members. Everyone knows the area, but only a select few know where the entrance to the tunnel is."

"Where is Orion going to stay?"

"There is no shortage of available houses, and when the new section of the village is completed and the furniture delivered, there will be an abundance of vacant houses even in the center of the village. I'm moving all the Guardians to the new homes."

"Exciting times. But what are you going to do with him in the meantime? Perhaps one of the homes in phase two would do. Is he used to luxury?"

"I don't know. But even if he is, it doesn't mean that I need to pamper him. What's good enough for my clan members should be good enough for him."

"What is he like?" Annani asked.

"He's okay. I had Edna probe him, and she didn't find anything that is cause for concern. Frankly, I'm starting to like the guy."

Orion was no Boy Scout, but he was a good male. He didn't use his powers to gain an unfair advantage, which was truly admirable since he answered to no one, and he cared deeply for his sister and her family, assisting them in any way he could.

"You have no idea how happy I am to hear that," Annani said. "I was afraid that you would regard him with suspicion like you did Kalugal."

"I'm still suspicious of that conceited know-it-all, but I also like him."

Annani laughed. "You like him because he smokes cigars and drinks whiskey with you. You found a partner in crime."

"Kalugal smokes *my* cigars and drinks *my* whiskey, but I don't mind. He's good company."

The guy was intelligent, well-read, easygoing, and he was good to his mate and to his men. That was good enough for Kian.

"Indeed. I am glad that you are getting along with your cousin, and now you have another one."

"Orion is not my cousin any more than Navuh is. Both are Ekin's grandsons, and Ekin was your father's half-brother, so that's a very distant relationship. And even though Kalugal and Lokan are the sons of Areana, calling them cousins is a stretch because you share a father and not a mother."

She sighed. "I like thinking of Lokan and Kalugal as close family. Fates know that these boys have no one else. Areana is locked up on the island, and Navuh regards them as potential enemies. We are the only ones who treat them like real family."

"True. I never thought of it from that angle."

"Well, now you do. Did Orion tell you anything about Toven?"

"Yeah." Annani wasn't going to like what Kian had to tell her about the god she used to be so fond of. "Orion met him only once, and at the time, Toven called himself Herman."

"Herman? Why on earth would he call himself that? Had he been hiding among the Germanic tribes?"

"It's possible, but he didn't tell Orion much." Kian repeated everything that Orion had told them about that fateful meeting with Toven.

"That does not sound like the Toven I knew. He must have been devastated when he learned the fate of our people. I, at least, had the Odus to keep me company. He had no one."

"He also lost his mate. I remember you telling me that he loved his wife and was faithful to her, but that they weren't truelove mates. Is that correct? Or am I confusing Khiann's parents' story with Toven's?"

"Both couples had good marriages despite not being truelove mates. That was why they could be separated for long periods of time without suffering terribly. Khiann's father was often gone for months, taking caravans to trade in faraway lands, and Toven was an explorer and a researcher. He was also gone for months at a time."

"Then Toven should have gotten over her death a long time ago."

"Perhaps he could not," Annani said softly. "He had been married for much longer than I had."

"Perhaps." Kian needed to change the subject before his mother started crying. As strong and as resilient as she was, it still pained her to talk about Khiann.

"I want to see Orion," Annani said.

"Of course you do. When should I expect you?"

"It will take Alena and me about an hour to pack and for the Odus to prepare the jet. The flight time is about five hours, so plan for Okidu to pick us up from the airstrip accordingly. Also, since there are so many houses available, have one prepared for us. We will be staying for a while this time, at least until Amanda delivers her daughter and probably a couple of weeks after that if not longer."

Ingrid would have a panic attack if he asked her to prepare two houses on such short notice.

"I'll see what I can do. If Ingrid can't manage a house for you right away, you can spend a couple of days with Syssi and me until the house is ready."

"I understand. But do the best you can. I would rather unpack once."

His mother had never packed or unpacked a suitcase, the Odus took care of that for her, but he wasn't going to point that out. "Naturally. I'd better let Syssi know that you will be joining us for dinner."

"Invite Orion to dinner as well."

He should have expected that. In fact, he should have thought of it himself. The problem was that the guy wasn't just any immortal. He was a compeller.

"We need to consider security, Mother. Orion is a compeller, and he's immune to compulsion by others. Even Toven couldn't compel him."

"Are you suggesting that I wear those earpieces?" Her tone was incredulous.

"I don't think we need to go that far. But instruct your Odus not to obey orders from you if they originate from Orion. I will also have the brothers attend dinner while wearing earpieces. They will know not to obey questionable orders from either of us."

"Sounds reasonable."

"We can discuss what to do about Toven when you get here."

"I want to find him, of course. Do you not?"

"I do, but even more important than that is finding his other children if he fathered any in addition to Orion and Geraldine. Those immortals could cause a lot of trouble, or worse, get caught."

"We can search for both," Annani said. "But we will talk about it over dinner tonight. I need to tell my Odus what to pack for me."

"Call me when you are within an hour of landing, and I'll send Okidu to pick you up. Syssi will need every spare moment of his help to prepare dinner for so many people."

"Who are you inviting other than the family and Orion?"

Kian loosed a breath. "If I invite Orion, I have to invite Geraldine and Shai, Cassandra and Onegus, and Roni and Sylvia. And since it's too early for me to trust Orion, I need Anandur and Brundar to be there with earpieces, but since I don't want him to think that I consider him a threat, I'll have them bring their mates along. The rest are the usual suspects—Amanda and Dalhu, Andrew, Nathalie, and Phoenix, and Jacki and Kalugal. Together with you and Alena, that's twenty-two people."

"Is your dining room large enough?"

The one in their new house was, but the crews were still putting final touches on it, and the furniture wouldn't arrive for another two weeks.

They might be able to squeeze twenty people into their current dining room, but perhaps it was better to move dinner to the backyard and bring in heaters. He needed to check the forecast to see if it was going to rain tonight.

"I need to talk it over with Syssi, and I should do that as soon as possible. Is there anything else you need to discuss with me before I go?"

"We can talk more when I get there. Goodbye, Kian."

"Goodbye, Mother. I'll see you tonight." He ended the call and then called Syssi.

She patiently listened as he gave her a quick summary of the day's events, the number of people they would be hosting tonight, and his suggestion to have the dinner in the backyard.

"Did you look at the forecast?" Syssi asked.

"Not yet."

"It might rain tonight. Maybe we should have it at Kalugal's place," she suggested. "I'm sure he wouldn't mind. Atzil can whip up a dinner for twenty with ease. He's used to cooking for a crowd."

"I'd rather cancel the whole thing than give Kalugal the satisfaction. Okidu can move the dining table into the living room and stick the living room furniture somewhere else."

"That could work."

"Thank you for doing this. I'll try to get home early and assist with whatever you need me to do."

She chuckled. "You have enough on your plate, and you shouldn't worry about me. I'll draft the queen of party organizing to help me prepare this lovely event."

"The queen is heavily pregnant. I doubt she can do much."

"She can conduct the orchestra from the couch. Amanda never does anything with her own two hands, but she's great at planning, organizing, and delegating."

14

ALENA

Annani opened the door to Alena's suite and rushed in, in a flurry of nightgown and robe. "Pack your things, Alena. We are leaving within the hour."

Alena's heartbeat accelerated. "What happened?"

Her mother smiled. "Kian is moving Orion to the village, and we are going to see him tonight at dinner at Syssi and Kian's house. I am so excited to meet Toven's son. Are you?"

With how fast her heart was racing, to say that she was merely excited would be missing it by a mile. Terrified would be more accurate.

Alena hadn't expected to have to face Orion so soon, or ever if she could help it. He was a compeller, a possessor of a rare paranormal ability that gave her the creeps, but he was also the most attractive male she'd ever seen a picture of, and she yearned to meet him in person. Those two opposing forces were sure to mess with her head, and it would have been best to avoid walking into that landmine.

Except, her mother wanted to see Orion today, so that was happening whether Alena was ready and willing or not.

"What is Kian doing as far as precautions?" she asked. "Orion is a compeller."

Annani waved a dismissive hand. "So is Kalugal, and no one wears those special earpieces around him anymore." She turned toward the door she'd left open. "And if we don't need them around Kalugal, who is the son of our arch-enemy, we definitely don't need to wear them around Orion, who is not."

They didn't know what Toven was up to, but Alena didn't point it out. There were other considerations that her mother had conveniently forgotten. "You compelled Kalugal not to use his powers on clan members. Are you going to do the same with Orion?"

"I might not be able to. He told Kian that Toven had tried to compel him to go away but was unsuccessful. I do not know how strong of a compeller Toven is, and whether I am stronger than him or not. I will need to test it."

Great, so that one kernel of hope was gone. If Annani could have compelled Orion not to use his compulsion on her clan members, Alena might have given him a chance, but now it was out of the question.

"I don't like it. I know that there is no way I can convince you to wear earpieces when you meet Orion, but I'm definitely going to do so. I'll text Kian and ask him to send a pair for me with Okidu."

Annani regarded her with her ancient eyes. "I am a compeller as well. Are you living in constant fear of me using my power on you?"

"Of course not. You're my mother, and I trust you."

"Why do you trust me?"

Alena rolled her eyes. "Because you love me, and you know how much I hate the very idea of compulsion. I know you will never use it on me or any of your children without their permission."

"I compelled you once. Did you forget?"

"That doesn't count. It was for an excellent cause, and it was a blanket compulsion that covered everyone in the clan. There was so much mistrust between Kian and Kalugal and between Kalugal's men and our clan that the only way they could coexist alongside us was if you compelled everyone to get along and not harm each other."

"Nevertheless, you felt the power of my compulsion. Was it so terrible?"

"It wasn't," Alena admitted. "From you, it felt like love. But it wouldn't feel like that from anyone else, and especially not from a male." She shivered. "It's vile. It's a violation of the worst kind."

Annani shook her head. "I do not know why you have such aversion to people who possess the ability. Like with everything else, it depends on how they use it. A male is typically stronger than a female, and he can force himself on her. Does the ability to do so make him vile? Of course not. If he uses his superior strength to rape and plunder, then he is evil. But if he uses it to protect those who cannot protect themselves, then he is a hero."

It was hard to argue with that logic, but Alena was well aware that her aversion to compellers wasn't entirely rational, and she didn't even know why. It wasn't like she'd ever been a victim of compulsion or even of hypnotism.

"You are right, Mother, but I still prefer to wear the earpieces, at least until I'm convinced that Orion is a good guy."

"Fair enough." Annani looked down at her robe. "Oh my. In all the excitement, I forgot to get dressed before leaving my suite."

As usual, she looked magnificent even when wearing a nightgown. Not that it looked any different than her dresses. It was silk—because she didn't like any other fabric touching her skin, purple—because it complemented her fiery red hair, and floor-length—because she didn't like her feet showing.

Evidently, everyone had their quirks. Alena's was an allergic reaction to compellers, and Annani's was embarrassment over her tiny, child-like feet.

"That's okay, Mother. No one noticed because your dresses look like nightgowns anyway."

"They do." Annani chuckled. "I like to be comfortable but still stylish." She cast Alena a motherly smile before opening the door. "Tell Ovidu to start packing. I want to leave as soon as possible."

15

ORION

After Geraldine, Cassandra, and their mates had returned, and Kian had left again, no one bothered to close the massive door to Orion's comfy prison.

Evidently Edna's favorable opinion of him had put the suspicious Kian at ease, and he had slackened security.

"I can smell food." The redhead pushed to his feet. "That must be Edwin with the delivery." He walked out of the room and a moment later returned with a bunch of paper bags in hand and Kian in tow.

Orion liked the casual way these immortals interacted. They called each other by their first names, and although the guards regarded Kian with respect, they also treated him as a friend or a family member rather than their boss.

Well, the redhead did. The blond was doing an excellent impersonation of a statue and was impossible to read, except for that one glimpse of emotion he'd shown when Edna explained what she'd been about to do.

The experience had been intrusive and a little uncomfortable, but it hadn't been as bad as Orion had expected. She'd handled him with care.

"After we are done with lunch—" Kian accepted a box

from the redhead "—we will head to the village." He leveled his intense eyes on Orion's. "I'm having a house prepared for you, so you can continue your reunion with your sister and niece from the comfort of your own home."

That didn't sound good.

Did Kian intend to keep him under house arrest?

"A whole house just for me? Can't I stay for a couple of days with Geraldine or Cassandra?"

"Perhaps during your next visit. Right now, the housing situation in the village is in flux, and the best solution is to give you your own place for as long as you want to stay with us. It's nothing fancy, but it's nearly brand new, and it's as nicely decorated as this place by the same talented interior designer."

That was a relief and a pleasant surprise, but he needed to make sure that he understood Kian's intentions correctly. "Thank you. That's very generous of you, but I can't stay for more than a few days. I have a business to run."

"I understand," Kian said. "As I told you, you're welcome to stay as long as you want." He opened the box and lifted a piece of eggplant with a pair of chopsticks. "Naturally, I count on you to keep our existence a secret just as you keep yours. The safety of your sister and niece depends on that." He put the piece of eggplant in his mouth.

"I would never do anything to jeopardize their safety, as well as yours and the rest of your people. I vow it on my life."

It was a shame that the lie detector guy was gone and couldn't vouch for the veracity of his statement, but it seemed that Edna's probe was enough to convince Kian of his good intentions.

"I count on it." Kian lifted another piece of eggplant and ate it.

Was he a vegetarian?

Orion had always been a carnivore and assumed that it was part of his unique physiology. His fangs, venom, and ability to thrall people and beasts alike were the traits of a predator, and by definition predators were meat-eaters.

Opening the box the redhead handed him, Orion was glad to find beef and broccoli. He looked at the tall guard. "How did you know what to order for me?"

The guy shrugged. "I didn't order it, Shai did, and the box had your name written on it."

"I told Shai what to order," Geraldine said. "More and more of my memories of you are slowly resurfacing, including the many lunches we had together. I even remember which dishes you used to order."

It was a nice feeling to have at least one person know and care about his preferences. Before, he hadn't dared to let her remember those things because her mind had been too fragile.

Casting a sidelong glance at her mate, Orion wondered if the guy was aware of the risk he and his people were taking by releasing Geraldine's memories. As long as she stayed in the village, that was okay, but if she ventured into the human world, she might forget not to say anything about immortals and their beautiful hideout.

"By the way," Kian said. "The Clan Mother is on her way, and you are all invited to dinner at my house." He smiled at Orion. "You are going to meet her much sooner than you hoped for."

He dropped his chopsticks into the box. "Tonight?"

"I told you that she's eager to meet you."

Geraldine put a hand on his arm. "You have nothing to fear from Annani. She is kind and friendly and much nicer than your father."

"That's not difficult to do." He gripped the chopsticks and lifted a piece of broccoli.

"Shai and I need to get a house of our own as well." Geraldine put her box on the coffee table. "And I need to start driving again so I can visit my friends. Shai is arranging a new fake driver's license and passport for me." She smiled at her mate. "I can finally leave the country and travel. I've seen nothing of the world yet."

Orion didn't know whether he should issue a warning or keep his mouth shut. Perhaps later, he would take Shai aside and tell him to proceed with caution.

Shai groaned. "I don't know if I can take a vacation that's longer than a couple of days." He cast a sidelong glance at Kian. "How are you going to manage without me?"

"I told you that you need an assistant, and I also asked that you put an ad on the clan's virtual bulletin board. I don't know why you're dragging your feet about that."

"What is it that you do, Shai?" Orion asked.

In all the commotion, he'd forgotten his original reason for following Shai. He still hadn't determined whether the guy was worthy of Geraldine.

Shai hadn't said much during the long hours that they had spent together, which was an admirable trait, provided that he did it out of respect and consideration and not because he had nothing to add to the conversation.

"I'm Kian's assistant." Shai avoided his eyes as if he was ashamed of his job.

"That's a very respectable position," Orion said and meant it.

"Shai is much more than that," Kian said. "I would have been lost without his eidetic memory."

Orion's appreciation for the guy ratcheted up by a few notches. "Do you remember everything?"

Shai nodded. "Word for word."

"What a great asset to have." Orion thought of all the ways a talent like that could be useful.

"Not as great as the power to compel," Shai said. "I would trade with you in a heartbeat, not because I'm power-hungry, but because it's a great defensive weapon."

"I'm glad that you think of my compulsion as a defense mechanism, but most people don't." Orion put the empty box on the coffee table. "They assume it's an offensive tool, which I admit it can be. But I would rather have your amazing memory and not be considered a threat." He pinned Kian with a hard stare. "As a compeller, I'm assumed guilty until proven innocent."

16

KIAN

As the SUV's windows turned opaque, Kian felt Orion tense.

"What's going on?" he asked.

"Nothing to be alarmed about. It's a little trick we use to make sure even our own people can't find the village."

Letting go of the wheel, Anandur turned around and grinned at Orion. "From this point on, the autonomous driving engages. It will relinquish control to me when we reach the parking structure."

"You can't be serious." Orion cast a glance at Brundar, who sat beside him in the back seat, but when the Guardian didn't respond, he turned to look at Kian. "Unless you keep your people underground in that village of yours, I'm sure everyone has already figured out where they live. All it takes is to look at the landmarks."

"True, but they can't find the entrance to the tunnel, which is the only way in," Kian explained with no small amount of smugness. "When we get there, you will feel the car enter an elevator, which will take it up to the parking level. From there, another elevator will take us to the surface. The only other way into the village is by parachuting from above, but thanks to clever camouflage and signal disruptors, no aircraft fly overhead. You would have to use a very large bird to get over the village, but since dragons are extinct, you're out of luck."

"I was under the impression that Dragons were a myth."

"It was a joke," Kian clarified. "The bottom line is that our village is very well-hidden."

"I have to admit that I'm impressed." Orion folded his arms over his chest. "Not by the technology but by the resources your clan has to command to afford a project like that. How rich are you people?"

"We're doing well, but our humanitarian efforts are a big drain on our resources. We've organized a charity to help with the costs and the donations help, but we still fund about half of the operations."

"What's your gig?"

Kian didn't like that word in reference to a serious problem like trafficking. Hadn't Geraldine or Cassandra told Orion about the charity gala where Onegus and Cassandra had met? The donations had gone to the rehabilitation center for the victims.

"We fight trafficking," Brundar said.

Orion was so startled by the Guardian speaking that Kian doubted he'd noticed that they'd entered the tunnel.

"Human trafficking?"

Brundar cast him an incredulous look and didn't bother to answer.

"Is there any other kind?" Anandur asked.

Uncrossing his arms, Orion leaned closer to the redhead. "What exactly do you do to stop it?"

"We raid the brothels, rough up the scum, free the victims, and leave enough evidence for the police to lock the scum up." Anandur smiled evilly. "Sometimes we get too rough and the scum expires, but oh well, shit happens."

"We also rehabilitate the victims," Kian added.

Orion was about to comment when the car rolled onto the elevator platform, and the thing lurched up. "It's like science fiction. I feel like I'm entering Batman's cave."

"Not quite." Kian chuckled.

When the elevator door opened, Anandur drove the SUV out and pulled into Kian's parking spot. "We are home."

Brundar opened the door, got out, and opened the trunk to get Orion's suitcase and carry-on.

After they'd collect his things from the Airbnb he had been renting, Orion told them about the pizza delivery guy he'd hosted for an evening against the guy's will. What Kian liked about the story was that Orion had compensated the Uber driver for his time and for the use of his car. Provided that it was true, and Kian had no reason to doubt it, Orion had done precisely as he would have, which made him like the guy even more.

"I can take these." Orion took the luggage from Brundar's hands.

The Guardian didn't argue and headed for the elevators.

As they stepped out of the elevator and entered the pavilion, Orion's eyes widened. "What's all this?" He motioned at the artifacts housed behind the glass displays.

"Our shared cousin, Kalugal, is into archeology. He's been searching for clues about the gods' civilization and collecting artifacts that pertain to them. I'm afraid most of these were smuggled illegally from the countries they were discovered in, but I can definitely turn a blind eye to that. Technically, they belong to us."

"What do you mean, shared cousin? Are we cousins?"

Kian led the way out the doors. "In a manner of speaking. Mortdh was Kalugal's grandfather, and Toven was Mortdh's brother. That's how you and Kalugal are related. Kalugal's mother is my mother's half-sister from the same father but different mothers, and that's how we are related. So, you and I might not be cousins, but we share Kalugal as a second or third cousin." Kian chuckled. "In the clan, we make it easy. Everyone is a cousin unless they are directly your sibling or an uncle or an aunt, and of course your mother."

Orion arched a brow. "What about fathers?"

"Up until recently, there were no fathers in the clan. But things are changing." Kian smiled proudly. "I'm a father, and so is Andrew, and also one of the Guardians. Another Guardian mated a widow with two children and officially adopted them. Kalugal's wife is expecting, and so is my sister Amanda. Hopefully, the clan will have many more fathers in the not-too-distant future."

17

ORION

"Get some rest," were Kian's parting words as he left the house that would be Orion's home for as long as he wished to stay.

The immortals' village was serene and beautiful, the only noises disturbing the quiet coming from the building project that Kian had promised to take him on a tour of.

"So, what do you think?" Cassandra sat down on the couch. "It's nice here, isn't it."

She and Geraldine had come along to see the house. Their mates had bid him goodbye outside the glass pavilion, and Orion assumed that they had gone to work.

"It's a slice of paradise." He walked over to the sliding doors and opened them. "I've never owned a house."

"Why not?" Geraldine followed him out into the backyard. "It's surely not due to lack of funds."

He shrugged. "I have apartments in different cities around the world, but I keep them more as an investment than personal residences. I'm always traveling and staying either in hotels or Airbnbs."

She glanced back at the living room where his suitcase and carry-on had been left next to the front door.

"For someone who lives out of a suitcase, you travel light."

"I don't need much."

He wondered whether the male he'd seen sitting on a bench across from the house was there to keep an eye on him.

Kian had done his best to make it seem as if he didn't consider him a threat, but Orion saw right through the act. The guy was right to be cautious, though. Orion meant none of them harm, but despite Edna's stamp of approval, Kian still didn't know him well enough to be sure of that.

The fact remained that he was a compeller, and apparently, it was a rare power that even immortals feared. That was why they'd been wearing specialty earpieces when they'd apprehended him. Kian hadn't, but his guards had, and Orion was willing to bet that the one sitting on the bench had them too.

"Do you want to shower and take a nap before dinner?" Geraldine asked. "If you need your clothes ironed, I can do that for you."

He wrapped an arm around her shoulders and kissed the top of her head. "I know how to use an iron. I've been a bachelor for most of my life."

She lifted a pair of sad eyes to him. "I remember what you told me about the woman you loved. Are you still mourning her?"

"I will never stop mourning her. Miriam was the love of my life."

"How long ago did she die?"

"Four hundred fifty-six years, two months, and three days ago." He walked back into the house through the sliding doors.

"That's a long time to mourn," Cassandra said. "This village is full of lovely immortal females who will be all over you once they hear that there is a new immortal bachelor in the village who is not Annani's descendant. Perhaps you should give them a chance."

Orion snorted. "Don't mind if I do. Vowing never to love again doesn't mean that I've abstained for all these years."

"Good. For a moment there, I thought that you had, and wouldn't that have been a great loss to females everywhere."

"I doubt that." He sat on the couch, taking Geraldine with him. "I'm not much of a catch."

He was old, and most people tried his patience. His encounters with women were purely physical, and he never spent the night with them.

The only one he'd ever woken up next to had been Miriam, the woman he'd been married to for thirty-three years, the woman who had known his secret but had taken it to her grave. She'd loved him with everything she had, and he'd loved her back just as much.

A love like that came once in a lifetime if one was lucky. There was no chance he could ever find someone to love like that again.

"Come on, Mom. Orion had a very tiring day. We should let him rest."

Geraldine rose to her feet. "We need to go grocery shopping. I opened the fridge, and there was nothing but beer and sodas in there."

That piqued Orion's interest. "There is beer?"

Cassandra grimaced. "It's probably Snake Venom. It's potent, which is why the clan males love it, but it tastes vile. I wonder who put it there."

"I bet it was Anandur," Geraldine said. "That's a sign that he likes you."

"I've heard of Snake Venom." Orion opened the fridge and pulled a bottle out. "Since you say that it tastes terrible,

I won't offer you a beer, but would you like some sparkling water?"

"I'm good." Cassandra walked into the pantry. "There are two boxes of crackers and two kinds of cereal in here. Do you want some crackers with your beer?"

"Why not." He popped the cap off and took a careful sip. "That certainly packs a punch."

"Men." Cassandra opened the box of crackers. "Don't tell me that you actually like it."

"It's not bad." He took another sip.

After the day he'd had, whiskey would have been better, but beggars can't be choosers, and this high-alcohol-content beer hit the spot.

Geraldine put a hand on his bicep. "Are you going to be okay here by yourself until Cassandra and I return with the groceries?" She fiddled with her necklace. "I also need to stop by the house and get a change of clothes. I can't go dressed like this to dinner with Annani."

He looked her over and saw nothing wrong with the outfit she had on. Geraldine had always been a smart dresser, even when finances had been tight and she'd made her own clothes. He would have gladly covered all of her expenses, but he couldn't have done that without leaving clues. The only safe way to help her had been anonymously buying her quilts.

"You look beautiful as always, but if you want to go home and change, don't hesitate because of me. I'm used to being alone." He turned toward the living room window and looked at the walkway, where the man still sat on the bench and pretended to watch something on his phone. "Besides, I have this guy to keep me company. If I get bored while waiting for your return, I'll join him on the bench and strike up a conversation." He smiled at Cassandra. "Maybe I'll ask him about the village's single ladies."

18

ALENA

As Okidu pulled the limo into its parking spot, Kian opened the back door for Annani and offered her a hand up.

"Good evening, Mother. How was your flight?"

"I took a nice nap." She kissed his cheek. "I was hoping for a vision of Toven, but evidently, I only get visions of my children."

Alena stifled an eye roll and took Kian's offered hand. "Good to see you, Kian." She kissed his other cheek. "How is our newest guest doing?"

Despite the butterflies flapping around in her stomach, she'd somehow managed a bored tone. If she didn't get a hold of herself and that schoolgirl crush she'd developed over a sketched portrait, she was going to embarrass herself.

It was difficult to hide attraction from immortals, but Alena was old and experienced, and she knew how to handle herself. She would do just fine, and no one would be any the wiser.

"After I brought him to the village, Geraldine and Cassandra stayed with him for most of the time, only taking a couple of hours off to get groceries. After they left, he took a long nap, showered, shaved, and got ready for dinner."

"How do you know all that?" Annani asked.

"I posted a Guardian in front of his house."

Annani leveled Kian with a hard look. "How would a Guardian who is outside the house know that Orion shaved? Did you put surveillance cameras inside to spy on him?"

"I did, but not in the bathroom. He must have heard the electric shaver. There is one in the living room, and the feed from it goes into the server for safekeeping. Unless he gives us a reason to suspect something, no one is going to watch it."

As Okidu, Ovidu, and her mother's three butlers each pulled a suitcase out of the trunk, Kian arched a brow. "Did you bring your entire wardrobe along?"

"We are going to stay for at least a month." Alena fell in step with him. "And you know Mother—she needs a different gown for every day."

Annani huffed. "My silk gowns do not take much space, and they do not weigh much either. Alena and I visited a baby store in Anchorage, and there were so many beautiful outfits for babies and toddlers and such marvelous toys that we ended up buying half the store. We have a lot of presents for all the little ones."

"Not just for the little ones," Alena said. "We got something for everyone. After all, we will be staying for the holidays."

Kian held the elevator door open for them. "Don't tell me that you got gifts for every clan member."

"I wish I could." Annani glanced at the Odus, who were staying outside to wait for the next elevator to arrive. "Alena and I would have needed many more suitcases."

The clan didn't celebrate during the various human

holidays, but since the newly transitioned immortals missed the end-of-year festivities they had been so fond of as humans, Annani had decided to start a new gift-giving tradition during the holiday season. Alena was still trying to figure out how to add more celebratory flair to it, a symbol like the Christmas tree or the menorah could have been helpful—something people could gather around.

So far, the new custom hadn't taken root, and only a few clan members exchanged gifts during the holidays, but if she came up with a party theme, perhaps more would join. It was a nice tradition.

As the elevator door opened and they entered the pavilion, looking at Kalugal's display of artifacts gave her an idea. Perhaps she should research Sumerian mythology and find a symbol her people would be comfortable with. Nothing came to mind readily, but it had been many years since she'd read the Sumerian legends.

The clan's large golf cart that was parked outside the pavilion doors was the size of a limo and could seat eight, or in their case, the three of them, the four Odus, and all of the luggage.

As Kian helped Annani up, Alena walked around to the other side and climbed in. They waited for the Odus to load the luggage and get in as well, and then they were off with Okidu driving the thing.

"Which home are we getting this time?" Alena asked.

"Shai's. I convinced him to get a new house for him and Geraldine in the newer part of the village, right next to the house Onegus and Cassandra are getting. Shai's roommate is moving in with Onegus's."

"Is it going to be ready on time?" Annani asked. "You did not know that we were coming until this morning, and then you were busy interrogating Orion."

"I owe Ingrid a big bonus for what I put her through. I gave her four hours to get Shai and his roommate's things moved to their new homes, and the house scrubbed clean and prepared for you and Alena. She mobilized several Guardians to help her with the task and was done in three."

"The woman is a miracle worker," Alena said. "She deserves a promotion."

"She's already got it. I let her use one of the houses in phase two as her headquarters, and I authorized her to hire five full-time employees to tackle the new homes in the last building phase. She's strutting like a peacock through the village, telling everyone about her new design center."

"I want to see it," Annani said. "Put it on my calendar, Alena."

She pulled out her phone. "You have Wednesday early afternoon open. Is two o'clock okay?"

Annani nodded. "Coordinate it with Ingrid."

"Of course." Alena added a reminder to call the designer later and put her phone away. "Before I forget, did you bring me the earpieces I asked for?"

"Yes." Kian reached into his pocket and handed her a clear box. "These are William's newest edition, and they are much better than the previous versions. They are smaller, so they are less obvious, and the AI filters the voices and slightly alters their frequencies in real time instead of translating them into machine voices. Before, everyone sounded the same, and it was disorienting and uncomfortable. With these, you will still recognize the voices and who they belong to, but they will sound a little different."

"Wonderful." She put them in her skirt pocket. "Will you be wearing a pair?"

Kian shook his head. "Anandur and Brundar will, and Okidu and Onidu will be there as well. That should be enough. Even if Orion had nefarious intentions, which Edna assured me that he doesn't, he wouldn't dare to use compulsion on you or anyone else during dinner. You really don't need the earpieces, but it's up to you."

She patted her pocket. "I'll use them. At least until we know for sure that he can be trusted."

"Fair enough."

Their mother didn't look happy about it, but she refrained from saying anything. They'd had that discussion before.

When Kian's phone pinged with a message, he pulled it out and read it. "Syssi says that Kalugal and Jacki are already there. And the brothers arrived with their mates even before I left to greet you."

Alena checked the time on her phone. "It's not eight yet." They still had eighteen minutes, and her family was not known to be punctual.

"Kalugal probably thought that he could share a cigar with me before dinner." Kian smiled. "I wonder if Orion likes cigars."

"You should ask him," Annani said. "Perhaps you could bond with him over whiskey and cigars as you did with Kalugal and Dalhu."

His lips twisted in a grimace. "I wouldn't call it bonding. Kalugal is just pleasant company, and so is Dalhu when he actually speaks. Orion seems to be a decent fellow, and he certainly knows how to tell a story. He's quite likable."

As soon as Kian had brought up Orion again, Alena's heart rate accelerated.

In mere minutes, she was about to come face to face with her silly crush, and it would take all of her self-control to hide her infatuation.

Kian frowned. "Are you cold, Alena? Your cheeks are red."

Mortified, she lifted her hands to her heated face. "I must be. My coat is in the suitcase. It's usually so warm here, even during the winter, that I thought I wouldn't need it, but it's colder than usual."

Annani cast her a curious glance. "The cold has never bothered you before."

Reminded of the theme song from *Frozen*, Alena was overcome by an urge to sing it. When the movie had first come out, she'd sung it over and over again, but never in public.

At first, she just hummed the melody, but as the song seemed to rise from inside her, demanding to be heard, Alena ignored her mother and brother's amused expressions and started singing loud enough for the entire village to hear. "Let it go, let it go, can't hold it back anymore—"

19

ORION

When a knock sounded on the door and Orion opened up, he wasn't surprised to see the guy who'd been sitting all day on the bench in front of the house.

"Good evening. I'm Mason, and I'm here to escort you to Kian's house." The guy extended his hand and smiled.

"Orion." He shook what was offered.

Mason had chin-length hair, which would never have been allowed in the human army or police force, but apparently these immortals were not sticklers for the rules. Besides, Mason had probably been chosen for the job because of his long hair. It served to obscure the special earpieces that nullified Orion's compulsion ability.

Evidently, Kian didn't want him to feel like he wasn't trusted but still considered him a threat.

What about thralling, though? It didn't require speech to be effective. It worked telepathically, so earpieces were useless against it. If he could thrall Geraldine, which he had done in the past, he most likely could thrall Mason as well.

Did Kian know that?

Since the Clan Mother had seen Geraldine's memories, they should have known that Orion could thrall immortals.

It was an inexcusable oversight, which made him wonder about the quality of the rest of the clan's security measures. Perhaps they weren't as thorough as Kian liked to think they were.

"Are you assigned to guard me?" he asked the guy.

Mason nodded. "I'm assigned to assist you in any way you require."

It was a nice way to put it. "But you're a guard, right?"

"Guardian."

"Like a Guardian angel?"

Mason chuckled. "I would like to think that I am, and sometimes the trafficking victims we rescue call us that." His eyes clouded with sadness. "When they are not too traumatized and don't think that every male is a monster." He loosed a breath. "Anyway, members of the clan's security force are called Guardians."

"I would like to hear more about those rescues. Would you like to come in?"

The Guardian lifted his phone and glanced at the screen. "Perhaps some other time. It's twenty minutes to eight, which gives us just enough time to get you to Kian's house in time for dinner without rushing."

"Then let's go." Orion stepped out and closed the door behind him. "Is it okay to leave it unlocked? I don't have a key."

"No one locks their doors in the village. There is no need."

Orion arched a brow. "Is everyone perfectly behaved?"

"I wouldn't say that, but no one enters someone else's house without permission or takes something that doesn't belong to them."

"So what's considered misbehavior?"

"Gossip is a big issue in a small community like ours, and since most of us are related, everyone thinks that they have the right to butt into everyone else's business."

The guy didn't realize how lucky he was to have a big family that gave a shit about him.

"That's not so bad." Orion cast the Guardian a sidelong glance. "Other than dealing with pesky relatives, do you like living here?"

The guy turned puzzled eyes on him. "What's not to like? Other than the damn gossip, the place is perfect."

"It looks new. Where did the clan live before?"

"The Guardians and some of the civilians lived in the keep, and the rest were scattered throughout. When the Doomers murdered one of ours who lived alone in San Francisco, Kian ordered everyone to move into the keep, but people weren't happy living in a concrete and glass tower, so he started the village project."

"Who and what are the Doomers?"

"That's a long story."

Orion lifted his hand and looked at his watch. "We have fifteen minutes."

"I guess that's enough. You are Toven's son, right?"

"Yes."

"The Doomers are the followers of his brother's son Navuh, who in some ways is worse than his father. He's not as powerful, but he's smarter and not as impulsive. He's the master of long-term planning."

"I thought that no one other than Toven and the two goddesses survived."

"Some of the immortals survived as well. Those who were in Mortdh's stronghold in the north escaped the nuclear wind, or so we think, about the wind, I mean. No one knows for sure what actually destroyed the southern region. It might have been a hydrogen bomb or something else completely."

Orion was about to ask about the bombing when he heard soft singing that quickly grew louder. The woman's voice was beautiful, powerful, defiant, sexy. It wasn't what most men would consider a siren's song, but it was to him.

He needed to find out who the woman behind the voice was.

"Who's the singer?" he asked Mason.

The guy chuckled. "I know only one female who can sing like that, but I haven't heard her sing in a very long time."

"Who is she?"

"Alena, Kian's elder sister. Most of the time, she's such a quiet, soft-spoken female—motherly, sweet, and gentle as can be. Until she starts singing." He cast Orion an amused glance. "We used to tease her that she could topple the walls of Jericho if they were still standing. Maybe that's why she stopped."

"That's a shame. She has an amazing voice." Orion stopped talking and listened.

The melody sounded familiar. He'd heard it before, but he'd never paid attention to the lyrics. This time he did because it was impossible not to when sung with so much emotion and with so much conviction.

It was about fear and isolation, about being tired of acting good while a storm was raging inside her, about refusing to bow to expectations, about letting go.

"She sounds frustrated," he murmured.

"Nah." Mason waved a hand in dismissal. "It's just a catchy song. The funny thing is that Alena kind of looks like Elsa. She's also blond and wears her hair in a thick braid." He chuckled. "And Alena also lives where it always snows."

"Who's Elsa?"

The Guardian stopped and turned to look at him with

amused disbelief dancing in his eyes. "Have you been living under a rock? Who doesn't know who Princess Elsa is?"

"A princess?"

"Yeah, not just any princess, a Disney princess or rather queen." Mason frowned as if it was an important distinction. "I think Elsa was a queen, not a princess."

"Oh." Orion finally got the reference. "She's a character from a Disney movie. I don't have children, so I don't watch those kinds of movies."

"They are not just for children." Mason resumed walking. "They are fun to watch at any age."

"I'll take your word for it."

20

ALENA

The song ended just as Okidu parked the cart in front of the house.

Kian clapped. "That was one hell of a performance. I haven't heard you sing in ages."

Alena shrugged. "My voice is not very good. It's just loud." Compared to her mother's voice, hers was like a trombone to a harp—loud and limited in range. "I use singing to relieve tension, and I usually do that in the shower in the sanctuary, where no one can hear me. I don't know what possessed me to bellow it over the entire village."

"You have an amazing voice." Kian helped Annani down. "You're just as good if not better than the original singer of that song."

She got down and followed them up the front steps. "That's nice of you to say, but it's not true."

Syssi threw open the door. "Alena, was that you singing?"

"Guilty. Mother said something about the cold never bothering me before, and that triggered the damn song.

When the movie first came out, I couldn't stop singing it. It's an earworm."

Syssi grinned. "I didn't realize it before, but that song could be about you. The snow princess who craves freedom and adventure."

That was why she'd been singing it so obsessively until she'd forced herself to stop. "It's just a song."

Annani embraced Syssi. "Alena doesn't think that her voice is good, and when I say that it is lovely, she tells me that I am hearing it with mother's ears. Perhaps if more people complimented her on it, she would sing more."

When they entered the living room, which had been transformed into a big dining room, Amanda, Jacki, and Kalugal gushed over her singing as well, and Alena wanted to hide somewhere until everyone forgot about it.

Thankfully, Dalhu didn't say a thing, but he smiled at her and nodded as if to say that he agreed with the others.

"Where did the living room furniture go?" she asked to change the subject.

"It's out on the back patio." Syssi walked over to the sliding doors and flicked the backyard lights on. "I just hope it doesn't rain. The patio is covered, but it's windy, and the wind will blow the rain inside."

"Let's cross our fingers that it doesn't." Alena pulled out a chair next to Dalhu, the only one who seemed safe not to start talking about her singing again.

"Anything new and exciting happen during the month we were gone?"

Amanda patted her very pregnant belly. "I grew to mammoth proportions. I have six weeks to go, but I think this girl is not going to wait. She's ready to come out."

"All in good time." Their mother put a hand on Amanda's belly.

"I'm finally showing." Jacki patted her small bump. "But I'm still good to go."

"Go where?" Syssi asked.

"To visit the Mosuo. Kalugal was busy and kept postponing it, but I convinced him that it had to be done now or not at all. I'm not traveling when I'm Amanda's size or after the baby is born."

Alena leaned over the table. "Do you know whether you're having a boy or a girl?"

Jacki nodded. "We are having a boy."

Next to her, Kalugal puffed out his chest and grinned. "Allegra and Amanda's daughters need a couple of boys to chase after them."

Kian growled, probably because he didn't want any boys chasing after his precious Allegra, but Syssi smiled. "Hopefully, another couple will conceive soon, and we will have another boy."

Annani lifted a brow. "Did you forget about Ethan?"

"Of course I didn't. We need one more boy for Phoenix."

When the doorbell chimed, Alena tensed. Was it Orion? Would she finally get to see him in person?

Holding her breath as Okidu rushed to open the door, she remained seated at the table and listened to him welcome the latest arrivals.

"Good evening, Mistress Geraldine, Master Shai. Good evening, Mistress Cassandra, Master Onegus. Good to see you, Mistress Sylvia, Master Roni."

One after the other, the couples entered the living room, and Alena rose to her feet to greet them. She was embracing Cassandra when the doorbell chimed again, and Okidu opened the door once more.

This time she knew it was Orion, felt it in her bones.

Alena shook her head. She wasn't superstitious, and her senses weren't that good. It was simply statistically probable that it was him.

"Good evening, Master Orion," Okidu said.

Rooted in place and holding her breath, Alena waited for him to emerge from the foyer, and when he did, the impact of his presence was even more powerful than what she'd been prepared for.

He was nearly as tall as Kian, perhaps a half an inch shorter, broad-shouldered but not overly muscled, and his face was just as perfect as Tim's drawing. But the portrait couldn't convey the power in the eyes that scanned the room and landed on her with the intensity of a heat-seeking missile.

21

ORION

She was beautiful, and Orion knew without having to be told that she was the singer he'd heard on the way.

The song might as well have been written about her.

A pale blue dress adorned her tall but very feminine body, and a thick blond braid was draped over an ample breast. Her shoulders were squared, her chin was up, and her stormy blue eyes gazed at him with an intensity that looked more like animosity than the admiration he was used to from females.

As Kian walked up to him, blocking his view of the snow princess, Orion couldn't help the urge to lean sideways so he could keep looking at her. Perhaps if he smiled, she would smile back, instead of looking as if she wanted to trample him under her feet.

"Good evening, Orion." Kian offered him his hand. "Let me introduce you to my mother, the goddess Annani." Following Orion's gaze, he turned to look at the blond beauty and smiled. "This is not Annani. This is my sister Alena."

It took a moment for the meaning of Kian's words to

sink in, and another split second for Orion to tear his eyes from the ice queen and look at her brother.

"I know." He plastered a smile on his face. "The singer with the lovely voice whom I heard on the way."

Behind Kian, Alena uttered a frustrated groan that didn't fit her royal demeanor.

Ignoring his sister, Kian led Orion to the head of the table, where a stunning beauty with a mane of red hair and a knowing smirk on her angelic face regarded him with amusement in her ancient eyes.

He bowed deeply. "It's an honor and a pleasure to make your acquaintance, Clan Mother." That was the title Mason had told him to use, and given her nod of approval, his greeting had been well executed.

"The pleasure is all mine, Orion." With a wave of her hand, she indicated her wish that he sit next to her.

A butler rushed over and pulled out a chair for him.

"Thank you," he told the guy before lowering himself to the seat.

Again, there was approval in her eyes. "Do you prefer Orion, or should I call you Orlando?"

"I go by Orion these days."

She nodded. "It suits you better than Orlando. You can call me Annani." She flashed him a bright smile. "After all, we are family. And speaking of family, let me introduce you to those you have not met yet."

When Orion turned to look at his dinner companions, he realized that Geraldine and Cassandra were there as well, and so was Roni, who he hadn't seen in years. Having been blindsided by the goddess's magnificent daughter, he hadn't noticed them before.

"You already know Kian," the goddess said. "And I do not need to introduce you to Geraldine and Cassandra and their mates, or to Roni, but the lovely lady sitting next to him is his mate, Sylvia."

"Hi." Sylvia smiled. "I'm so excited to meet you."

"So am I," Roni said. "You might know me, but I don't know you. Did we meet before I turned immortal? Have you thralled or compelled me to forget you?"

Orion shook his head. "I've watched over your family from afar."

"So you never thralled or compelled my mother?"

"I did not."

"Let us continue with the introductions," Annani said. "You can discuss family matters with Roni later."

Orion bowed his head. "My apologies, Clan Mother. Please, continue."

She smiled, her eyes sparkling with amusement and mischief that belied her age. "The lovely blond beauty you could not take your eyes off of when you walked in is my eldest daughter Alena."

"Enchanted." He turned to look at her and dipped his head.

She'd chosen the farthest seat from him on the other side of the long table, and he had to crane his neck to look at her above everyone's heads.

"Nice to meet you," she murmured so quietly that he wouldn't have heard her if he were human.

Where was that powerful voice that had carried over the entire village?

The goddess frowned, but then shifted her gaze to a stunning, very pregnant brunette. "This is my youngest daughter, Amanda, and her mate Dalhu."

The guy nodded his hello but didn't smile. Amanda grinned and waved. "We'll talk later. I have so many questions."

It seemed that Amanda was the opposite of Alena—a confident extrovert who didn't take no for an answer.

"And this is Syssi." The goddess took the hand of the

smiling woman sitting next to her son. "My favorite daughter-in-law."

"I'm your only daughter-in-law," Syssi said before turning to him. "Welcome to the clan, Orion."

"Thank you, but I'm not going to stay long. I have a business to run and more siblings to look for." He turned to Kian. "I appreciate your offer to help me search for them."

"The one who can help you the most is Andrew, my brother-in-law. You met him this morning."

"The truth detector."

"That's me." Andrew turned to the brunette sitting next to him. "This is my wife Nathalie, and that's our daughter Phoenix."

The little girl, who apparently had been hiding from him behind her mother's side, peeked her dark-haired head out. "Are you my uncle?"

As he glanced at Andrew for directions, the guy nodded and mouthed, "Just go with it."

"Yes, I am."

"Can you play horsey with me after dinner? Uncle Kian gets tired too fast, and Uncle Anandur says that I'm too big for playing baby games. Uncle Brundar doesn't like to play kids' games at all, and Uncles Shai and Onegus never come to family dinners." She eyed Onegus as if assessing whether he would be a willing victim.

Andrew stroked his daughter's silky dark hair. "Don't pester Orion, Phoenix. He just got here."

She pouted. "Okay. He can be my horsey next time."

"It will be my pleasure." Orion winked at the child.

22

ANNANI

Annani observed Orion's interaction with her family and could not find fault with a single thing.

Toven's son was behaving perfectly. He was polite, well-spoken, charming, and utterly unintimidated by her or Kian.

It rankled a little that he did not regard her with the same awe and reverence as others who had met her for the first time, but then she was not the first god he had met, and according to Kian, Orion's single encounter with Toven had left him unimpressed.

What a shame.

Toven used to be such an upstanding god. He was as brilliant as Ekin and as dedicated as his father to the improvement of human society. What had happened to him?

Perhaps loneliness had driven him mad.

Fates only knew what would have happened to her if not for her seven Odus and the kernel of hope that the soothsayer had planted in her heart.

The Odus had ensured her survival in more ways than just keeping her safe and nourished. They had kept her company when she had not wanted to engage with the primitive northern tribe that had accepted her as their goddess, had helped her build a proper shelter and had kept it warm and clean. But none of that would have sufficed if not for the hope that one day Khiann would return to her in one form or another. Without that hope, her will to live would have winked out.

After five millennia, that hope was nothing more than a dim flicker, but in the past, it had gotten her over the hardest times. Then her children had been born, and then her grandchildren, and their children and grandchildren and so on, filling the empty spaces in her heart with love and joy. Not fully, there would always be a large hole that only Khiann could fill, but enough for her to enjoy living even without her beloved.

Could Orion be Khiann's reincarnation?

Annani cast him another glance. He was very handsome and charming and intelligent, but he did not spark anything in her. She had met human males who had excited her more.

Alena, on the other hand, was completely smitten with Orion and fighting it with everything she had, unable to get over her aversion to compellers long enough to judge the male for everything he was aside from that.

Perhaps he could win her over. It would require patience and understanding that not many males were blessed with, but if Orion was as taken with Alena as she was with him, he would put in the effort.

If not, he probably was not worthy of her.

Closing her eyes momentarily, Annani prayed to the Fates, wishing that Orion and Alena were truelove mates. With all her siblings happily mated, Alena felt left out and wondered whether the Fates did not deem her worthy. It was absurd for her to think that, and it pained Annani that her daughter believed it.

With her thoughts wandering Annani had forgotten that she had not finished introducing her family to Orion, and Kalugal seemed upset, probably thinking that she had overlooked him, or worse, not considered him part of the family.

"My apologies, Kalugal. I should have introduced you first. After all, you and Orion are cousins."

"No need to apologize, Clan Mother." He put on one of his winning smiles. "I can introduce myself." He shifted his eyes to Orion. "I am Kalugal, grandson of Mortdh, your father's brother, and sitting beside me is my better half—my wife, Jacki."

Orion's smile was wide and genuine as he answered, "Well met, cousin Kalugal and the fair Jacki. I feel blessed that my sister and I, as well as my niece and my nephew, have become part of such a big and wonderful family of immortals."

Looking at Annani, he put his hand over his heart. "It has been a difficult and stressful day for me. But now that I know who your people are and understand that they had no choice but to approach me with caution, I'm just grateful to be here. Knowing that my sister and I are not alone in the world has eased something inside of me. So even when I go on my travels, collecting antiques and finding buyers for them, it will no longer feel as if I'm flying solo. I have a people I belong to."

Annani was not the only one who wiped tears from her eyes. Nearly every female at the table did the same thing, with Alena being the most notable exception. She did her best to pretend that Orion was not there.

It was such strange behavior for her. Alena was usually easygoing, mellow, and accommodating.

"Fates willing," Kian said. "We will find more of your siblings." He reached for a bottle of wine and uncorked it. "Let's make a toast."

On the other side of the table, Anandur uncorked another bottle of wine, and together he and Kian poured wine into everyone's glasses.

"To family." Kian lifted his goblet.

"To family." Orion clinked his glass with Kian's.

23

ALENA

Thankfully, once dinner was over Orion had gone outside with Kian and the other guys to smoke, and Alena could finally take a full breath and remove the annoying earpieces. They distorted everyone's voices and had gotten uncomfortable after a while. How did Anandur and Brundar tolerate wearing those things?

"What's gotten into you?" Amanda asked quietly. "You've been on edge the entire evening."

"I don't know what you're talking about." She smiled at her sister. "How is my niece doing in there?" She put her hand on Amanda's belly.

"She's kicking up a storm, but don't change the subject. There is definitely something going on for you to sing your heart out like that." She lowered her voice further. "Is Mother getting on your nerves?"

Alena's eyes darted to Annani, who was busy cooing to Allegra and oblivious to everyone else.

"Not at all," she whispered. "In fact, I'm a little worried about her. She hasn't come up with any risky shenanigans lately."

"Maybe that's the problem." Amanda rubbed slow

circles over her belly. "Without Mother providing excitement, you're bored, and the tedium is getting to you."

There was some truth to Amanda's observation.

Alena winced. "Way to make me sound pathetic. I need my mother to stir things up to make my dull life exciting."

Involuntarily, her gaze shifted to the glass doors and to the men outside, or rather to one man. Perhaps that was why she was fascinated with Orion. He was dangerous, and that made him thrilling—sexy.

It was the bad-boy allure that she hadn't understood before.

Damn, she needed to stop right away. During dinner, she'd masked the scent of her attraction to him by keeping herself angry. Anger was a potent emotion, even stronger than arousal, and the scent it emitted was dominant.

Amanda chuckled. "Oh, I get it now. You've been cruising on neutral for so long that you don't know what to do when someone shakes up that equilibrium. A certain someone who's about six foot three inches tall with lips that are just begging to be kissed, not by me of course, because I'm taken, but they could be all yours."

"Stop it," Alena hissed.

The men were all outside except for Roni, whose ears had perked up the moment Amanda started her teasing about Orion. Syssi was pretending that she didn't hear a thing, and perhaps she didn't since the cappuccino machine was making all those grinding and thumping noises, and Callie and Wonder were busy discussing Callie's plans for opening a gourmet restaurant in the latest section of the village.

Cassandra and Geraldine, however, had heard every word and were eyeing her with curiosity.

"Oh, come on." Amanda tried to cross her arms over her belly, which put them right under her chin, so she gave up and put her hands on the table. "Since when are you so prissy? What's wrong with Orion?"

"He's a compeller."

"He's a good man." Geraldine came to his defense. "And he's been so lonely for so long." She sighed. "He lost the woman he loved and has never recovered from the loss."

"That's so sad," Amanda said.

It shouldn't have pained Alena to hear that Orion had loved someone so dearly and had lost her, but it did. Not because she was jealous or begrudged him the love, but because she wished he hadn't gone through the heartache.

He'd had no one to guide him, no one to tell him to keep his relationships with human women purely physical. She could imagine him as a young man, yearning for the love and connection with another and thinking that he could somehow make it work.

Kian had fallen into the same trap despite their mother's warning, and it had scarred him for life. Perhaps if he hadn't married Lavena at nineteen and then had to leave her a year later pregnant with their daughter, he wouldn't have become so grumpy and cynical.

"Poor guy," Alena murmured.

Roni groaned. "If it's going to be one of those talks, I'd better join the guys outside." He rose to his feet.

"Coward," Sylvia chided him playfully.

Leaning down, he kissed the top of her head. "You can come along."

"I want to hear the story about Orion's great love. You can go."

"I don't remember the details," Geraldine said after Roni closed the sliding door behind him. "Or perhaps Orion didn't tell me more than what I remember." She lifted her hand to her temple and rubbed it. "It was a long time ago. I asked him if he had someone special in his life, and he said that he had once, but after he lost her, he vowed never to love again because it was just too painful. When I asked if she had left him, he said that she had died, and he looked so sad that I didn't want to pry and ask him how it happened. Now that I know he's immortal, I assume that she died from old age."

"That's not likely," Cassandra said. "He couldn't have stayed with her for so long without her discovering who and what he was."

"Don't forget that Orion is a compeller," Alena said. "He could've compelled her to keep quiet about his fangs and everything else that was different about him."

"That's true," Cassandra agreed. "But even if they kept moving, people would have wondered about a young man married to a much older woman."

Alena shrugged. "He could have compelled their neighbors to ignore that as well. A powerful compeller can get away with almost anything."

24

ORION

In Kian's backyard the air was fresh, and the cool night breeze crisp and soothing on Orion's frayed nerves.

He'd done okay, his mask of composure never once faltering under the goddess's intense gaze.

She'd asked him many questions, for which his answers had hopefully been truthful. Orion couldn't remember half the things he'd said because his attention had been split between Annani and Alena, most of it commanded by the goddess's intriguing eldest daughter, who hadn't spared him a single look all throughout dinner.

His eyes had darted to her numerous times, but she hadn't even turned her head in his direction. It had been more than indifference—it had been hostility.

For some reason, Alena did not like him.

Was she a contrary person? Was that why she was the only one of Annani's children who was still single?

Was it by choice?

He'd garnered that she was the goddess's companion, so maybe she didn't wish to settle down with a male. Or perhaps she just hadn't found the right one yet?

He shouldn't be having these thoughts about her. A magnificent female like her deserved much more than he could offer, which was passion and perhaps occasional companionship, but not love. His heart had been buried with Miriam, and he'd vowed never to love again.

Except, a small voice at the back of his head whispered that Miriam wouldn't have wanted him to be alone. She'd actually said it on her deathbed, beseeching him to move on and live his life. He'd promised that he would, and he had. He'd built a profitable business, he traveled all over the world and met interesting people, and he shared his body and his passion with numerous females. Miriam hadn't been specific, so technically he hadn't defied her deathbed wish by avoiding relationships and therefore love.

He had a life, but he hadn't moved on.

Perhaps it was time to fulfill that part of Miriam's wish.

He'd been devastated by pain and grief when he'd made that vow, and he never wanted to experience such devastation again. But Alena wasn't human, and if he allowed himself to love her and she loved him back, they could have eternity together.

Yeah, no.

It hadn't escaped his notice that in addition to the two Guardians, Alena was the only one at the dinner table who was wearing earpieces.

No one else deemed him a threat, not even the goddess, who'd said she was going to test her own power of compulsion on him at some point. Although, after he'd warned her that it wouldn't work because he would obey her every wish regardless of whether it was imbued with compulsion or not, she might choose to forgo the test.

"Orion." Kian motioned to the humidor on the coffee table. "Pick a cigar."

The living room furniture had been moved to the back

patio to make room for the large dining table. The men had spread out, with Kian and Kalugal sharing the couch, Andrew and Dalhu each commandeering an armchair, and Shai, Onegus, and the Guardians making do with outdoor chairs.

Roni had stayed inside, saying that he wasn't a fan of cigars.

"Which one do you recommend?" Orion sat between his cousins.

It wasn't the most comfortable seat, but his other option was a chair next to the Guardians, and that would have sent the wrong message.

"They are all superb," Kian said. "You can't go wrong with any of them."

Orion picked a short one that was aptly named Short Story by Arturo Fuente. "I'm not much of an expert. The last cigar I smoked must have been twenty years ago."

"Then you should take it easy," Kalugal advised. "You might get lightheaded."

As the patio doors opened and his grand-nephew stepped out, Orion took a quick glance inside, his eyes searching for a long blond braid. He saw her sitting between her sister and Geraldine, her pale cheeks slightly flushed as if she was embarrassed about something. The faint splash of color made Alena look young and innocent, but he knew both to be untrue. As the goddess's eldest daughter, she might be twice as old as he was, and he doubted she'd retained any innocence after living that long.

"Did they kick you out?" Anandur asked Roni.

"Nah. They started talking about mushy stuff that made me uncomfortable." He sat next to the Guardian. "Sylvia says that I'm on the spectrum because I can't handle emotions, but that's not true. I love her. Isn't that enough?"

Anandur clapped him on the back. "Your brain is

mostly made of code and numbers. There isn't much left to process anything else."

"True," Roni admitted. "If all people have about the same number of neurons and synapses, then when most of them are taken by something a person is passionate about, other areas suffer."

"You should ask Amanda." Andrew crossed his arms over his chest. "Maybe each person has a different number of brain cells and connections between them. After all, some people are smarter than others, right?"

Orion wondered if the same was true for various paranormal talents. Did his ability to compel rob him of intelligence or some other ability he might have possessed? And why should Roni ask Amanda? Was she an expert on the subject?

"Amanda is a neuroscientist," Kalugal said. "She researches paranormal abilities."

"Did I ask that out loud?"

"No, but you were frowning, so I assumed you were wondering about that." Kalugal smiled condescendingly. "How old are you, Orion?"

"Over five hundred years old. Why?"

"If Andrew told Roni to ask William about neurons and synapses, what would you have thought?"

Orion guessed where Kalugal was going with that question, and he didn't like that the guy was making assumptions about him. "Who is William?" He pretended not to catch Kalugal's drift.

"It doesn't matter. He's a male."

"So what?"

"You would have assumed that William knew something about the brain that others didn't, but you wouldn't have assumed that about a beautiful woman like Amanda."

"Is that so?" Orion arched a brow. "Are you a mind reader?"

"No, I'm a compeller like you." Kalugal grinned. "I wonder, though, which of us is more powerful."

25

KIAN

Kalugal and Orion were about to engage in a pissing contest, and Kian wasn't going to do anything to stop it because he wanted to find out who was more powerful as well.

"I didn't know that you were a compeller." Orion turned to look at Kalugal. "Kian only told me that you're an archeologist."

"That's just a hobby of mine. My business endeavors are varied, and I was born with the ability to compel, which has proved very useful over the years."

"Yeah," Kian grumbled. "To get insider information and make a fortune on the stock market."

"It also saved my life," Kalugal countered. "It allowed me to escape my father."

His father was Mortdh's son, and therefore Orion's first cousin. Or was it second because Mortdh and Toven shared only a father and had different mothers?

"Excuse me." Orion pushed to his feet. "The smoke from your cigars and my own is too much for me."

The guy had probably been uncomfortable sitting

between them and turning his back to one in order to look at the other.

Lifting one of the outdoor chairs, Orion brought it over and set it down next to Dalhu's armchair.

"I'm getting bits and pieces of information, and it's all becoming a soup in my head. I need someone to explain things to me in order. Who are the main players of the immortal world? Who were the gods? What did they do before Mortdh killed them?"

"That's a lot of information to cover in a short time." Kian took a puff of his cigar. "What do you want to know first?"

"Let's start with compulsion. Can't all immortals do that to some extent? Can they compel humans? I know that Geraldine didn't have the ability even before the accident, but I assumed it didn't manifest because she'd never needed it."

"All immortal males can thrall," Onegus said. "The females can as well, but since they have less need for it, not many bother to learn how. Compulsion is a rarer ability, and even more so the ability to compel other immortals. That's why Brundar and Anandur are still wearing earpieces. We would like to think of you as family, but trust takes time to build."

"What about Kalugal? Do you wear earpieces around him too?"

Kalugal chuckled. "They were much more careful with me when we first met, and they didn't trust me until the Clan Mother compelled me to do no harm to her clan members. For some reason, you've gotten the red-carpet welcome."

Kian arched a brow. "Some reason? You are Navuh's son. He's not. That's why."

Kalugal hitched his brow even higher. "You've just met

him this morning, and you don't know a thing about him. He could be an ax murderer."

Andrew's shoulders started shaking, and then a laugh bubbled out of him. "I don't know why everyone is afraid of ax murderers as if any others are less deadly. Dead is dead."

"The conversation has just turned too morbid for my taste." Roni rose to his feet and walked over to the bottle of whiskey Kian had left on the dining table. "If you don't mind, I'll pour myself a glass."

"You can go back inside," Shai suggested. "I'm sure the ladies are not talking about anything gruesome or morbid."

"No, thank you. I want to find out who is the stronger compeller."

"So do I," Kian said. "Let's test it." He leveled his eyes at Orion. "After that, I'll tell you everything you want to know." He lifted his cigar. "Or at least as much as I can squeeze in as long as my cigar lasts."

"Then let's make it quick." Orion turned to Kalugal. "Give me your wallet."

The order had been directed at Kalugal, but Kian found himself reaching into his pocket, and he saw Roni do the same.

"No." Kalugal grinned at Orion. "I'm immune to your compulsion. Let's reverse the roles, shall we?"

"Do your worst," Orion challenged.

Kalugal took a puff of his cigar, pretending to consider that. "Since you are not a clan member yet, I'm not bound by Annani's compulsion to do you no harm. Are you sure that you want me to do my worst?"

"It was a figure of speech." Orion took a look around the backyard. "Thankfully, you can't tell me to jump off a cliff because there are none."

"Actually, there is one, just not in Kian's backyard. But I would never do that." Kalugal smiled evilly. "What I want you to do, Orion aka Orlando, is to stand on one foot and quack like a chicken."

Orion grinned. "It's quack like a duck, but I'll do neither. I'm immune to your compulsion as well."

Kalugal didn't look happy. "That only proves that we are immune to each other's compulsion. It doesn't prove who is stronger."

"Does it matter?" Orion asked. "I hardly ever use my ability, and only when it's either necessary or deserved."

"Same here." Kalugal tapped on his cigar to dislodge the ash. "My interest is more general, and it has to do with my father's legions of warriors. He has them all under his compulsion, and I admit that I'm not nearly as powerful as he is, so I can't wrestle control over them from him. I wondered whether you could."

Kalugal had never shown any interest in the island or taking down Navuh. Had it all been a lie?

"What sparked this sudden interest?" Kian asked. "You said over and over again that the island is of no interest to you."

"My only interest in the island has to do with my mother, but she does not wish to be freed. At this point, it's a purely hypothetical end-of-days kind of scenario. If anything happens to Navuh, for whatever reason, the outcome would be disastrous. Without his control, his warriors would spread out like a plague over humanity. I'm not powerful enough to contain them all, but perhaps Orion is."

26

ORION

"How many warriors are we talking about?"

"Twenty-some thousand," Kalugal said. "My father has them recite devotions several times a day, which is how he reinforces the compulsion."

"I don't think I can compel so many at once, nor do I want to. Politics was never something I wished to get involved in."

"It's more than politics," Kian said. "But I doubt you are powerful enough. Power grows with age, and Navuh is even older than Annani. Not by much, but he obviously inherited his father's ability, which was formidable."

"He's also smart," commented Amanda's mate. "And careful. Anyone who thinks that they can take that island from him is fooling himself."

Given Kian's somber expression, he shared Dalhu's opinion.

"What about the goddess?" Orion asked. "If she's powerful enough to compel Kalugal to behave, then she should be able to control those warriors."

"I will never risk it," Kian said. "I don't want her

anywhere near that vile island or Navuh. He has her sister. That's bad enough."

Orion cast a sidelong glance at Kalugal. "Is your mother under your father's compulsion? Is that why she doesn't want to be freed?"

"It's complicated." Kalugal puffed on his cigar. "She claims that he doesn't compel her. She's convinced that they are truelove mates, and that without her, he would become an even worse monster than he is now. It might be true, or it might be all in her head."

"Perhaps things have changed since you escaped."

"We found a way to keep in touch with her," Kian said. "My mother talks with her twice a week, and Areana hasn't changed her mind about Navuh. From what the other compellers we have report, you can't compel someone to love you or feel any other emotion toward you. You can only compel her to stay with you. Is that your experience as well?"

So, they had other compellers in addition to Kalugal, just not as powerful.

"I've never tried to compel anyone to love me. The only woman I've ever loved didn't need to be compelled, and after she died, I did my best to prevent anyone from falling in love with me again."

"I'm sorry." There was genuine compassion in Kian's eyes.

Orion nodded. "So am I. But it is what it is. My love couldn't prolong her human life."

Even after over four centuries it still hurt to think of her, but now was not the time to show weakness, and Kian's cigar was one-third shorter than it had been when he'd made the bargain with him. "I fulfilled my part, and now it's your turn. I need a comprehensive overview of the immortal landscape —history, politics, ongoing conflicts, and future prospects. I need to familiarize myself with this new world I find myself in." He leaned down and reached for Kian's lighter. "Do you think you can fit all that in before your cigar is done?"

Kian examined his Fuentes whatever-the-name-was and smiled. "It has an hour left in it, and I will be done long before that."

Andrew pushed to his feet. "I'll leave you to it. Phoenix is making faces at me through the sliding door."

They all turned to look, Orion included, and everyone smiled at the little girl standing on the other side of the glass with her tiny hands pressed to the door and making funny faces at her daddy.

Lucky guy.

Orion kept watching as Andrew opened the door, flung his daughter into his arms, and started kissing her cheeks. Giggling, she cupped his face and kissed him back. The happiness on her face was heartwarming.

"Adorable child." Orion turned back to Kian. "I still remember Cassandra at that age. She was always such a serious girl. I guess having a mother who needed constant help wasn't easy. I wish I could have hired a nanny for her."

"Why didn't you?" Shai asked. "You could have taken them both with you and compelled them not to say anything about your special abilities. In fact, they didn't even have to know that you were immortal. Don't get me wrong, I'm glad that you didn't, but I'm just curious."

"Cassandra was human, and I didn't know that she could one day turn immortal. I wanted her to have a normal life, which she wouldn't have had with me. I traveled a lot, for my business and in search of my other possible siblings." He took a tentative puff on his cigar. "I still don't understand how the bite can induce a Dormant into immortality and where and how to find Dormants."

27

KIAN

"You wanted a comprehensive overview, so I'll start at the beginning, but I'll try to squeeze as much as I can into the time we have." Kian tapped his cigar over the ashtray.

"The gods were a small group of either refugees or exiles from a different place in the universe. We don't know where they came from or why. For a while, I entertained the idea that they might have been a divergent species of humans, survivors of a different epoch, perhaps pre-diluvial. But Kalugal and his brother Lokan gleaned some more information from Navuh, who'd learned it from his father, which made that theory obsolete. Now, the leading theory is that the gods were genetically enhanced humanoids, and that humanity was actually created by them as a race of servants."

"That explains why humans are so easily led by the nose," Roni said. "They were engineered to follow and not ask too many questions."

Kian grimaced. "You sound like Navuh."

"Did he say that?"

Kalugal nodded. "Same exact words."

Roni shrugged. "We know that he's not stupid."

Orion frowned. "Doesn't Annani know where her people came from?"

"Her parents didn't tell her," Kian said. "The younger generation of gods were kept in the dark, so to speak, because the original settlers didn't want their children to know about their bloody history. They tried to create a utopia for the gods and for the humans they were in charge of, establishing just laws and practicing an assembly-style democratic rule combined with a kind of monarchy. The position of head god was hereditary, but the ruler couldn't make any major decisions without getting approval from the gods' council. Some decisions could be passed by a simple majority, while others required a unanimous vote."

Orion nodded. "Toven told me that his brother was sentenced to entombment by the council of gods for murdering another god. To avoid the sentencing, he attacked the assembly and killed them all, perishing alongside them."

"That's correct. A decision that grave required a unanimous vote, which was why all the gods attended the assembly and could be destroyed in one fell swoop. It also meant that Toven voted to entomb his brother for the crime of murdering my mother's truelove mate—her husband, Khiann."

Orion's eyes widened. "Toven didn't tell me that." He frowned. "But you are not a god, so Khiann wasn't your father."

"He was murdered mere months after they were mated. There wasn't enough time for my mother to conceive." Kian took another puff of his cigar. "But I'm getting ahead of the story. Mortdh was a powerful god, and he didn't want to answer to Ahn, the ruling god and my mother's father. He built a stronghold in the northern part of the region and amassed power. Hoping to keep Mortdh from starting a war, Ahn promised him Annani's hand in marriage. Once Ahn stepped down, his daughter would have become the next leader, and as her mate, so would Mortdh. Ahn believed that would assuage Mortdh's aspirations for rulership in the interim."

"Was he wrong?" Orion asked.

"Annani believed so. She was convinced that once they became the ruling couple, Mortdh would get rid of her. He wouldn't have been satisfied to rule at her side. He wanted to rule supreme. My mother is a very smart lady, so I believe that her assessment of Mortdh was correct. She's also cunning. She could have invoked her right to choose a mate and break off the engagement that way, but she knew that would offend Mortdh's honor and would result in a war. If she found a truelove mate, though, war could be averted. Or so she hoped."

When Orion frowned again, Kian lifted his hand. "To refuse the gift of a truelove mate was to offend the Fates, and no one, including Mortdh, could officially go against the Fates' decree. He would have lost popular support, and since he was a savvy politician, she hoped that would stay his hand."

"Good plan," Orion said. "But isn't finding a truelove mate a difficult thing to do?"

"It is," Kian agreed. "Khiann was a childhood crush of Annani's, and she decided that he was the one. She pursued him and convinced him to ask for her hand."

"Your mother is beautiful. She probably didn't have to work hard to convince him."

Kian smiled. "Her beauty aside, when my mother decides on something, no one and nothing can stand in her way."

Orion shook his head. "Let me guess. Mortdh was offended anyway and murdered Khiann."

"Mortdh felt humiliated, but more than that, he was furious about losing his shot at the throne. He tried to murder Khiann covertly, but the men who accompanied him on his murderous mission betrayed him and testified before the gods' council, sealing his fate. My mother sat in the assembly until the sentencing was passed. But while the gods debated how to bring Mortdh to justice, news arrived of him preparing forces to march against them, and Annani realized that she was in grave danger. If he attacked and won, he would make her life a living hell to punish her for humiliating him. So, she snuck out, loaded her servants and a few belongings on her flying machine, and escaped."

"My father said that he'd gotten bored with the endless discussions, and he snuck out as well. I wonder if he noticed that Annani had done that first."

"He might have thought that she was too upset to attend. She told me that she'd cried a river during the proceedings."

"What about her sister?" Orion asked. "Kalugal's mother?"

"When Annani broke off the engagement, Ahn offered Mortdh his other daughter, Areana. Reluctantly, Mortdh accepted the offer, but Areana wasn't the one he wanted. She was Ahn's daughter with a concubine, not his official wife, so she was not in line to rule even though she was older than Annani, and she was a widow."

"Did Annani have any other siblings?"

"No. Which meant that if anything happened to Annani, Areana could become the next ruler of the gods. That was the consolation prize that Ahn dangled in front of Mortdh."

"If Annani had the right to choose her mate, I assume that Areana had that right as well. Why did she agree to marry Mortdh?"

"Because she wanted to please her father," Kalugal said. "He never thought much of her, and when he summoned her and asked her to take Annani's place, she agreed, hoping he would finally appreciate her." He grimaced. "Mortdh was insane, but Ahn was an asshole. He treated my mother badly, barely deigning to acknowledge her as his daughter because she was a weak goddess."

"How did Areana end up mating Mortdh's son, though?" Orion asked.

"Turns out that Navuh had a crush on my mother, which she hadn't been aware of," Kalugal said. "My father wasn't a god, so she never considered him as a contender even though he was Mortdh's official heir and the most powerful immortal in existence. Besides, she mourned her first husband many decades after his passing and turned down full-blooded gods, so he never dared to approach her. She agreed to wed Mortdh out of duty and considered it a sacrifice for her people. Mortdh left Navuh to escort Areana to his stronghold in the north, but when she asked to stay a little longer to attend Annani's wedding, Navuh agreed. After the wedding, she left with an escort of Ahn's men, but Navuh intercepted her on the way, one thing led to another, and they became involved. When news of Mortdh's demise along with the other gods reached the north, Navuh took Areana as his mate and hid her from the world, claiming that he was protecting her from his immortal warriors. He told her that they were overcome with grief and rage and would want to take it out on the last remaining goddess. Most of them had families in the south."

"Why would they be angry at her?" Orion asked. "None of it was her fault."

Kalugal shrugged. "Navuh probably made it up. As Mortdh's only son, he inherited his father's stronghold, which already had several thousands of immortal warriors, and as the most powerful immortal, his rule was uncontested. But Areana was a full-blooded goddess, and even though she was less powerful than him, she outranked him. He didn't want anyone to know that he had a goddess in his harem. Navuh kept his father's immortal concubines in there for show, but he never graced their beds. He has remained loyal to my mother, which is proof that they are indeed truelove mates."

"Annani wasn't even sure that her sister had survived," Kian said. "She lived with terrible guilt for thousands of years, thinking that if Areana made it to the north, she was suffering endlessly at Navuh's hands. We've discovered only recently that Areana has been living like a pampered queen in the lap of luxury, but that's a story for another time."

"It's a good story, though." Kalugal smiled. "Remind me to tell it to you some time."

28

ORION

"What are you doing tomorrow?" Orion asked.

"In the morning, I'm in the office." Kalugal stubbed out his cigar. "But I would love for you to come visit Jacki and me in our home in the evening." He turned to Kian. "How about the entire family comes over to dinner at my place? You haven't seen it yet."

"You keep saying that it's not ready. I was waiting for an invitation to a house-warming party."

"Where do you live?" Orion asked. "I'm not sure I'm free to come and go as I please yet."

"I live right here in the village. My men and I have our own section, which we just recently moved into. I'm still waiting for some artwork and furniture to arrive, but Jacki is pestering me to invite everyone over even though some pieces are still missing."

Orion shook his head. "Your story and how you ended up with Annani's clan is another missing puzzle piece, but you can tell me all about it tomorrow. I think Kian skipped over the part of how the immortals came to be. If the stories of the Bible reflect reality, then I assume that at some point the gods decided to slum it with humans."

Kian nodded. "In the beginning, unions with humans were indeed prohibited. But there weren't enough gods to provide genetic diversity, and combined with their extremely low fertility rate, they feared eventual extinction, so unions with humans were sanctioned, provided that they were consensual. I guess that the creatures they'd created to serve them turned out to be much smarter than the gods had originally planned, and to the gods' credit, they acknowledged that and treated humans with kindness and respect."

"I'm glad to hear that, although I have my doubts. Perhaps that's how they wanted to go down in history."

"It's possible," Kian agreed. "My mother's version of the gods' era might be somewhat embellished to make them look better than they actually were. But let's continue with how the immortals came to be. Compared to the gods, human fertility was robust, and many immortal children were born, but when those immortals took human lovers, their children were born human, or so it initially seemed." Kian took a small puff of his cigar.

The thing was down to less than one-third of its original length, and Orion was running out of time, but it wasn't a big deal. Kian could continue the story at Kalugal's tomorrow.

"I assume that those children had the godly genes, but they were inactive," Orion said.

"Precisely. They discovered, probably by chance, that a venom bite could activate those genes and induce transition into immortality, but only for the children born to female immortals. The children born to immortal males and their human mates didn't possess the godly gene."

Orion rubbed a hand over his jaw. "Maybe the children of the males have the genes as well but require a different mode of activation?"

For a long moment, Kian just looked at him with a deep

frown. "You know what? You might be onto something. We've always taken it for granted that the children of the males didn't have the genes because that was what the gods believed. But what if they were wrong?"

Anandur shifted in his chair. "I hope they were right because it would really piss me off if they weren't."

From the corner of his eye, Orion saw Shai close his eyes and wondered why Anandur's words had upset him.

"Why wouldn't you want the gods to be proven wrong?" Orion asked Anandur.

"Because that would mean that hundreds of clan males were deprived of the joys of fatherhood based on a false premise."

Kian lifted his hand. "Even if the children of the males have the gene and there is another method of activating them, we couldn't have discovered it up until very recently. Genetic sequencing wasn't developed enough, and the equipment needed was too pricey even for the clan's deep pockets. We might have the ability to test it now, though. William is searching for bioinformaticians to recruit for another project we are working on, and once he gets a team together, he and Bridget might be able to finally identify what makes us different. Once they do, we could possibly find out whether children born to male immortals with humans have the gene."

"We have no children to test," Onegus said. "Nowadays, everyone uses birth control, and the chances of immortal males causing unintended pregnancies is practically nonexistent."

The topic was fascinating, and Orion was surprised that no one had thought of testing children of the males before, but given the state of Kian's cigar, he didn't have much time. Some of his questions could wait for tomorrow, but there were several he didn't want to wait to hear the answer for.

"How does the venom bite activate a Dormant?"

"We don't know," Kian said. "What we found out was done through trial and error rather than a scientific study. We know that for an adult female Dormant to transition the venom bite is not enough, and insemination is needed to boost the effect. For a male, the venom bite suffices, probably because it's done during a match and the composition of the venom is more potent when its production is triggered by aggression as opposed to sexual arousal."

"What about younger Dormants?"

Kian winced. "Boys and girls can be activated once they reach puberty, which is about the age of thirteen, and at that age, the venom is enough, and sex is not required. For very young girls, being around my mother is enough. Phoenix is already immortal."

"What about very young boys?" Orion asked. "How come being around the goddess doesn't activate them? Was it even tried?"

"Of course it was, but for some reason, it didn't work."

29

SHAI

Hope surged in Shai's heart.

Kian hadn't dismissed Orion's idea out of hand. He'd actually planned on having William and the new team of bioinformaticians identify the immortal gene and then search for it in children born to immortal males and human females.

What if Rhett could turn immortal?

What if he had the godly genes and William's team found a way to activate them? That seemed like a much easier problem to solve than not having the genes in the first place.

It would probably take a long time for the research to be done, but Rhett was still young. He still had time.

It was ironic that Orion, who didn't know anything about immortals aside from his own experience, would ask the question no one else had thought to ask.

But it also made sense.

Only someone without preconceived notions could challenge a belief that had been held for thousands of years.

The problem was finding children of immortal males to

test. When the time came, and they searched for test subjects, Shai would have to reveal the secret he'd kept for nearly twenty years and accept whatever punishment Edna or Kian decided on.

If there was even a sliver of a chance of Rhett becoming immortal, Shai would do whatever it took to make it happen.

"That's so odd," Orion murmured. "Why would being in the goddess's presence activate the little girls but not the boys?"

Kian leaned forward and stubbed out his cigar. "As I said. I don't know." He rose to his feet. "We should go back inside."

Orion followed him up. "I still have so many questions, but I guess I can save some for tomorrow." He smiled at Kalugal.

"Or I can stay out here with you. Would you mind entertaining me until you're done with your cigar?"

"By all means." Kalugal motioned to the seat Kian had vacated.

Uttering a groan, Kian walked over to the table and refilled his glass of whiskey. "I'd better stay and make sure he's not feeding you embellished stories."

Kalugal arched a brow. "Why would you think that? Have I ever told you untruths?"

"You're prone to exaggerations. I want Orion to get the facts as best as we know them."

Kalugal regarded him with thinly veiled amusement. "What's gotten you riled, cousin? It couldn't have been me because I hardly said a word."

"It wasn't you." Kian downed the whiskey in one go and didn't offer an explanation for what was bothering him.

The air between the two seemed to crackle with tension, and it seemed to affect Orion.

"My apologies for bringing up a painful subject,"

Orion said. "It must be difficult for the immortal males who were not blessed with immortal mates to be denied the joys of fatherhood. That brings me to the next question, which is why so few males are fathers. Is there a prohibition on mating within the clan for genetic reasons?"

The guy was smart to figure that one out, or perhaps Cassandra and Geraldine had told him that during the long hours they'd spent with him.

"Annani's descendants are considered closely related and therefore forbidden to each other," Kian said. "And until recently, we didn't know of any immortals aside from the Doomers, who are all male and are our sworn enemies."

"I assume that you're referring to Navuh's followers," Orion said.

"DOOM is the acronym for The Devout Order Of Mortdh Brotherhood," Kalugal clarified. "The clan nicknamed them Doomers."

"Why are they all male?" Orion asked.

"Because my father doesn't allow the females born to Dormants to be induced and transition into immortality. He doesn't want them to lose their human fertility. He needs them to keep producing children for his army and his breeding program. The boys are induced and join the warrior ranks, and the girls join their mothers as breeding mares."

Orion's eyes blazed with inner fire, and when he opened his mouth, Shai saw that his fangs had elongated. "That's despicable."

"I agree." Kalugal puffed on his cigar. "That's why I was curious about your powers. If you happen to be as powerful as my father, perhaps you could do something about it."

Just like Kian, Shai wondered about Kalugal's sudden

interest in the welfare of the island's population. He hadn't shown concern for them before.

"You mentioned that they live on an island. Where is that?" Orion asked.

"A small rock somewhere in the Indian Ocean. They manage to hide their existence well, but we found out where they are. Nevertheless, we can do nothing to liberate the Dormants and other humans they hold captive. We don't have the military power, and we can't just blow the place up because not everyone on that damn rock deserves to die, and least of all my mother."

"Of course." Orion pushed a dark strand of hair behind his ear. "Perhaps if we combined our powers we could overthrow your father."

"I wish it were that simple." Kalugal sighed. "It's not enough to eliminate him. Someone has to take control over those hordes of warriors and keep them contained. That means staying on that godforsaken island and ruling over scores of hoodlums and emotionally handicapped Dormants and humans. Who wants to do that?"

"Your brother," Kian said. "Lokan, Kalugal's brother, is also a compeller, but not as strong. He can only compel humans, and he has aspirations for the island and dreams of turning it into a utopia."

"He's a dreamer, all right," Kalugal said. "I'm not a pessimist, but I consider myself a realist, and I don't see a solution to the island's problem that will not result in thousands of lives lost."

"What does Navuh do with all those warriors?" Orion asked.

"He used to instigate wars and send them to fight on the side of his protégés," Dalhu said. "Now he uses them to sell drugs and run prostitution."

Orion's fangs descended even lower. "Is he involved in trafficking?"

"Of course," Kalugal said. "The island serves two purposes. One side is home to the Brotherhood, and the other is known as Pleasure Island. It's the most exclusive brothel in the world, serving the super-rich, powerful, and depraved. Lately, though, my father has started inviting brains to the island. He finally realized that brute strength was no longer the best qualifier for his soldiers, so he's working on improving the stock, breeding brainiacs. I think that's why it has been so quiet lately. Navuh is not in a rush, and he can afford waiting a couple of decades to build a smart army and amass weapons. In the past, even the thousands of immortal soldiers were not enough to take over the world, but with today's technology, it can be achieved with a much smaller force of smart cyber warriors."

So that was why Kalugal was suddenly interested in taking over the island.

"I don't get it." Orion looked between Kian and Kalugal. "If it's a known brothel, the island's location can't be secret."

"Windowless private transport planes." Kian looked like he'd lost the last of his patience and was on the verge of exploding. "I'm going inside," he proclaimed and strode toward the sliding doors.

This time, they all rose to their feet and followed him.

30

KIAN

Kian was bristling with anger, mostly at himself. Kalugal's comment about Navuh's future plans was nothing that hadn't occurred to him before, but the issue that Orion had raised had not.

Why hadn't he thought to ask his mother to run a test on a child of an immortal male?

Her blood could potentially be the other method of activation, and if it wasn't, it would not harm the child either. They should have given it a try a long time ago, as soon as Annani and Alena had found out that it activated the girls.

He felt like punching a wall, and he probably would have if he didn't have a house full of guests. His mother and sister had been sitting on this secret for two thousand fucking years.

Kian hadn't known. His mother had shared the secret only with Alena because the first child they'd tried it on was hers. He'd found out when Annani had given Syssi a small amount of her blood to help her pull through her transition.

And what about Bridget and William? The two big

brains on his council? Why hadn't it occurred to them that the children of immortal males could have the genes but needed a different method of activation?

They shouldn't have blindly accepted that the method the gods had discovered over five thousand years ago was the only one.

Except, those two didn't know about Annani using her blood to activate the little girls, so they could be forgiven, but not his mother and sister, and not he.

Most likely it wouldn't work, but until they tried and failed, the guilt was going to eat him alive. Not that it wouldn't if it worked. He would live with the guilt for not trying it sooner for the rest of his immortal life.

Syssi walked up to him and wrapped her arm around his middle. "What's wrong?"

He couldn't tell her the secret of Annani's blood, but he could tell her about Orion's theory.

"Orion offered a fresh perspective on Dormants. We accepted the gods' conclusion that only the children of immortal females carried the dormant godly genes, and therefore could be activated. We didn't consider that the children of the males might carry the genes as well but require a different method of activation. If that's true, I will never forgive myself for not investigating it sooner."

His mother turned to look at him. "I assure you that the gods tried everything they could think of to activate the children of the male immortals. My aunt and uncle were relentless in their research, and they found no way to do it."

Alena, knowing what he knew, looked just as disturbed as he was. "What possible other method that we haven't tried yet could there be?"

Was that her way of telling him that she didn't think Annani's blood could activate the children of the males? Had they tried?

He couldn't ask her in front of everyone, but the first chance he got, he was going to have a private talk with her and Annani.

"We didn't have a way to do that before," Amanda said. "But with how fast the field of gene editing is growing, we might be able to turn anyone immortal in the not-so-distant future."

Kian arched a brow. "Are you serious?"

"We are not there yet, and it might take a couple more decades, but I'm hopeful." She turned to Shai. "You said that you read some articles on the subject. And since you remember everything you read verbatim, you can probably explain it better than I can."

Shai shook his head. "Remembering is not the same as understanding, and I'm not a scientist. Perhaps it would be better if you do that."

"Not really." She leaned back as much as her belly allowed. "Because you are not a scientist, you will explain it in laymen's terms, and everyone will get it."

"Very well." Shai walked over to the other side of the table so everyone could see him. "New genome editing technologies allow scientists to change DNA, by adding, removing, or altering genetic material at specific locations in the genome. The newest technology was adapted from a naturally occurring genome editing system in bacteria. The bacteria capture snippets of DNA from invading viruses and use them to create DNA segments called CRISPR arrays. Those arrays are like an instruction manual to defend the organism when the same virus invades it again. When it does, the bacteria produce RNA segments from the CRISPR arrays to target the virus's DNA and cut it apart, disabling it."

Annani tilted her head. "I understand how it can be used to fight viruses, but how can it turn a human into an immortal?"

"Currently, scientists use that mechanism to fight diseases," Amanda said. "But it can also be used to modify genes. They use the cell's own DNA repair mechanism to add, delete, or replace genetic material with a customized DNA sequence. At this time, the editing changes are limited to somatic cells, which means that the changes only affect certain tissues and are not passed from one generation to the next. Because of ethical concerns, changes to genes in egg and sperm cells and to embryos are illegal in many countries, but that's where the juice is, that's where the answers to what makes us immortal are hidden, and that's how we will be able to transfer our enhanced genes to the next generation."

Cassandra nodded. "I've read that soon genes could be not only altered but built from scratch by artificial intelligence. That whole field of research seems like science fiction to me."

Kian hadn't understood half of what Shai and Amanda had said, but he'd gotten the gist of it. Since he suspected that the gods themselves had been genetically engineered, he believed that when the genes responsible for their longevity and various other enhancements were identified, regular humans might one day be turned immortal.

The potential was exciting for the clan but terrifying on a global level. What if everyone lived forever? Immortals didn't multiply as fast as humans, but their numbers still grew.

If all of humanity became immortal, even given the same low fertility rate as the clan immortals, there would be a population explosion. Kian didn't want to imagine the terrors that would bring about.

31

VROG

Vrog pulled on the T-shirt Vlad had loaned him. He'd been given clothes by the Guardians in the keep, but most were too loose on his slim frame. His son's shirt was a little tight, and it reminded him of the way he used to look when he was Vlad's age.

He hadn't been much older than his son when he'd fathered him, and in retrospect, he was less mature.

Vlad was a pensive young man, a good son to his mother, and a good mate to Wendy. He was also hard-working, kind, and intelligent.

Vrog was so undeservedly proud of him. Other than contributing his genes, he hadn't done anything. Worse, he'd demanded that Stella abort the pregnancy. He was so ashamed of it now but was too much of a coward to apologize to both mother and son.

Perhaps he would do that over dinner.

Wendy had invited Richard and Stella, the sweet girl intending to bring their ragtag family closer, but Vrog doubted Richard would be on board with that. The guy would celebrate the day he left the village and returned to his school.

The truth was that he missed the place, missed the students and even the chatty Doctor Wang. Vrog was respected there, even admired, and for a good reason. He was the founder, the one who kept the thing running like a well-oiled machine. Without him, the school would not collapse right away, but it would deteriorate over time. An organization was only as good as the people running it.

It always started at the top.

In the village he was a nobody, and that wasn't going to change. They didn't need him, and he had nothing to contribute.

Stella and several of the others had talked about him founding a school in the village, but it would take a long time and many more children before the clan would need one.

With a sigh, he pulled the T-shirt down to smooth out the wrinkles, opened the door, and headed toward the living room.

"You look awesome," Wendy said. "I knew Vlad's shirt would fit you. You guys are almost the same height, and you are both slim."

He smiled and took the dish she handed him. "Where should I put it?"

"On the table."

Vlad was in the kitchen, an apron tied around his waist, flipping steaks over the griddle. "I left yours almost rare." He lifted an overflowing platter to show Vrog. "This is all for you."

"Thank you." He had to find a way to pay for the extra food he was consuming, but he knew that they wouldn't hear of it, and he didn't want to offend them.

As the doorbell rang and Wendy rushed to open the door for Stella and Richard, Vrog took in a deep breath.

"I brought a casserole." Stella handed Wendy a glass dish.

"And I brought wine." Richard walked in with a bottle in each hand and cast Vrog a semi-friendly look. "You drink wine, I hope."

"I do." Vrog took the plate of steaks and put it on the table. "Vlad was kind enough to prepare nearly rare steaks for me. I don't know how to repay his and Wendy's kindness."

"Oh, stop it." Wendy slapped his arm. "We are a family. When Vlad and I come to visit you in China, you will return the favor."

"I will. That's a promise."

"And when is that?" Richard pulled out a chair for Stella. "I mean, when do you plan to go home?"

"Soon." Vrog took a seat across from the guy. "I just want to spend a few more days with Vlad and Wendy."

"You can stay as long as you like." Wendy put a salad bowl on the table and sat down. "I need more time to find you a good match."

That got Richard smiling. "I know just the lady for you."

"Who?" Wendy asked.

"Ingrid."

Stella winced. "Really? Is that your idea of a joke, Richard?"

"What's wrong with Ingrid?" Vlad asked. "She's a very talented lady."

"She was Richard's first immortal lover, which is why he's suggesting her."

"Well, yeah." Richard's expression was the picture of innocence. "I know her, and I know what she likes. I think she'll like Vrog." He smiled evilly. "She's not very picky."

"Richard!" Stella admonished.

"What?"

"That was offensive."

He snorted. "Ingrid was with me, so when I say that

she's not very picky, I'm also insulting myself, and therefore it shouldn't be taken as an insult."

"I'm not offended," Vrog said. "And if Richard thinks that the lady will find me agreeable, then I'm more than willing to make her acquaintance."

Vrog didn't care if the woman was a bombshell or a hag. He just wanted Stella and Richard to stop fighting because of him. He'd done enough damage already, and he was there to make amends, not to cause more strife.

32

RICHARD

Richard was starting to warm up to Vrog. The guy was polite, deferential, and did his best not to step on anyone's toes.

Perhaps he wasn't so bad.

After all, Vlad was one of the best people Richard knew, and half of his genes had come from his father, so there was that.

The guy could eat, though. Vlad took after Vrog in that regard too. They both were skinny and yet consumed huge quantities, however in Vrog's case, it had been almost exclusively meat. Vlad enjoyed carbs like any normal human.

When the pile of steaks on Vrog's plate was demolished, the guy put his fork and knife on top of it, reached for the napkin, and dabbed at his mouth like some damn aristocrat. "I remember Stella mentioning that you guessed Vlad's origins during a virtual adventure you both participated in. Could you tell me more about it?"

Richard lifted a brow. "You told him about that?"

"It's not a secret." Stella shrugged. "Many people know about our virtual adventure, and most everyone knows about Emmett confirming Syssi's amazingly accurate depiction of the Kra-ell."

Vrog gaped at her. "Is Kian's mate a seer?"

"She has visions," Stella said. "But the odd part is that she originally came up with the Kra-ell story for the virtual adventure company, and she was convinced that it was a product of her imagination. But she described a female-dominated society that was nearly identical to the Kra-ell, and she even named her imaginary people Krall. Coincidence? I think not. Anyway, William, who is the clan's tech genius, wanted us to test the program because Richard was still human back then, and he needed a human test subject. I chose the Krall adventure, but it turned out very differently than what I expected."

As Stella dove into the story, Richard was reminded of details he'd forgotten. It had been one hell of an adventure, and even though it had been terrifying and heart-wrenching at times, he liked the role he played and what it had shown him about himself.

He was damn proud of the hero act he'd pulled off.

The only thing that he didn't remember fondly was the damn fish stink during their escape from the Krall territory. They had been smuggled out in a fishing boat, hidden under a tarp, and he could still smell it.

"Why are you grimacing?" Wendy asked.

He waved a dismissive hand. "The experience was amazing, but it was too damn realistic. We escaped in a fishing boat through the Arctic Sea, freezing our asses off, and dying from the smell of rotten fish."

Vlad chuckled. "But you had your happy ending—a small house with a white picket fence and a vampiric, blood-sucking baby boy."

"That was how Richard guessed my secret," Stella said. "Subconsciously, I must have included clues about Vlad's heritage when I filled out the questionnaire."

Richard leaned back and puffed out his chest. "Yeah, a blood-sucking little Vlad was a big fat clue. Everything about the adventure was fun, though. I got to play the hero, rescue the woman I love, and come out in one piece."

"That sounds amazing," Vrog said. "Do you think Kian will allow me to experience a virtual adventure like that?"

"I don't see why not." Vlad uncorked one of the wine bottles.

"You'll need a partner," Richard said. "The Krall adventure is not a solo experience. But don't worry, the software will find your perfect match." He winked. "Who knows, maybe it will be Ingrid. I wonder if she's filled out the questionnaire."

Stella elbowed him in the ribs. "You've been with so many of the clan females. Can't you think of anyone but her?"

"She deserves a break. But it's not up to me, is it? Let the computer match up Vrog with the best female for him."

Vrog was watching their argument with a puzzled expression on his face. "You told me that bonded mates can't feel attraction to anyone other than their partner. How come Richard sampled so many different females?"

Richard winced. It was better to get it over with and tell the guy about his first job in the village before he heard it from someone else.

"I wasn't as lucky as you. When I arrived in the village, I was a human who was potentially a Dormant, but after several failed inductions, I lost hope of transitioning, and I knew that my days in the village were numbered. Then Amanda came up with the idea to sell my stud services in daily auctions to speed up the process of finding my one and only. And that's how I became the clan's gigolo."

"Is that how you found Stella?"

She snorted. "No. I would never buy a male's sexual favors in an auction. The Fates steered us toward each other, but I was too hardheaded and judgmental, and I didn't snatch up Richard when I first met him." She smiled at him apologetically. "I'm sorry. If I hadn't run off the first time we met, you would have been spared all that hard work."

"Did any of the ladies conceive?" Vrog asked.

Richard shook his head. "I know it's sacrilege to say this in the clan, but I'm glad none did. I only want children with Stella."

33

ALENA

Kian's accusations hurt.

After implying that Annani's *presence* might have activated the children of immortal males, he'd started on the boys born to immortal females, saying that he didn't understand why what worked for the girls didn't work for them.

What did he think? That they hadn't tried to use Annani's blood to activate the boys?

Alena couldn't believe that her brother could be so dense.

Neither she nor Annani would have been able to look Amanda in the eyes if they could have prevented Aiden's death and hadn't.

Even after all these years, Alena still teared up whenever she thought of her sister's grief. There was nothing worse for a mother than losing her child, and she prayed to the Fates she would never have to experience it herself.

"It is getting late." Annani rose to her feet and put her hand on Alena's shoulder. "We should head home." She shifted her gaze to Shai and smiled. "Thank you for letting us have your house on such short notice. It must have been a hassle to move your things so quickly."

"My pleasure, Clan Mother." He inclined his head. "I was glad for the excuse. Without it, Ingrid would have dragged her feet about getting Geraldine and me a new house. She has her hands full these days.

"Congratulations." Annani turned to Geraldine. "Are you staying in the village tonight?"

She nodded. "I waited for Orion to show up, and now that he is here, I can finally move in with Shai. For now, I just brought one suitcase, but later we will get the rest of my things and put the house up for rent."

Alena snuck a quick sidelong glance at Orion to see if Geraldine's words had angered him, but he had a small smile on his face, just a curve of one side of his lips that made him look even more roguish.

From the fond way he regarded his sister, niece, and nephew, it was obvious that he cared deeply for them. That was one point in his favor.

He was also so damn handsome, which she shouldn't give him points for because his looks had more to do with who his parents were and not with anything he had done. He seemed to be a good guy, though, and he wasn't intimidated by her big, overbearing family, which earned him two more favorable points.

Perhaps he was worth taking a risk on.

Except, his compulsion ability was worth at least five unfavorable points, which brought his balance down to a negative two.

Alena lifted a hand to her ear, realizing that she'd removed the earpieces when he'd gone outside and forgotten to put them back in when he returned. As a surge of fear speared through her, she had to stifle the urge to stick her fingers in her ears.

"May you enjoy many happy years in your new home,"

Annani said. "It amuses me to think that our bodies outlast the houses we build. Even our castle in Scotland, which is only a few centuries old, is crumbling and needs constant repairs, while our bodies still operate at optimal levels." She smoothed a hand down her hip. "We owe our thanks to those genetic engineers who perfected our genome. Perhaps the next step should have been to engineer self-repairing houses."

As a quick look at Kian revealed that his mood hadn't improved, Alena wondered if he was still thinking about the possibility of the children born to male immortals having the godly genes.

His frown was so deep that his brows were nearly touching.

Syssi leaned her head on his arm. "I thank God, the Fates, and the universe every day for the gift I was given. I get to spend eternity with the man I love and with our daughter. I hope we will have more children, but even if Allegra is the only one, I will still consider myself blessed beyond measure."

Kian's expression softened, and his forehead smoothed out. "So do I." He kissed the top of her head before pulling out of her hold. "I need to escort Annani and Alena to their new home, but I won't be long."

As if they needed him to escort them. He probably wanted to talk to them in private

"Thank you." Annani reached for Syssi's hand and pulled her into her arms. "It was a lovely evening."

"Tomorrow at our place," Kalugal said. "Everyone is invited, including Andrew and Nathalie and their adorable little girl who needed to go to sleep." He waved a hand around the room and everyone gathered. "It's not an official housewarming party, so don't bring gifts. I'll remind Andrew and Nathalie to bring Eva and Bhathian along." He turned to Orion. "You'll get to see all the little ones we currently have in the village. Eva and Bhathian have a little boy." He put his hand on Jacki's small belly. "Soon, there will be two more. Our son and Amanda's daughter."

Alena snuck another glance at Orion, curious to see his reaction to the pitiful number of children the clan had.

His face was surprisingly unguarded for someone who had walked the planet for over half a millennium, and his expression was more contemplative than sad or puzzled.

"When are you planning on having the official party?" Onegus asked Kalugal.

"Are you asking in your capacity as the chief? Or do you just want to know?"

"Both. But I was wondering what's taking you so long. You moved into the house over two weeks ago."

"Jacki and I are waiting for the last of the furnishings and decorative pieces we ordered. Hopefully, everything will arrive by the time we return from our trip."

"What trip?" Kian asked.

"I told you that I arranged to do some digging in the Mosuo territory. Jacki wants to see an archeological dig, but I don't want to take her to Egypt, where it's hot and humid. The Mosuo live around Lugu Lake, which is located in a high plateau amidst the Xiaoliangshan hills of Western Yunnan and enjoys temperate weather."

"I'm excited," Jacki said. "I just wish we had some company. I enjoyed our trip to Scotland so much. Does anyone want to join us?"

"When are you leaving?" Kian asked.

"Wednesday." Kalugal wrapped an arm around his wife's shoulders. "If any of you want to come, let me know, and I'll get Phinas to reserve rooms in the hotel."

Alena would have loved to go, but as usual she could only go where her mother wished to visit. And even if Annani was as intrigued by the Mosuo as Alena was, there was no chance Kian would allow them to join Kalugal without him being there and at least fifty Guardians to watch over them.

"How long are you going to spend there?" Shai asked.

"A couple of weeks," Jacki said. "But we might shorten or lengthen the visit depending on what we find."

"I hope that you are taking some of your men with you," Kian said. "I don't know how safe it is, especially since you are looking for clues about the Kra-ell."

"I'm taking Phinas and two more men. That still leaves plenty of space on my jet." He looked around the assembled company until his eyes fell on Alena. "How about it? Are you in?"

"I wish I could, but I'll have to take a raincheck."

34

ORION

While everyone was saying their goodnights and thanking their hosts for dinner, Orion wondered whether Mason would be outside waiting to escort him back to the house.

The guy had acted as if he'd been there to help Orion, but as evidenced by the earpieces the guy wore, it was obvious that his job was to guard the *dangerous* compeller.

Evidently, Alena viewed him as a threat as well.

Why, though?

Kalugal was probably just as powerful a compeller as he was. Did she wear protective earpieces around him also?

If compulsion was such a rare ability, it wasn't likely that Alena had encountered a nasty compeller and had a bad experience. Perhaps it was just a subconscious fear, like some humans feared snakes even if they'd never seen one.

Orion grimaced. That wasn't a good comparison.

"We can walk you back to your house," Geraldine offered as they stepped out onto Kian's front porch. "That's where our new house is, right next to Onegus and Cassandra's."

"Sylvia and I are in the second phase as well." Roni led the way, going down the steps.

As Orion had expected, Mason was waiting for him outside.

"I see that you have a full escort." The guy pushed his hands into his jeans pockets. "I guess you don't need me." He nodded to Onegus and the others. "I'll see you tomorrow morning."

"Good night, Mason." Orion had hoped to grill the Guardian about Alena and get as much background information on her as he could, but it would have to wait until tomorrow.

As the seven of them started toward their section of the village, Orion fell in step with Onegus. "So you are the chief of security here."

"I am."

"And you are also Cassandra's mate."

"I am that as well."

Orion smiled. "We are family. Do you really need to waste a Guardian on me? I'm not a threat to anyone here."

"I don't think that you are, but I'm a cautious fellow, and I just met you earlier today. Besides, you can use Mason or any other Guardian I post in front of your house as your personal tour guide. Their instructions are to be friendly and helpful."

"Mason followed your instructions perfectly." He cut a glance at the chief. "Can I ask you a question about Alena?"

Onegus narrowed his eyes at him. "What do you want to know?"

"What does she have against compellers? Did she have a bad experience with one?"

"Not that I'm aware of. We are all wary of compellers, especially powerful ones that can compel immortals."

"Your Clan Mother is a compeller."

"Annani never uses her power on us. The only exception was when Kalugal and his men joined the clan. There was a lot of mistrust going both ways, and everyone agreed that the only way to solve that was to have Annani compel everyone to do no harm to one another. We knew she was going to do it, we knew why, and everyone agreed that it was necessary. No one's will was taken away from them."

"Could the goddess compel me to do no harm as well? It bothers me that Alena regards me as a threat."

"You like her," Cassandra said. "And she likes you."

That was news to him. "She does?"

Grinning, Geraldine nodded. "We overheard her talking with Amanda. She didn't admit anything, but Amanda thought that she liked you."

Roni groaned. "You sound like a bunch of middle schoolers. She likes me, she likes me not," he taunted.

"I have no problem admitting that I'm intrigued by the lovely Alena. I just want to figure out why she was the only one other than Kian's bodyguards who was wearing earpieces."

"Alena is Annani's eldest daughter," Shai said. "And she deserves only the best."

"Are you implying that I'm lacking in any way? I hate to use the term, but I'm a demigod just like her."

"You vowed never to love a woman again. Alena deserves a male who will give himself to her fully, while you can only give her your body."

Cassandra snorted. "Alena might look all prim and proper, but she didn't produce those thirteen children by immaculate conception. She must have hooked up with many human males to do that. So why not Orion?"

Orion was still stuck on the number. "Thirteen children? How is that possible? Aren't immortals supposed to be nearly infertile?"

"Alena is a miracle," Onegus said. "If not for her fertility, the clan wouldn't exist. Sari has no children, Amanda lost her first son and is only now pregnant with her second child, and Kian's children would have been born human if he didn't find Syssi who was a Dormant and turned immortal. Alena is the de facto mother of the clan."

"Does it bother you?" Geraldine asked softly. "That she has so many children, and grandchildren and so on? Nearly every member of the clan is her descendant."

"Why would that bother me? I'm just awed." He shook his head. "Thirteen children. That's a lot even for a human."

"And yet, she's never been in love," Shai said. "Her entire life is about duty to her mother and to the clan. Ponder that when you lust after her."

"Shai!" Geraldine slapped his arm. "Why are you being so mean to Orion?"

He chuckled. "I'm not being mean, I'm giving him advice. If he breaks Alena's heart, what do you think Kian would do to him?"

35

ALENA

As they entered Shai's former house, Alena was impressed with the cleaning job the Guardians and the Odus had done.

The place was sparkling clean, and everything looked brand new. They must have polished the wood, vacuumed the couches, and sprayed fresh scent all over the place.

There were only two bedrooms, which didn't leave room for the Odus, but since they didn't need to sleep or rest, they also didn't need beds. Still, she would have felt better if they had a place of their own and didn't have to spend the night sitting quietly in the living room.

She looked at Kian. "Do you have anything you can give our Odus to do during the night? They can clean up the office building or do some gardening."

He shook his head. "I prefer for them to stay with you and guard you. But if you want to send a couple of them to our house, they are welcome to stay with Okidu in his room."

"That would be lovely." Annani walked over to the couch and sat down.

Immediately, Oridu rushed to her. "Does the Clan

Mother require refreshments?"

"I could use a cup of tea, thank you." Annani looked at Kian. "Can I offer you some?"

"Yes, please." He sat on one of the armchairs facing the couch.

"Please make tea for the three of us, Oridu."

He bowed. "Right away, Clan Mother."

As Alena joined Annani on the couch, Kian cast a quick look at the four Odus gathered in the kitchen. "I assume that all of them are safe to talk around?"

"Of course," Annani said. "They will never repeat a word."

"What Orion said about activating the children of the males got me thinking. Did you try the same method you use to activate the daughters of our females on the sons?"

"Naturally," Annani said. "After the experiment worked with the first baby girl, Alena and I tested it on every new child born to her, boy or girl. Unfortunately, my blood did not induce the boys' transition, but fortunately, we had you to activate them."

He let out a breath. "That's a relief but also a disappointment. I wish that what Orion said was true, even if it worked only on the males' daughters. I would hate myself if we didn't try." He smiled. "It's not like there would have been many who needed your special blessing."

Annani nodded gravely. "If you find a child sired by an immortal male with a human, I am willing to give it a try. The worst that could happen would be a boost of health for the child."

Kian leaned back and crossed his legs at the ankles. "Sometimes it takes an outsider to ask a question that those on the inside never thought to ask. We took for granted that the gods had determined that the children of immortal males didn't carry the immortal gene, and we never thought to question that assertion. Now that we are on the cusp of developing tools that would allow us to play with the genome as the gods did, I wonder if we should."

Alena chuckled. "This gives the phrase 'playing God' a whole new meaning."

"Thank you." Annani took the cup of tea Oridu handed her and took a sip. "The gods tampered with the human genome, enhancing it just enough to create servants who were intelligent and obedient. But humans did not turn out exactly as they had intended. In a way, they were like today's artificial intelligence. They learned fast, and every generation was smarter than the one before it. Soon, they became just as intelligent as the gods, and since they multiplied rapidly as they had been designed to do, they became a threat."

"The law of unintended consequences," Kian said as he put his teacup on the coffee table.

Annani nodded. "Even though most humans were obedient and easy to control, some of them were ambitious and had minds of their own. Those outliers made the gods realize that they could not regard humans as mindless servants, and they enacted laws to govern them that mimicked their own. In the end, the gods were not destroyed by humans as they had originally feared, but by one of their own. Nevertheless, Mortdh would not have been able to amass power if not for the immortals and humans he commanded. So in a way, my father was right about humans posing an existential threat to the gods."

"What are you trying to say, Mother? That we need to be careful about tampering with genes?" Kian crossed his arms over his chest.

She shrugged. "I was just thinking out loud. This is not an easy issue that can be resolved over a cup of tea. There are pros and cons to be weighed, both moral and ethical, and the real danger is that you can never be sure of what that tampering will produce."

36

VROG

Vrog had spent half the night thinking about the Kra-ell virtual adventure, and the other half dreaming about it. It had been a damn sexy dream, and when he woke up, he was determined to try it out.

He found Vlad in the kitchen, kneading dough.

"What are you making?"

"Wendy's favorite breakfast, lunch, and dinner. Beignets."

"I don't know what that is." Vrog pulled a mug out of the drying rack and filled it with coffee from the coffeemaker. "I've spent a lot of time thinking about that virtual adventure that Stella and Richard talked about. How difficult do you think it would be to arrange one for me?"

"Not difficult at all. I can take you to William after breakfast."

"It's Saturday. Does he work on weekends?"

"To William, the lab is not his workplace. It's his home. He's always there. Anyway, he'll give you a questionnaire to fill in, run it through the program, and hopefully, your perfect match will be somewhere in the village and interested in the same adventure."

"So it's an inside program. I can't be matched with a human female."

"You can." Vlad rolled out the dough. "You can go online and buy an adventure package in the Perfect Match studios. I think they have one in Beverly Hills, which is not too far from here. They can match you with a compatible human, but they are pricey. The one in the village is free."

"Price is not an issue, but I prefer to be matched with an immortal female. How does it work? Would I know who she is?"

Vlad shook his head. "Couples can choose to go together and have a joined virtual adventure. But if you want to find your perfect partner, it's anonymous. If you like her very much, you can put in a request to meet her, but she's not obligated to agree." He smiled shyly. "In fact, there is no guarantee that she is indeed a she. Unless you specify that she must be female in real life, you might get matched with a male who wants to play the part of a female. But if he's your perfect match, then hey, why not, right?"

Vrog stared at his son, not sure whether Vlad was serious or pulling his leg. "The computer will not match a straight male with a gay one because that wouldn't be a perfect match. It would be a mismatch."

Vlad laughed. "Yeah, you are probably right. Unless the straight guy is secretly gay, that is. Not everyone is brave enough to admit their desires."

"True." Vrog took a sip from his coffee. "But I don't have these kinds of secret desires. I have others."

"Oh yeah? Like what?"

"Like the kind a father doesn't discuss with his son."

Vlad's amusement faded. "I don't want to hurt your feelings, but it's easier for me to think of you as a friend or a distant relative. Perhaps that will change in the future, but for now, that's the best I can do."

It hurt, but Vrog appreciated Vlad's honesty. "That's better than thinking of me as your enemy."

"I'm glad you're not taking it to heart. I like you, just not as a paternal figure." Vlad smiled again. "And since we are friends, you can tell me about your secret desires, if it's not too kinky, that is. I'm a simple guy with simple tastes."

Vrog was relieved to hear that. "So am I." He shifted on the stool that was too short for his long legs. "I always wondered how it would feel to be with a Kra-ell female. I would like to experience that at least once in my life."

Vrog's heart ached at the thought that they might be gone. He hadn't loved Jade or any of the others, but he'd admired and desired them. He'd hoped that his loyal service would earn him an invitation to one of their beds, but they had either been killed or abducted before it could have happened. Now, his only option was to experience a Kra-ell female in a fantasy that would probably not reflect reality.

Then again, if the creator of that fantasy was a seeress, she might have pierced the veil and seen a real Kra-ell coupling.

"I heard that they are vicious," Vlad said. "Why would you want that?"

"I'm just curious."

37

ALENA

In the morning, Alena emerged from her bedroom, dreading breakfast with her mother.

Last night, she'd ducked into her room as soon as Kian had left, thus avoiding Annani's interrogation about her reaction to Orion. There was no doubt in her mind that Annani had known precisely what was going on.

They'd spent over two thousand years together, but although her mother could read her like an open book, the reverse was not true. The only thing predictable about Annani was her unpredictability, and that she was sure to surprise Alena with yet another one of her schemes that walked the razor-thin line between daring and reckless.

Perhaps that was the secret juice that kept Alena from going crazy.

Her childbearing years were long behind her, and the sanctuary, although beautiful, was stifling. If not for their frequent trips and her mother's shenanigans, the tedium would have been unbearable.

"Good morning, Alena." Annani put the newspaper down. "Did you sleep well?"

"Not really." Alena pulled out a chair and sat down.

Ovidu rushed over and poured her a cup of coffee. "Would you like an omelet, mistress?"

"Yes, thank you." Alena stirred cream and sugar into her coffee and took a sip.

Annani observed her for a moment before saying, "I want to discuss with you our plans for celebrating the holidays."

That was good. As long as her mother didn't bring up Orion and Alena's attitude toward him, she was willing to talk about any topic under the sun.

"What do you have in mind?"

"You said that we needed to choose a symbol for our holiday celebrations, and I found the perfect solution not just for one annual celebration but for two." Annani smiled triumphantly. "The summer and winter solstices. They are not directly related to any religion but rather symbolize the changing of seasons and celebrate nature. What do you think?"

"I think that you are brilliant, Mother, and I love the idea. Except, what actually symbolizes the solstices?"

Annani waved a dismissive hand. "I am sure that you will come up with something by Monday evening. I want to host the close family for the winter solstice celebration. You will handle the decorations, the Odus will prepare the feast, and we will hand out presents."

"A wonderful idea, Mother."

For a few moments they sat in silent companionship, with Alena thinking about winter theme decorations and where she could get them before Monday evening, but then Annani smirked, and Alena braced for what she knew was coming.

"Orion is very handsome," her mother said.

Here it comes. Alena stifled a groan and nodded. "Mm-hmm," she agreed noncommittally.

Annani smiled knowingly. "It is obvious that you find

him attractive. Why do you try to hide it? You are not a bashful girl."

Alena snorted. "You are the only one who still calls me a girl. I'm ancient, Mother. And bashfulness has nothing to do with it."

"Then what does?"

"I've already told you why he can't be a contender for me." She braced her elbows on the table, which she knew annoyed her mother, but she didn't care.

"His compulsion ability should not be a deterrent." Annani cast her a stern look. "You cannot condemn Orion for something he was born with, and you offended him by wearing those ear contraptions throughout dinner. I saw him casting quick glances at you, and whenever he did, he had a hurt look in his eyes."

Alena hadn't noticed, but she didn't doubt her mother's observation.

"Maybe he was constipated."

"Alena!" Annani admonished. "Immortals do not suffer from that malady, and furthermore, this is not a topic that should be mentioned while eating." She waved a hand. "You should go over to his place and make amends."

"We didn't quarrel, so there is nothing to make amends for."

"You could be more friendly. Invite him for a walk, show him the village, or take him to the café."

Alena narrowed her eyes at her mother. "Why are you pushing me at him?"

Annani sighed. "No matter how old you are, I am still your mother, and I want what is best for you. The Fates sent Orion to us for a reason, and I do not think that they intended him for another female. He might be your one and only."

"If he's the one the Fates chose for me, then they have a really sick sense of humor. Compellers make my skin crawl, and that's who they send me? What did I do to deserve that punishment?"

"You are being childish, Alena, and it does not suit you. I want you to go to Orion's house and invite him for a walk. It is not a mother's suggestion. It is the Clan Mother's directive."

Her mother had never pulled rank on her or any of her other children. Well, she had done so once when Kian had wanted to marry Lavena and Annani forbade it. He'd done it anyway and suffered mightily for it.

Her mother had been right then, so maybe she was also right now.

"Here is your omelet, mistress." Oridu placed the plate in front of her.

"Thank you." Alena unfurled the napkin and placed it over her lap. "I'll do as you ask, Mother. I'll invite Orion on a walk around the village." She would do so while wearing earpieces, but Annani didn't need to know that.

The question was what to wear to control her raging attraction to him.

A chastity belt?

Perhaps Merlin could brew her a potion that suppressed desire.

Her mother smiled benevolently. "Thank you for being so agreeable, Alena. I assure you that you will not regret it."

"I know." Alena smiled sweetly. "But don't expect some grand romance to come out of it. I'm just going to take him on a walk so he doesn't think I hate him."

38

KIAN

Annani's front door swung open just as Kian was ascending the stairs, and Alena walked out with Ovidu in tow.

The Odu bowed and kept the door open for him. "Good morning, Master Kian."

"Good morning." Halting on the mid stair, Kian waited for Alena to reach him. When she leaned to kiss his cheek, he noticed that she was still wearing the earpieces he'd given her the day before. "Going to see Orion?"

She leaned away to look at him. "How did you know?"

He pointed to her ear. "Unless these are a new fashion accessory or you forgot to take them out and slept with them in, Orion is the only reason for you to wear them."

Last night, when he'd escorted Alena and Annani home, Kian had been too consumed with his seething anger over their presumed oversight to notice, but he doubted she'd left them in.

Wincing, Alena lifted a hand to her ear. "These are too uncomfortable to forget about. Mother thinks that I was rude to Orion, and she wants me to make amends by inviting him for a walk around the village. I'm to give him a tour."

"Amends, eh?" He shook his head. "She's playing matchmaker."

"I know. But it's easier to do what she wants than argue."

Kian snorted. "I know what you mean. You are an angel to put up with her for all these years."

"Not so loud." Looking over her shoulder, Alena cast a furtive glance toward the open door. "She might hear you," she whispered.

He hadn't said anything that their mother wasn't aware of, but it was offensive nonetheless, and he didn't wish to hurt her feelings.

"You're right." Kian climbed the last stair. "Enjoy your walk with Orion."

"I'll do my best."

When he walked inside, he found Annani sitting on the living room couch with a newspaper spread out in front of her.

"Good morning, Mother." He leaned to kiss her cheek.

She beamed at him. "I am so glad you came." Folding the newspaper, she put it on the coffee table.

"You texted me and asked that I come over." He sat next to her. "I am not in the habit of refusing your summonses."

"Those are not summonses." She looked at him down her delicate nose. "Those are invitations."

"You told me to come alone."

"I did not want to bore Syssi with what I needed to discuss with you. I know that she likes to stay in bed on Saturday mornings."

"That she does. Only now, she brings Allegra to our bed in the mornings so we can cuddle with her. Not that our daughter is far from us during the night. Syssi still keeps her in a bassinet next to our bed."

Annani tilted her head. "Does it not interfere with certain activities?"

Kian stifled a chuckle. "From time to time, we roll the bassinet to Allegra's room and turn the baby monitor on."

His mother frowned. "Only from time to time?"

"A couple of times a day."

She smiled. "That is much better."

"Now that we are done discussing my sex life, what did you want to talk to me about? And does it have anything to do with you sending Alena to invite Orion on a walk?"

"I have no secrets from Alena, so no, there is no connection. She has a strange aversion to compellers, and I figured that the best way for her to get over it was by exposure. That is what they recommend for children who are afraid of dogs—get them accustomed to a cute little puppy, then to a medium-sized friendly dog, and eventually a big one."

This time Kian couldn't stifle the laugh bubbling out of him. "So if Orion is the puppy, who is the big dog?"

"Well, that would be Navuh, but I do not wish Alena anywhere near him. I will be satisfied if she is comfortable with the puppy."

"Orion is no puppy. He's cultured and polite, but don't mistake it for weakness."

Annani smiled. "I certainly hope that he is no weakling. Alena would trample all over him if he were."

That was a surprising thing for his mother to say about his sweet, even-keeled older sister. "She would never do that. Alena is pure heart."

"She is also an immortal female who is a demigoddess." Annani flipped a strand of her hip-length hair over her shoulder. "We are predatory by nature, and we want our males to be strong, so we test them, push them, and if they yield too easily, we lose interest." She smiled. "Perhaps we have more in common with the Kra-ell than we would like to believe."

Kian nodded. "It occurred to me that we might share a common ancestry, with the Kra-ell being a more primitive version of us."

"Or they might be us before the enhancements. They have shorter lifespans, do not heal as fast as we do, and they cannot activate their Dormants. All that talk about the scientific advancements in genetics got me thinking about them and their plight. Genome editing might provide a solution for them as well as for the children of immortal males."

"Is that what you wanted to talk to me about?"

"It was one of the topics. Is there anything we can do to hasten the progress?"

"We don't have any special knowledge to contribute. We helped along with technology, but that was thanks to Ekin's tablet and William's ability to figure out the information contained in it. Regrettably, the tablet didn't contain any information or instructions on genetics."

"But Okidu's journals do. When I heard the talk last night about genome editing, that was the first thing that came to my mind."

"William is searching for bioinformaticians to assemble a team that will help him tackle the journals. We don't know how much of the information contained in them will be helpful in that regard. Those are instructions on how to build Odus, not how to turn humans into immortals."

"Are we talking months or years?" Annani asked.

"I can't even answer that. We will know more once William and his team make some initial progress."

"I understand." She shifted her legs and adjusted the skirt of her dark-green gown. "The other thing I wanted to talk to you about is searching for Toven. Orion must have some clues that can point us in his direction."

"He mentioned a journal that he'd pilfered from Toven. Monday, I'll ask him if he will allow us to make a copy. I hope he has it with him."

"Why wait until Monday? Why not do that today or tomorrow? I have plans for Monday that I also need to discuss with you."

"Patience, Mother." He leaned closer to her and kissed her cheek. "Orion needs to get to know us better before he trusts us with that journal."

Her eyes blazing mischief, Annani smirked. "Why do you think I sent Alena to invite him on a walk?"

He arched a brow. "Because you wanted her to get over her aversion to compellers?"

"Well, that too," Annani agreed. "And I also think that they would make a nice couple. Orion is so ruggedly handsome, even more so than Toven. His mother must have been a very beautiful human."

"I suppose so." Kian leaned back and crossed his legs at the ankles. "So, what plans did you have for Monday, Mother?"

"Oh, yes." Her eyes sparkled. "Alena and I decided that the clan needs more celebrations, but since we have no official holidays, we would adopt a human one that is not tied to any particular religion. Starting with this Monday, we shall celebrate every winter and summer solstice."

"That's a great idea, but we can't arrange a clan-wide celebration in one day. Is it important to have the party this Monday?"

"That is the date of the winter solstice, so we cannot celebrate it a week later, but what Alena and I have in mind for this year is just a small family gathering. We will host a family dinner and distribute the gifts we brought with us. However, for the next solstice celebration, we will plan ahead and make it a grand event."

39

ALENA

When Alena neared Orion's house and didn't see a Guardian in front of it, two warring emotions ran through her, one right on the heels of the other.

The lack of a Guardian meant that Orion had gone out, and the Guardian had followed as he'd been instructed to do.

It was a relief not having to face him, but it was also a disappointment.

All that prep and pep talk on the way had been wasted, and she would just have to do it all over when Annani sent her again later.

"Shall I knock on the door, mistress?" Ovidu asked.

"I don't think Orion is home."

The Odu tilted his head. "I can hear two males conversing inside."

Perhaps Shai or Onegus were visiting him, and Onegus had dismissed the Guardian or had sent him to get something. In either case, she could turn around and tell Annani that Orion was busy.

Except, that was not going to fly with her mother.

Annani would demand to know what Orion was busy with, and unless Alena knocked on that door and heard from him why he couldn't join her on a walk, her mission would not be deemed completed.

"I'll do it." Alena ascended the stairs. "You can wait for me on the porch." It was weird enough that she was showing up on Orion's doorstep uninvited. Having her butler with her would make it even more awkward.

She could have left Ovidu home, but he was an added layer of protection that she wasn't willing to forgo. Orion could physically overpower her and pull the earpieces out, the Guardian assigned to him might not reach them in time to help her, and Ovidu might be the only one who could save her mind from being overwhelmed by Orion.

She had to admit that it was an absurd scenario, but she wasn't taking any chances with a compeller.

Damn, she was overthinking this. It was only a walk through the village. He wasn't going to kidnap her even if he wanted to.

It wasn't a big deal, and she should relax.

"As you wish, mistress." Ovidu dipped his head and sat down on one of the two wicker outdoor chairs.

They were a deviation from Ingrid's usual decorating style. Most other homes in the village had either a wooden bench or loveseat swing on their front porches. Ingrid's idea had been to promote neighborly feelings, but most people didn't use them, preferring their private backyards.

Aware that she was letting her mind wander to buy herself another moment before knocking, Alena took a deep breath, plastered a pleasant smile on her face, and knocked.

When the door opened, though, revealing Orion in a pair of sweatpants and an unbuttoned shirt, Alena reconsidered her previous assessment.

Orion was a big deal and then some.

His bare chest was a work of art, hairless and tan and ripped with lean muscles, which hadn't been as noticeable under the dress shirt he'd worn the day before.

"Alena." Even with the damn earpieces distorting his voice, the way he said her name was like a soft caress over the most intimate places on her body.

But that was all he said and then he just stared at her as if he was as lost for words as she was.

"Hi," she finally managed to say. "May I come in?"

"Forgive me." With the spell broken, he shook his head and opened the door all the way. "I was just stunned to see you on my doorstep. What a pleasant surprise."

Mason, who was apparently the Guardian assigned to him, rose to his feet and smiled. "Good morning, Alena."

What was he doing inside the house? Wasn't he supposed to sit on the bench outside and do his best to be unobtrusive?

"Good morning." She forced a smile back.

"I invited Mason for a cup of coffee." Orion hurriedly buttoned up his shirt. "I hope that's okay, and he's not going to get in trouble for coming in."

"Not at all. It was nice of you to invite him."

"Can I offer you a cup as well? It has just finished brewing."

"Thank you. That would be lovely." The fake smile remained on her lips as her mind processed the scene she'd walked in on.

Mason was a handsome guy, and Orion had invited him in while wearing a pair of sweatpants that hung low on his hips, an unbuttoned shirt that left his magnificent chest bare, and no shoes on his sexy feet.

Had she been pining after a guy who was not interested in females?

"Please, take a seat." Orion motioned to the couch.

"Perhaps I should leave," Mason said.

"Don't leave on my account." Alena sat down. "The three of us can have coffee together, and then we can all go on a tour of the village, which is why I'm here this lovely morning. Ovidu is waiting outside." She'd felt compelled to add the last sentence, so neither Orion nor Mason would think she was there for the same reason Mason was.

The Guardian's expression turned rightfully doubtful, but he didn't say a thing.

Alena didn't live in the village, so although she knew the place well, she wasn't the best choice of a tour guide.

"Who's Ovidu?" Orion asked.

"My butler. The Clan Mother asked me to show you around." That should suffice as an explanation, and it was also the truth.

Alena wasn't there because she wanted to seduce Orion. Mason could have him.

Was she disappointed?

A little.

A lot.

"Why is he waiting outside?" Orion asked. "Invite him in."

"He's perfectly fine on your front porch."

Evidently, no one had told Orion about the Odus, and he assumed Ovidu was a clan member.

Well, in a way, he was, especially after Okidu and Onidu had rebooted and had become sentient. She still had a hard time wrapping her mind around that and even a harder time deciding whether she wanted Ovidu to reboot as well.

For a moment, Orion didn't move, looking at her as if he was waiting for her to change her mind about inviting Ovidu in, but when she didn't, he shrugged. "I'll get the coffee."

As he ducked into the kitchen, Mason and Alena sat in

awkward silence, and when he returned a few moments later with a tray, they were both relieved.

Orion set down the mugs, cream, and sugar on the coffee table, but he didn't join her on the couch. "I would love to go on a walk, but I need to get dressed first. I was told that there is a café in the village, so perhaps we can stop for breakfast there." He smiled apologetically. "When I woke up this morning and saw Mason sitting outside on the bench, his breath misting because it was so cold, I took pity on him and invited him to share breakfast with me, but you came before I had a chance to make it."

Why had he felt the need to explain? Was he embarrassed about getting caught with Mason in the house?

A sidelong glance at the Guardian confirmed that he still looked like he would rather be anywhere but there.

Alena didn't know Mason well, but she'd never heard anything about him being into males, and Orion's invitation might have put him in an uncomfortable spot. In fact, he was probably grateful to her for showing up and saving him from having to reject unwanted advances.

As Orion sat down on the armchair next to Mason's, Alena cast another quick look at the Guardian, but he didn't seem bothered by Orion's proximity.

Perhaps she was reading the situation wrong?

She turned to Orion and smiled. "You are used to being around humans who are bothered by cold temperatures. We are immortals. The cold doesn't bother us as much. Nevertheless, it was nice of you to invite Mason in."

A smile bloomed on Orion's gorgeous face. "Right, you sang to that effect." He rubbed a hand over his stubbled chin. "The cold never bothered me anyway," he sang the line in a lovely baritone.

"You have a good voice."

"Not as good as yours."

Mason downed his coffee in one go and pushed to his

feet. "I'll be outside keeping Ovidu company." He rushed out before either of them had a chance to stop him.

"Was it my singing?" Orion asked.

She laughed a little too merrily to cover her embarrassment. "I think it was me." She took a sip of the coffee and then rose to her feet. "Why don't you get dressed, and I'll see what I can make you for breakfast."

The horrified look on his face was hilarious. "I can't have the Clan Mother's eldest daughter making me breakfast."

"Why not?"

"It's just not right."

"What's not right is me taking you out on a walk on an empty stomach." She waved him off. "Go already. I don't have all day."

"Yes, ma'am."

40

ORION

Orion felt like pinching himself to make sure that he wasn't dreaming.

Alena, the goddess's eldest daughter, was in his kitchen making him breakfast.

Did she even know how to cook?

She had a butler, who she'd left outside to wait for her.

It must be a dream.

Last night, after he'd returned to his temporary abode, he searched the village streaming service for that song she'd sung and found the animated movie. He'd watched it from start to finish and had listened to that song two more times.

The fairytale ice princess looked a lot like Alena, with the same big blue eyes and the same blond braid that she wore draped over her ample chest. Well, Alena's chest was ample, while the Disney princess's was less so. The other difference was that Alena was not icy.

In fact, he had a feeling that under her amiable expression and the quaint dress, there was a wild, passionate female just itching to get out.

Smiling, he looked at the suitcase that he'd left open on the floor and debated what to wear.

Alena's style was simple, old-fashioned. She hadn't bothered with anything fancy for dinner at her brother's house either, and this morning, she wore a long-sleeved cream-colored dress with small pearl buttons down the front and a flowing calf-length skirt. No makeup, no heels, and no jewelry except for a thin gold chain draped around her neck, the pendant dipping between those ample breasts.

She was a breath of fresh air—beautiful without putting any effort into it, direct and assertive despite her soft appearance, and she had an amazing singing voice to boot.

A true princess.

Pulling on a pair of slacks, Orion zipped them up, added a belt, a button-down that was his least formal, and pushed his feet into a pair of loafers.

A quick pass with the shaver got rid of his morning stubble, and a splash of cologne completed his primping. He tucked his useless phone in one pocket and his wallet in the other, more out of habit than expecting to have any use for either.

His phone had no reception in the village, and he didn't know whether the café accepted cash or credit cards. Perhaps it was free to clan members.

When he walked out of the bedroom, he was greeted with a pleasant smell of toast and eggs. It evoked a bittersweet feeling, the homey smells reminding him of Miriam—the only woman who'd ever cooked for him.

"Just in time." Alena waved a spatula in the direction of the kitchen counter.

Orion pulled out a stool and sat down. "Given that you have your own butler, I'm surprised that you know your way around a kitchen. Is he a new addition to your staff?"

"I've had Ovidu since I was born. He was my nanny."

Alena transferred the omelet she'd made onto a plate and added toast, a container of butter, and another of jam.

Orion frowned. "How is that possible? You were Annani's firstborn. The clan didn't exist yet, and there were no other immortals."

"The Odus were Annani's servants, and she took them with her when she fled to the north." She pointed to his plate. "Eat. It's getting cold."

"I'm waiting for you."

"I've already had breakfast." She poured coffee into two fresh cups, set them down on the counter, and sat down on the stool he'd pulled out for her.

"I remember now Kian mentioning something about your mother loading her servants onto her flying machine. For some reason, I assumed that they were human females, ladies-in-waiting sort of servants. I should have known that they were immortal. She wouldn't have taken humans with her."

Had those servants fathered her children? Was that the reason she'd taken them along?

"They were neither." Alena cradled the coffee cup between her palms. "I hope Kian doesn't consider this classified information, but the Odus are a very advanced sort of cyborg."

"The Odus?"

She nodded. "That's what their kind is called, but Annani didn't like to refer to them as things, so she gave each one a distinct name. Her servants are Oridu, Ogidu, and Oshidu. Mine is Ovidu, Kian's Okidu, Amanda's Onidu, and Sari's is called Ojidu."

"I can't wait to meet your Ovidu. Does he look humanoid?"

She laughed. "Did Annani command all of your attention last night, so you didn't notice the servers? Those were Okidu and Onidu. They made all the food, set the table, served the meal, and cleaned up afterward."

"Impossible." He shook his head. "I remember thinking that they looked old for immortals, so I assumed that they were humans."

"We don't have humans in the village. Well, except for a couple of Dormants that is. And the construction workers..." she chuckled. "I guess we have plenty of humans in the village, just not as household staff."

"Who made the Odus?"

"We don't know. We assume that they were created on the gods' home planet and that their owner sent them to Earth to save them. Annani's father-in-law found them in the desert, and his son Khiann offered them to her as an engagement gift."

"Save them from what?"

Alena rolled her eyes. "Finish your breakfast, and I'll tell you on the way. We are supposed to be going for a walk."

Right. It was probably considered improper for her to be alone with him in his house. Nowadays, no one followed those outdated propriety rules, but Alena had been born in a different era, and so had her brother, whom Orion really did not wish to piss off.

41

ALENA

As Alena and Orion walked out the front door, Mason and Ovidu rose to their feet.

"You can take a break, Mason." Alena smiled at the Guardian to put him at ease. "Ovidu will suffice as my chaperone." She winked at him.

The guy hesitated, his hand closing around the phone in his pocket.

"You don't need to call Onegus to ask his permission. Tell him that I authorized your break." She made her tone just a smidgen stricter than usual to let him know it wasn't up for discussion.

"Yes, ma'am." Mason planted his butt back on the chair.

"Go home, Mason. I'll call you when I return Orion safely to the house."

Reluctantly, the Guardian obeyed.

"Shall we?" She descended the stairs.

Following her down, Orion offered her his arm as if they were a couple in the Victorian times about to stroll through a city park.

Heck, why not.

She threaded her arm through his. "This will give people the wrong idea, you know."

"In what way?"

"They will assume that we are a couple."

"And that's bad?"

"No. It's just not true."

He cast her a roguish smile. "It could be true."

"Is that an offer?"

"I would very much like to get to know you better, Alena. I will consider it an honor if you accept my suit."

That was ridiculously old-fashioned but kind of sweet. The question was whether he'd meant it.

What about Mason?

Had she seen what hadn't been there?

Probably.

Orion seemed very focused on her, and his offer indicated that he was interested in more than just friendship. Then again, she'd started the flirtatious conversation, so he might have felt obligated to continue.

"Well?" Orion said. "I'm still waiting for an answer."

Alena flashed him a smile. "I'm old, but I like to think of myself as a modern female. You don't need to announce your intentions and get my permission."

That was a very noncommittal answer, and she was proud of herself for coming up with it.

Orion sighed dramatically. "There are advantages and disadvantages to the old customs, and to the new. In the old times, the guesswork was taken out of courtship. A lady either rejected a gentleman's suit or accepted it and things progressed from there. Nowadays, there are so many variations of possible relationships, or rather encounters. I had one lasting relationship a long time ago, and too many brief encounters. It's a novelty for me to court a lady."

"That's more than I had." Alena was curious about that

one lasting relationship Orion had, but she didn't want to pry. If he wished to tell her about it, he would. "I only ever experienced encounters."

"And yet somehow you produced thirteen children. I'm told that for an immortal female, that is considered miraculous."

He'd sounded sincere, but just to be sure she snuck a sidelong glance at him to examine his expression and was relieved that he looked impressed rather than put off.

Alena had never told any of the human males she'd hooked up with about her children or any other personal details, keeping the encounters purely physical. To shield her heart and avoid false expectations, it was better to share with them as little as possible.

It felt uncomfortable to speak to a stranger who knew things about her because someone had told him. If she found out who that was, she would give them a piece of her mind. But it could have been anyone. Even Geraldine and Cassandra, who were new to the clan, knew about her children.

"My mother was also super fertile for a goddess. She had five children, while most of the goddesses she'd known had been lucky to have one. I probably inherited my super fertility from her, and my human side made me even more so."

"Your sisters were not so blessed." Orion halted. "Hold on. It just dawned on me that you said five. Annani talked about four children."

"Lilen was killed in battle. He was born between Kian and Sari."

Even though it happened centuries ago, it still hurt to talk about him.

"I'm so sorry." Orion put a hand over the one she put on his arm, the weight and warmth of it surprisingly comforting.

"It was a long time ago, and it plunged our mother into the depths of depression. She only managed to climb out of that black hole of despair when Sari was born. She was such an adorable baby. Kian and I doted on her. I guess we also needed help to get over our grief."

Orion nodded. "I know what you mean. I carried my grief around for a long time. I still do, but it's not as heavy as it used to be before I found Geraldine. For a while, life seemed a little better, a little brighter, but then she had a terrible accident, and I was terrified of losing her as well. Thankfully, she made it, and then Cassandra was born, and life got better once more." He flashed her his sexy roguish smile. "It's getting so much brighter now that I will soon need to wear shades."

Alena laughed. "It's winter, so we can get away with not wearing them. But summers in Southern California are brutal on our eyes. The sun is blinding."

He tilted his head. "So sensitivity to the sun is a common trait among immortals?"

"Only first-generation immortals like us. Although Amanda is less sensitive than Kian and I are, and Sari lives in Scotland, where the sunlight is manageable even in the summer."

Orion stopped and looked at the house they'd passed. "Did you notice that we are walking in circles? Isn't that the house I'm staying in? They all look alike, but I think that I would know the difference."

"You are right." Alena chuckled. "I wasn't paying attention, and I let you lead the way. What a lousy tour guide I am."

The roguish smirk was back. "On the contrary, you are the best guide I've ever had."

As she pondered what he meant by that, Orion lifted his head and sniffed the air. "I can find the way to the café if that's where you wish to go."

"You can smell it from here?"

He tapped his nose. "I adopted the name Orion for a reason. I'm a hunter."

Oh, boy, she was in trouble.

The predatory gleam in his eyes awakened the attraction she'd managed to suppress by convincing herself that he wasn't interested in her. But there was no way he'd missed the flare of desire that had shot through her a moment ago.

She needed to cloak herself in anger once more, but as hard as she tried, she just couldn't summon it.

Letting out a breath, she tugged on his arm. "Lead the way, oh mighty hunter."

42

ORION

The village café was teeming with people who said hello, nodded, smiled, and waved, and none of it was fake or forced. Alena was well liked, and because he was with her, everyone was friendly toward him as well.

After waiting in line with everyone else to get their cappuccinos and pastries—no special treatment for the goddess's daughter—they'd had to wait for a table to become available.

When a couple got up and waved Alena and him over, Orion had a feeling that they had done so out of respect for her.

"Thank you." She smiled as the male held the chair out for her.

"Have a lovely day," his partner said.

"I'm amazed at this place." Orion set down their tray. "The vibe is so positive." He took another look around. "Is it always this pleasant?"

"I don't know about always, but it is when I'm here. Not because of me, but because of my mother. Annani's presence in the village is a mood booster for everyone." Alena lifted her cappuccino cup and took a sip. "Being around her is like being plugged in. Didn't you feel that yesterday at dinner?"

The truth was that he'd been so preoccupied with thoughts of the demigoddess sitting across from him that his attention had been divided between her and Annani, which had probably diminished the impact of the goddess's electrifying personality.

"The Clan Mother is awe-inspiring." He said what he thought she'd expected him to say.

Alena smiled behind her paper cup. "For some reason, you didn't seem as impressed or awed as others upon first meeting her. Is it because you've already met a god?"

Orion thought back to his one meeting with his father. "Frankly, I was so angry at him that I didn't feel awed at all. He acted like a bastard and tried to get rid of me. I had to follow him and force my way into his house for him even to deign to talk to me."

"He didn't exude power?"

"Not like your mother. Even in my distracted state, I felt that Annani was a powerhouse."

"Why were you distracted?"

He smiled. "Why do you think?"

A lovely blush colored her pale cheeks pink. "You tell me." She still tried to hide behind that paper cup, holding it between her palms right in front of her face.

"I heard an enchanting siren's song on my way to Kian's house, and then I met a beautiful demigoddess, whom I recognized right away as the singer of that song. However, unlike most of the people at dinner, who were comfortable with me and didn't fear my evil compulsion power, she wore earpieces and did her best to ignore me. While her mother introduced me to my dinner companions, I kept thinking about the lovely demigoddess and stealing covert glances at her, hardly paying attention to the most powerful being in the world."

Alena's blush deepened. "I have an irrational fear of having my will taken away from me and my mind not being my own. I'm sorry if the earpieces offend you, but building trust takes time."

"What if I vow never to compel you for any reason?"

She looked into his eyes, assessing him, but even though he assumed the most innocent expression he could muster, Alena shook her head. "How can I be sure that you will keep your vow? You are very charming, and I like you, but I don't know you."

She was right. He'd vowed never to love again, and here he was, courting the goddess's daughter as if he could offer her everything she deserved, including his heart on a platter. Evidently, he wasn't very good at keeping his vows.

Except, that vow had been different. He had known then as he knew now that Miriam would have never wanted him to take it.

The vow not to use compulsion on Alena was simple and easy to keep.

"I can swear on my sister's life. You know how much Geraldine means to me."

Alena looked at him, her eyes stripping him bare. "I believe that you mean it, but you can't really make that vow. What if I hold a knife to Geraldine's neck, and the only way you can stop me is to compel me?"

"That's the silliest argument I've ever heard. You would never do that."

Putting her cup down, she leaned closer and assumed what she must have thought was an evil expression. "How do you know? You've just met me. I could be a psychotic killer."

Orion laughed. "I'm willing to risk it."

Alena threw her hands in the air. "I'm not the sweetheart that everyone thinks I am." She let out a breath. "I'm so tired of this role. I'm over two thousand years old, and I need a change of pace. Heck, I need a major makeover."

Leaning toward her, he reached for her hand. "You're perfect the way you are, but if you are not happy, make whatever changes that will make you so."

She loosed another breath. "I don't know where to start."

"Go out with me."

Alena waved a hand at their surroundings. "I am out with you."

"I mean on a proper date that is not in the village—a restaurant, a show, a movie, dancing—whatever is your fancy, I'm your man. Provided that your brother doesn't object, that is."

"Kian? He has no authority over me. I can do as I please."

"I know that you can, but I'm not sure that I'm allowed to leave the village. Kian has a Guardian watching me twenty-four-seven. I don't know if he'll allow me to go out with you."

"Let's check." She pulled out her phone from a pocket in her dress. "When do you want to go?"

"Tomorrow, if that works for you. Tonight, we are invited to Kalugal's."

"Thanks for reminding me." She cast him a small smile. "I forgot about that."

43

KIAN

Kian had spent over an hour with his mother, listening to her stories about how smart Toven was, and how she couldn't understand how he'd changed so much. With Alena gone on a walk with Orion, he hadn't wanted to leave Annani alone until her second guest of the day arrived, but the moment Ella and Julian had shown up, he'd bid everyone goodbye and rushed home.

What the hell was Annani going to do if Alena mated Orion?

Their mother needed a companion, someone to take with her on her travels, someone to talk to. She didn't do well on her own.

Did she expect Alena and Orion to live with her in the sanctuary?

Did she delude herself that Orion would happily give up his freedom and his business endeavors to travel with her and Alena all over the world?

Kian wouldn't put it past her. She'd coerced Wonder to move in with her and bring Anandur along, but the two had been so miserable there that she had to let them go.

Perhaps the best solution was for her to move into the village.

The sanctuary had been built a long time ago, before the village existed, and Annani loved it, but maybe it was time for a change.

They could convert the sanctuary into a vacation destination for the clan, or have people live there in rotations throughout the year, just to keep it from falling apart. A lot of resources had gone into building it, and it could prove essential in case of an emergency—a fallout shelter of sorts.

His phone rang as Kian was ascending the steps to his front porch, and as he pulled it out of his pocket, he was surprised to see Alena's contact on the screen.

Kian frowned. She almost never called him, and she was out on a walk with Orion. That could only mean trouble.

"Are you all right?" he barked into the receiver.

"I'm very well, thank you. Orion wants to take me out on a date, and he asks if he's allowed to leave the village."

Letting out a breath, Kian opened the door and walked inside.

His knee-jerk instinct was to decline the request, but he had no real reason to do so. Orion was not a prisoner, he was a guest, and he was not a bad choice for Alena, provided he wasn't hiding some dirty secrets or dastardly plans. But since Edna had cleared him, Kian had no excuse to veto the date other than his overprotective instincts. When it came to his mother and sisters, and even more so his wife and daughter, he was extremely risk averse.

If he said no, Alena would go over his head to Annani, and their mother was going to overrule him. His best course of action was to allow it but to insist on precautions.

Kian walked over to the couch and sat next to Syssi.

"Orion is not a prisoner, and if he wants to leave, he can. But since you are going with him, you'll have to take at least one Guardian along."

Smiling, Syssi put down her tablet and leaned her head on his shoulder.

"Really?" Alena's tone was incredulous. "I don't need a chaperone, Kian."

Syssi chuckled and mouthed, "She doesn't."

"Not my rules, Alena. Mother's. I'm not allowed to go anywhere without two Guardians either."

"Amanda doesn't have to, and neither does Sari. Mother is worried about you because you are a potential target, but no one outside the clan even knows that I exist."

He sighed. "Humor me, Alena. We've known Orion for all of twenty-four hours. I'd rather err on the side of caution."

"Fine. We will need a car, though. Neither of us has one."

"Okidu can take you with the limo."

"I don't want to be driven around in a limo. Can we borrow your SUV instead?"

"When and for how long?"

"One moment." Alena muted the phone and came back a moment later. "We will leave the village Sunday at around noon and come back late in the evening."

"That's a long date."

"If that's a problem, I can ask Amanda if I can borrow her or Dalhu's car."

"She can have mine," Syssi offered.

He kissed the top of her head. "You can have the SUV. My only plans for tomorrow are to spend time with my wife and daughter, so I don't need the car. But Okidu will drive it, and you're taking Mason or one of the other Guardians with you."

"It's not going to be a very romantic date with a butler

and a Guardian tagging along, but I'm willing to compromise." She chuckled. "I know that you regard this as a big concession on your part, so thank you. I want you to know that I appreciate it."

"You're welcome. I hope you'll enjoy your date." He ended the call and put the phone in his pocket.

"Alena and Orion," Syssi murmured. "They make a good couple."

"Annani thinks so as well."

"And you don't?"

"I think it's too early for matchmaking. Orion seems like a decent fellow, and Edna approved of him, but we know very little about him. If he proves to be as good as he seems, then he is probably the best match for Alena. A mating between them could also benefit the clan. If we ever find Toven, a union between Orion and Alena will ensure cooperation between him and Annani. An alliance with a powerful god like him could prove invaluable to us."

Syssi lifted her head off his arm. "From what Orion told us, his father doesn't care much about him or anyone and anything else. He might not give a damn about Orion and Alena's mating. He just wants to be left alone."

"Tough luck. Annani wants me to find him. I need to schedule a meeting with Orion and Onegus and talk strategy. Annani also wants us to find Toven's other children."

"If he had any," Syssi said. "Most gods didn't have more than one or two children. Your mother was very fertile for a goddess."

"You're probably right, but she wants us to help Orion search for them, and what Annani wants, Annani gets."

44

ALENA

Alena put the phone away and smiled apologetically. "I'm sorry about the escort. But just so you know, Kian is usually much more suspicious and careful about newcomers. That he agreed to let you take me out at all is a big deal. In fact, I'm sure he wouldn't have if not for my mother being here and pushing for us to get together."

She shouldn't have said that.

Orion looked like he'd just won the lottery. "Is she now?"

Alena shrugged, affecting nonchalance even though she knew that he could see through it. "She's interested in an alliance with your father. This is purely political maneuvering."

That was partially true, but not entirely. Annani thought that they were a good match, and she wanted to see all her children happily mated. But had she thought it through? Did she realize that she might lose her companion?

Orion put his large hand on top of hers. "I don't care what your mother's or brother's reasons are. I only care about yours. Do you want to go out with me because you like me and want to get to know me better, or are you doing it to please your mother?"

It would have been easy to tell him that she was doing it for Annani or for the clan, but that would be a lie, and it would hurt his feelings.

Letting out a breath, she pulled her hand from under his. "I like you, or at least the version you've shown me so far. But I've lived a long time, and I know better than to base my opinion upon first impressions. In my experience, there is almost always something rotten just underneath the surface, and often it's enough to just lightly scratch the decorative veneer to reveal it."

He gave her a roguish smile, his lips curving on one side of his mouth and creating a dimple in his cheek. "I might not have lived as long as you have, but I have spent most of it interacting with humans, so I assume that the sum of my experiences is greater than yours. And yet, I don't second guess my first impression of you. I know that nothing ugly is hiding under the surface."

Her gut instinct said the same about him, but Alena wasn't her mother, and she didn't act on impulses or feelings. She weighed each decision logically. That was why she was such a perfect companion for Annani.

Alena was the counterbalance, the voice of logic, and her mother relied on her to push back against schemes that were too dangerous.

Still, she didn't want Orion to feel guilty until proven innocent. The earpieces that she was still wearing were offensive enough.

She gave him an encouraging smile. "My gut tells me that you are a good male, but I'm a cautious female. Given my position, I have to be."

He seemed confused, but a moment later, his eyes started glowing as if what she'd said either angered or excited him. "Do you mean your position as the goddess's eldest daughter? Are you targeted by your enemies, the Doomers?"

Understanding dawning, her heart warmed. He'd thought that she was in danger, and his protective instincts had flared.

How sweet.

"Didn't you hear my conversation with Kian? The Doomers don't even know that my sisters and I exist. They are only aware of Kian, and not even by name."

The glow in his eyes dimmed. "So what did you mean by position?"

Should she tell him? What would he think of her spending her life as a mere companion? She wasn't a leader like Kian and Sari, or a scientist like Amanda. She was just a mother, and her mothering days were long gone.

"I'm Annani's companion," she said quietly.

"You are her right-hand daughter, then, her second-in-command. That makes you a target for your enemies whether you realize it or not."

Alena chuckled. "I'm nothing as important as that. Our mother leaves the management of the clan to Kian and Sari, who act as regents on her behalf. She seldom interferes in day-to-day matters, but she stays informed. My job is to keep Annani company so she won't be alone and also to keep her out of trouble. She's quite impulsive and adventurous, and she often disregards safety. My siblings count on me to rein her in."

"Do you enjoy it?"

She flipped her braid back. "It's never dull with Annani around. She keeps me on my toes and generates excitement the equivalent of a rollercoaster ride or a NASCAR race. I'm the opposite of her, and we balance each other well. Without Annani, my life would probably have been very boring."

45

ORION

Orion had a feeling that Alena didn't think much of her position as Annani's companion.

"You're very fortunate to have such a wonderful relationship with your mother. My father doesn't want me in his life at all."

She lifted her eyes to him. "If he had offered you a position as his companion, would you have taken it?"

He took a couple of seconds to think it over. "If what he did was interesting, involved a lot of travel, and wasn't evil, then yes. I would have loved to have the opportunity to spend time with him, learn from him. Alas, that wasn't meant to be."

"I'm sorry he was such a jerk to you. But it's his loss." She lifted her paper cup and drank the last few drops. "We've been hogging this table for too long. People are waiting for us to leave."

Orion doubted that was the reason they were being gawked at, but since he preferred to have this talk with her in a more private setting, he rose to his feet and collected their cups and plates. "Are you up for another walk?"

She followed him up. "Your house is twenty minutes

from here, and I promised Mason to escort you back, so we are walking."

"If you're tired, I can find my way back on my own." He tossed the paper things into the recycling bin and the leftovers into the trash.

"I'm not tired." She waited for him to put the tray away. "I enjoy talking to you."

His heart soared like a schoolboy's. "I'm glad." He offered her his arm.

Her butler appeared out of nowhere and started trailing them.

"Where has he been all this time?"

"Helping Wonder and Wendy clean up," Alena said. "The Odus don't get tired, and they like being useful."

Since the Odus were machines, and therefore had no likes or dislikes, he assumed that she'd meant that they'd been programmed to be helpful. Or maybe they did have preferences?

"You still didn't tell me what the Odus' previous owner saved them from."

When she hesitated for a moment, he suspected that she didn't want the butler to hear, and when she looked over her shoulder, his suspicion was confirmed. "No one knows for sure," Alena said quietly. "We have a theory that is based on a vision, so it's not entirely reliable, but on the other hand, so far Syssi's visions have never been proven wrong, so what she saw might be a true account. It's also substantiated by some other bits and pieces of information that my mother learned from her husband. I will tell you about it later, though. It might be upsetting to you-know-who."

"You said that he's a cyborg. Does he have feelings?"

"That's also a complicated story that I would rather tell you some other time."

"On our date?"

She leaned on his arm and whispered, "Only if he and the Guardian Kian assigns to us are far enough not to overhear." She lifted her head and smiled conspiratorially. "Tonight at Kalugal's might be a better idea. We are invited, but the Odus are not."

"Excellent. But as curious as I am about your butler, I'm much more curious about you."

"I think we've already covered my entire life. Would you like me to take you on a tour of the village's gym and training center?"

"Certainly, and on the way you can tell me more about your children. Do any of them live in the village?"

"Just one at the moment. The rest are either in Scotland or in the sanctuary."

"Where is the sanctuary?"

She tensed. "That's a well-guarded secret. So much so that neither I nor Kian nor my two other sisters can find the place. The only ones who know are Annani and the Odus, who fly us back and forth. But since no one can torture the information out of them, the secret of the sanctuary's location is safe."

"What about hacking into their brains? I'm told that there is no computer in existence that can't be hacked."

Alena snorted. "Perhaps if the gods landed on Earth and captured the Odus, they could hack into their stored data. But no human or immortal can penetrate a computer brain created by alien technology from alien materials."

"Fascinating, but we are back to talking about the Odus when I want to talk about you."

"I'm not nearly as interesting as they are."

"I disagree." He slowed his steps. "Did you have feelings for any of your children's fathers?"

Did she even know who they had been?

"Yes." She smiled. "Feelings of gratitude for the gift of motherhood—to the Fates for blessing me with an incredible fertility for an immortal female, and to the men for contributing their genetic material. Each of my children is a unique individual, and they are all good people thanks in part to the upstanding human males I chose to father them."

He tilted his head. "How did you know that the men you chose were good people if you only met them once?"

A soft blush bloomed on her cheeks. "I've never taken a male to my bed without vetting him first. For me, choosing the right males with the right traits was more important than physical gratification. Besides, the Fates made me fertile for a reason, and I like to believe that they had a hand in each one of the conceptions, allowing only the best to take root."

"So it was all about duty? About creating the clan?"

"Oh, no." She laughed. "I love children, and during the years they were growing up, I was the happiest and the most fulfilled."

"How far apart were your children born?"

She sighed. "It's strange, but I delivered all thirteen during the first five centuries of my life. After that, my fertility apparently ran out, which shouldn't have happened to an immortal whose body doesn't age." She looked at him from under lowered lashes. "And it wasn't for lack of trying. I wouldn't have minded having a hundred children if I could."

46

GERALDINE

Geraldine huffed out a breath and sank onto the couch. "I forgot how tiring it is to move."

Cassandra sat down next to her. "That was actually easy. We only brought over clothing. We still need to pack the artwork and all your knickknacks."

"The exhausting part is not hanging my things in the closet. It's the emotional drain." Geraldine sighed. "I'm going to miss our old house, which isn't old at all. It was brand new when you bought it, and it symbolizes so much." Tears gathered in the corners of her eyes. "You bought it after your big promotion. It was your way to show that you'd made it, that you'd succeeded, that you'd proven yourself."

"It's just a house, Mom." Cassandra draped her arm over Geraldine's shoulders. "You've always told me that a home is where your loved ones are, and since we are here, this lovely new house is our home. It's next door to Onegus and me on one side and Orion on the other. It doesn't get any better than that."

"Yeah, it does. If Darlene transitions and moves here as

well, it will be even better. Since Orion is not staying, she can move into his house."

"Maybe he will stay," Onegus said. "He's just gotten here, and he seems very interested in Alena. They went on a long walk this morning, then spent over an hour in the café, and they are going on a date tomorrow."

"Awesome." Cassandra pumped her fist in the air. "Nothing like a good woman to help a guy make up his mind about staying."

"Alena doesn't live in the village," Shai pointed out. "If they bond, he will have to move with her to the sanctuary."

Cassandra shrugged. "Then we need to convince Alena to move into the village. I'll start the campaign tonight at Kalugal's."

Shai's expression remained doubtful. "Alena is the Clan Mother's companion. She can't leave."

"The Clan Mother will have to find a new companion," Geraldine said. "As a mother, she needs to think about her daughter's happiness first." She lifted her eyes to Cassandra. "It was difficult for me when you moved out, but I dealt with it because I wanted you to have a life with Onegus."

"Oh, Mom." Cassandra leaned and kissed her cheek. "I love you."

"I love you too, sweetheart." Geraldine scrunched her nose. "Are you busy tomorrow?"

"I don't have any plans other than playing house with Onegus. Why?"

"If I want to be able to visit my friends, I need to start driving again, but I haven't driven in so long that I've lost my confidence. Can you take me out for a spin tomorrow?"

"Sure thing. We can drive to the mall and pick up stuff for our new houses. I want to replace Ingrid's artwork with something more exciting."

Geraldine winced. "I'm not ready for such a long drive.

I need to start on a deserted road where I can't hurt anyone."

"I'll take you," Shai said. "I've put in an order for a clan car for you. It should get here in about three weeks."

"Thank you." Geraldine rose to her feet, walked over to him, and kissed him lightly on the lips. "Why didn't you tell me sooner?"

"The order went out only yesterday, and I thought to surprise you when the car got here, but since it's such a long wait, you would've asked about it eventually, and I would've told you anyway."

"That's so sweet of you." She kissed him again. "I need to come up with a good story to explain to my friends why they can't visit me in my new place."

"You can use the same story—" He stopped himself. "You know, the one about your fiancé working for a reclusive billionaire who demands that his employees and their families live on his estate, but doesn't allow visitors."

That was the story Shai had told Rhett, but Cassandra and Onegus didn't know about the son he'd kept a secret for nearly twenty years. It was so sad that Shai had to be a lawbreaker to be part of his son's life. The stupid law that prohibited immortal males from sharing the lives of their children had to go.

Perhaps she could mention it tonight to Kian or even the goddess herself. But if she did, they might wonder why. She could make it sound like a random thought, and with her fragile mind, no one should think much of it. They would just assume that she'd gotten confused.

Except, it would stress Shai out, so maybe she shouldn't.

"When is Orion taking Alena on a date?" Cassandra asked. "I mean, what time?"

Onegus arched a brow. "Why?"

"I just thought that if Orion is busy with Alena, we can

call Darlene and invite her to have lunch with us. I spoke with her yesterday, and she said that Leo wasn't back yet. His business trip got prolonged."

"What does that have to do with Orion?" Onegus asked. "Do you want her to meet him?"

"No, not yet." She turned to Geraldine. "I didn't make any plans with Darlene because I knew that you wanted to spend as much time with your brother as possible before he left, but since he's going out on a date with Alena and won't be here anyway, we can move our plans regarding Darlene a step forward."

47

KIAN

"Kalugal's mansion is so impressive," Syssi said as Okidu drove the large golf cart over the bridge into Kalugal's section of the village.

"What you see is just what's above ground," Kian said. "Most of the structure is underground, and it's much grander on the inside."

"I know." She smiled at him. "I have seen the blueprints. But I didn't see the façade Gavin designed. He did a magnificent job of making the visible section impressive despite its modest size and security limitations. Hiding the structure from passing aircraft is one heck of an architectural challenge."

Syssi's comment on security had Kian seeking out the hidden cameras aimed at the bridge, but he couldn't detect them even though he knew they were working just fine. William's crew had done a good job of making them invisible.

If Kalugal had discovered them, he hadn't done or said anything about them. They were still transmitting images twenty-four-seven to the clan's security center. But that was the extent of what Kian had done to keep an eye on his cousin and his men. There were no Guardians posted on or near the bridge, and there was no gate either.

Only a small fraction of the security measures he'd originally planned for the place had ended up being implemented.

During the months it had taken to complete the building project, Kian's mistrust of Kalugal had significantly lessened. He no longer worried about his cousin making a move against the clan, but that didn't mean that he knew what Kalugal was up to. He and his men spent long hours in their city office building, including Saturdays and some of them even on Sundays.

That was a significant departure from the days of Kalugal not having enough work to keep his men busy.

It occurred to Kian that he had a new tool in his arsenal to use to find out what Kalugal was working on.

Orion was not bound by Annani's compulsion, and he was a powerful compeller who could ask one of Kalugal's top men a few questions on Kian's behalf. He wouldn't dare to refuse the request, especially now that he was interested in Alena and needed the clan's help to search for his father and siblings. The guy had a lot to gain by helping out.

Furthermore, as long as Kian didn't use the information against his cousin or his men, getting some questions answered was not a violation of the accord.

Kalugal, however, might be of a different opinion.

When Okidu parked the golf cart behind the smaller one that Anandur had driven over, Kalugal and Jacki came out to greet them. The couple waved hello at the brothers and their mates and then walked over to the larger cart.

"Good evening, my dear family." Kalugal rounded the vehicle to where Annani was seated and offered her a hand to help her down. "Welcome to our home, Clan Mother."

"Thank you." She took his hand and let him assist her. "It is very impressive."

Kalugal offered his hand to Alena next.

"Give me both hands," Amanda told Dalhu. "I'm a whale. I need a crane."

"You're not a whale, but you have a crane." He put his hands under her armpits and lifted her down.

"Where are the little ones?" Jacki asked as Andrew and Nathalie got out of the long limo-style golf cart.

"Ella, Wendy, and Lisa are watching Allegra, Ethan, and Phoenix. We decided to get babysitters and have us a grownup evening." She winked at Syssi.

When everyone disembarked, Okidu got back behind the wheel and drove to pick up the second group of guests.

"Aren't they too young to take care of babies?" Kalugal asked.

Syssi winced. "Phoenix and Ethan are not a problem, but I'm worried about Allegra. She's still so tiny."

"Don't worry," Amanda said. "Ella has plenty of experience babysitting. She helped Vivian raise Parker, and he grew up to be a fine young man. Besides, you're five minutes away. If Allegra gets fussy, Ella can call you, and you can rush over."

"Yeah, you're right." Syssi forced a smile. "I should trust her."

Syssi had wanted to leave Allegra with Okidu, but Kian still didn't feel comfortable doing so. He trusted Okidu, but not a hundred percent. Not enough to leave his vulnerable little daughter with him.

Jacki and Kalugal led them up the steps, and as Kalugal opened the massive front door, he turned to his wife. "Should we wait with the grand tour until everyone arrives?"

"We can do two tours." Jacki put a hand on his chest.

"I'll lead the first one while you wait out here for the others and give them a tour when they arrive."

Kalugal didn't look happy, and Kian knew why. He wanted to show off, and he wanted to see Kian's reaction to the extravagant opulence.

Heck, why not.

He didn't mind letting the guy enjoy his moment.

"How about we take a tour of the grounds while we wait for the others," Kian offered. "And then both of you can share the joy of giving everyone a tour of the interior."

Kalugal looked to his wife for approval of Kian's plan.

She nodded. "Good thinking. We will do it your way."

48

ALENA

As Orion and the other guests arrived, Alena's heart did a happy flip and started beating like a frantic butterfly.

After they were done saying their helloes, and Kalugal led them inside his mansion, Orion fell in step with her.

"Did you get any rest?" he asked.

"My mother had visitors, and my presence was required."

"You must be tired."

"Not at all."

She'd spent the afternoon smiling and nodding and pretending to listen, while replaying her morning with Orion in her head and going over their conversation so she wouldn't forget any of it.

"How about you? How did you spend your afternoon?"

"I watched *Frozen* again."

She chuckled. "You didn't."

"I did, and I enjoyed every moment of it." He leaned closer to whisper in her ear. "I want to hear you sing it again, preferably just for me."

Was he actually interested in hearing her sing, or was it a sexual innuendo?

"Aboveground, we have the entry, the family room, the secondary kitchen, and the staff bedrooms." Kalugal headed toward a wide staircase that led to the lower level. "The main living quarters are underground. But don't worry, it's not stuffy or dark. We have motorized skylights that can be opened to allow fresh air in, and there is plenty of natural light."

Kalugal's house was amazing, and it reminded Alena of the sanctuary, just without the indoor tropical paradise built under a dome of ice.

If someone flew a drone high over his house, they would only see treetops. Just as in the rest of the village, clever mirror placement multiplied the visual greenery and hid the rooftops. If the drone flew lower, under the tree canopies, it would see an average-sized home with expensive finishes, manicured grounds, and what looked like reflective tiles embedded in the ground in between shrubs and bushes and flower beds. Those tiles were actually the skylights, coated with reflective material and angled so they reflected the greenery.

It was just as luxurious as the sanctuary, but not nearly as large. Then again, the only people living in the house were Kalugal and Jacki and a staff of two, while the sanctuary was home to over seventy people.

"Here is our home gym." Kalugal pushed the double doors open. "It includes a lap pool a hundred feet long—that's two-thirds of a regulation Olympic pool."

"I'm impressed," Orion said. "But what do you need a private pool for? The one in the clan's training center is true Olympic size, and it's available to everyone."

"I like my privacy." Kalugal put an arm around Jacki's rounded middle. "And I don't like anyone gaping at my wife while she's in a bikini."

"Kalugal is a snob," Kian murmured next to Orion. "And he's a competitive bastard. Since I have a lap pool in my backyard, he needs to have a bigger one."

Alena stifled a chuckle.

"Are we done?" Amanda asked. "It's not easy walking around with this belly."

"Yes, of course." Kalugal led them out into the wide hallway. "Just one more room to see." He pushed another set of doors open. "Our twenty-four-seat home theater. After dinner, we can come here and watch a movie."

"You must be doing very well for yourself," Kian said. "This must have cost a fortune, and you also doubled your donations to our cause, for which I haven't thanked you yet. Your contribution is much needed and appreciated."

"You're very welcome." Kalugal cut a sidelong glance at Annani. "But that was Jacki's doing. She convinced me that if I expect my good fortune to continue, I need to contribute some of it to a good cause. The two causes I chose were the clan's fight against traffickers and another organization that fights world hunger." He puffed out his chest. "Frankly, I didn't think that donating would make me feel so good. I started the donations as a bribe, and I didn't expect to keep making them for long, but Jacki was right when she said that it was the right thing to do. I feel like I'm making the world a little better and paying forward the good fortune I've been given." He smiled lovingly at his wife.

Annani put her hand on his arm. "Areana will be so proud of you when she hears this. I assume that you did not tell her yet because she did not mention your increased contributions when we talked last week."

"What I want to know," Kian grumbled, "Is how you make all that money. Is it all stock market gains?"

"In a way, but not exactly. I'll tell you about it over cigars and whiskey after dinner."

49

ORION

Kalugal put his fork down and wiped his mouth with a napkin. "I would like your honest opinion, Orion. Now that you can compare Atzil's cooking to the Odus's, whose is better?"

The dinner served by Kalugal's cook hadn't been as fancy as the one served by Kian and Amanda's butlers, but the food was tasty in a hearty way that he preferred.

"It's a matter of taste." Lifting his wine goblet, Orion took a sip while catching a glimpse of the cook's white apron peeking from behind the opening to the kitchen. "I enjoyed Atzil's cooking more because I prefer simpler, heartier dishes. The Odus prepared a sophisticated meal, which probably appealed more to others."

Kian chuckled. "You're a politician, Orion."

"I told the truth and nothing but the truth. But if we are already talking about the Odus, I would like to know what their previous owner saved them from by sending them to Earth." He shifted his eyes to Syssi. "Alena told me that you had a vision about that."

As all eyes turned to Alena, the silence around the table was deafening.

"Was that supposed to be a secret?" she asked. "Because no one told me that it was."

Kian was shooting daggers at his sister, but he didn't say a word.

"It is not a secret," Annani said, defusing the tension. "My father-in-law found the Odus in the desert, and they immediately recognized him as their master." She looked at Orion. "They had been programmed to find a god and become his or hers, but other than that, all their other previous programming had been wiped. They only retained basic functioning and learning capabilities. My father-in-law told Khiann that the Odus had been created to be servants. He hinted that they had been misused in warfare and that the winning side decided to decommission them, and the technology of how to make them was erased. We speculate that the owner of the seven did not wish to see them destroyed and sent them to a distant colony of the gods where he believed they would be appreciated."

Syssi put her napkin over her plate. "In my vision, I saw scores of Odus being loaded into shuttles. Nothing was said in that vision, so I don't know for sure that they were being loaded to be ejected into space, but the feeling was somber, depressing."

"Perhaps they were loaded on the shuttle to be sent into battle," Orion suggested.

"Perhaps." Syssi lifted her wine goblet. "That would be a somber event as well."

Kian still looked as if someone had pissed in his soup, and Orion had a strong feeling that it was in his best interest to steer the conversation away from the subject of the marvelous Odus. For some reason, Kian either didn't like talking about them, or he didn't want Orion to learn too much about them.

Not that he could blame the guy. A greedy person

might decide to steal one of those amazing creations and sell it to the highest bidder. Human AI was nowhere near as sophisticated, and companies working on developing it would pay many millions to put their hands on a perfectly functioning cyborg so they could reverse engineer it.

Assuming an amiable expression, he turned to their host. "Something you said during the tour intrigued me. You said that you started donating to the clan's humanitarian cause as a bribe. Was that in exchange for Kian allowing you and your men to live in the village?"

Kalugal looked at his wife, who smiled and nodded, and then at Kian, who shrugged. He took Jacki's hand, lifted it to his lips, and kissed it. "I did that to win Jacki's love."

"He kept me as a hostage," Jacki said. "He scared the hell out of me just to verify that what Kian had told him was true, and to make amends and convince me to give him another chance, Kalugal made me a deal. For every day that I agreed to stay with him, he would donate twenty-five thousand dollars to the clan's charity."

Orion arched a brow. "That's a lot of money. He must have done something really bad."

"Oh, he did." Jacki cast a mock stern look at her husband. "But he apologized profusely and paid for it dearly, so I forgave him."

50

KIAN

After coffee had been served, Atzil's chocolate soufflé had been devoured, and Annani had invited everyone present to celebrate the winter solstice at her place, Kalugal rose to his feet. "Whoever wants to join Kian and me for whiskey and cigars out in the gazebo, please follow."

As usual, the ladies were happy to see them go. Kian could only imagine what they talked about when the men were not around, but he didn't care as long as Syssi enjoyed herself. She loved being a mother, but he'd noticed that she'd become restless lately, and this outing without Allegra was good for her.

For a change, she could spend time with her friends, not as the hostess but as a guest and without having to keep an ear on the baby monitor and rush out the moment Allegra uttered a sound.

Kalugal led them up the stairs and into his garden, which was walled off by greenery rather than a fence. A gazebo on a raised platform was already set up with a couple of bottles of superb whiskey and a box of cigars, the fire pit in its middle warming up the night's chilly air.

"I hope you approve." Kalugal opened the lid. "I got us genuine Cohibas from a reliable source. Those are not fake, my friends. Enjoy."

Seated around the fire pit, each holding a cigar in one hand and a glass of whiskey in the other, they took a few moments to savor the tastes, the smells, and to compliment their host.

It was decadent.

Kian had never felt like a privileged rich male when he smoked in his modest backyard. It felt like a well-earned reward after a long day at work, or when he had guests over, a way to be a good host and connect with his male friends.

At Kalugal's though, everything was grand, over the top, and screamed money.

Taking one more puff, Kian turned to his cousin. "So, what's your money-making secret?"

"I've always been good at spotting opportunities." Kalugal puffed on his cigar. "But I have to admit that I was a little slow to jump on this one." He smiled at Kian. "But not too late to make a fortune."

He had their attention.

"You do like drama, cousin. Enough with the intro and give us the juicy details."

Looking even smugger than usual, he lifted three fingers. "Blockchain technology, cryptocurrency, and Web 3.0—the new true global democracy."

Kian shook his head. "Cryptocurrency is unreliable. It has nothing to back it up. It's just an imaginary construct and it can disappear into the thin air it has been created from."

Kalugal smiled indulgently. "I was of the same opinion when I first read about it, but I've since changed my mind, and I'm a much richer man for it. Especially since I minted one of the most popular coins, and it's selling like crazy."

The guy was a gambler, and minting his own coin was a genius move, but he could lose all that money just as fast as he'd made it. Besides, Kian was sure that cryptocurrency wasn't the only thing keeping Kalugal busy these days.

"Good for you." Kian took a sip from his whiskey. "But I'm not a gambler. I'm not investing in cryptocurrency."

"You'll regret it." Kalugal smirked. "The dollar is just as imaginary a construct as crypto, but unlike crypto, the government does whatever it wants with it. When they print money, they devalue the worth of what's in your bank, and there is no way to bounce back from that. That money will never regain its worth. Crypto is volatile now, but it will eventually stabilize, and the government can't put its greedy paws on it."

"I'm glad that it's working for you, and I appreciate the doubling of your contributions, but for now, I'm not ready to jump in."

"You don't have to invest in cryptocurrency. There is a lot of money to be made by investing in companies that develop blockchain technology and the new internet. That's more up your alley as an investor. Although, I know that you prefer a more hands-on approach. You don't like just putting in money, you like developing the technology."

Kian nodded. "You got me pegged, cousin. I find it much more satisfying to be part of the creative process."

"What is Web 3.0?" Orion asked. "I didn't even know that there was a Web 1.0 or Web 2.0." He smiled apologetically. "I was never tech-savvy."

"Web 1.0 was the beginning of the internet," Shai said. "Users passively surfed for information but didn't generate content. In Web 2.0, users generate content and interact with sites and other users through social media. I don't know much about Web 3.0, though. Is it run by artificial intelligence?"

"Web 3.0 is the new democracy," Kalugal said. "Currently, the internet is dominated by tech giants who censor users and exploit their data for profit, selling it to advertisers and to other more nefarious parties. There is hope that Web 3.0 will have a decentralized infrastructure. A lot of it will run on blockchain, which means that the data will belong to the users, and they will be compensated for it, not the tech behemoths."

"A brave new world," Anandur teased. "I want to learn more about it."

"That's a smart man." Kalugal waved his cigar in Anandur's direction. "Crypto currently represents seven percent of all global currency." He cast Kian a sidelong glance. "Do you really think that it's going to disappear? Just think how much more you'll be able to do for the clan and for the humanitarian causes the clan supports with the fortunes you can make if you jump on this spaceship before it breaks orbit and shoots for the stars."

"Nice analogy," Shai said.

Kian leveled his eyes on Kalugal. "What I want to know is what you're going to do with all that money."

"Conquer the world, of course." Kalugal laughed. "Money makes the world go round, right? So those who have the most of it determine which way it spins and at what speed."

51

ALENA

"Thank you for a fantastic evening." Alena kissed Jacki's cheek.

"I'm glad everyone enjoyed themselves." Kalugal walked them out the door.

Up front, Okidu and Onidu were waiting with the golf carts, but Alena wasn't ready to call it a night. She and Orion had barely exchanged a few words throughout the evening, and the morning they'd spent together seemed like it had happened days ago.

"Alena?" Kian turned to her after helping Annani into the cart. "Are you coming?"

"I'd rather walk some of this off." She patted her belly and smiled at Orion in a blatant invitation. "Anyone want to join me?"

He dipped his head and offered her his arm. "It will be my pleasure to walk you home."

Kian's grimace was enough to scare off the most ardent suitor, but Orion wasn't easily deterred and kept his expression neutral under her brother's hard stare.

Alena had known that Kian wouldn't approve. Other than Anandur and Brundar, they had no other Guardians with them, and Ovidu had stayed in the house, so there was no one to chaperone her. But she didn't need to be guarded from Orion, and she wasn't asking Kian's permission.

"Anandur will go with you," Kian said.

The Guardian didn't look happy, and she couldn't blame him. He wanted to go home to his mate instead of performing a needless task because Kian was an overprotective brother.

"Orion will suffice as Alena's escort, Kian." Their mother's tone brooked no argument. "I am sure he can handle any night prowler that might slither into our very safe village." She winked at Alena.

As a blush warmed her cheeks, she didn't know whether to be angry at her mother or grateful. Annani's wink and smile sent a clear message that she didn't expect Alena to arrive at their house anytime soon.

Orion bowed his head. "I'll guard Alena with my life. Goodnight, everyone." He didn't wait for a response before leading Alena out of Kalugal's front courtyard.

"I'm sorry about that," she said quietly. "It's nothing personal against you. He would have done the same with any male other than a clan member." She let out a breath. "Kian is trying to adapt to the times, but he is still such a damn chauvinist. If the roles were reversed, and I was a clan male and you a newfound immortal female, he wouldn't have been worried one bit."

"I don't think that's true. Kian is more worried about me than others because of my compulsion ability." He cast her a bright smile. "Thank you for not wearing the earpieces tonight. I take it as a vote of confidence and trust in me."

She reached into her pocket and closed her hand around the two small devices. Coming here tonight, she hadn't planned on being alone with Orion, and she'd been sure he wouldn't use compulsion with Annani around, but now that they were alone, a sliver of fear crept into her heart.

"I have them in my pocket," she admitted. "But I'm not going to put them in. I trust you."

He stopped and turned to face her. "You can't imagine how much that means to me. You can be absolutely sure that I will never compel you to do anything."

"What if I ask you to do it?"

"Why would you?"

Smiling, she threaded her arm through his and resumed walking. "Amanda once asked Kalugal to compel her not to crave cheese. She's a vegetarian, but she wanted to go full vegan like Kian."

"Did he do it?"

"He wasn't happy about it, but after some convincing, he did, and it worked. Amanda couldn't touch cheese for days. But then she got tired of it and asked our mother to remove the compulsion."

Alena had told Orion the story as a subtle hint that she wasn't completely helpless against his compulsion. If need be, Annani could free her from it.

"Your mother must be more powerful than Toven, both in ability and in strength of character. After the demise of the gods, he allowed ennui to overtake his soul, while Annani found a worthy goal to keep her going. I kept watching her tonight and admiring how lively and passionate she is. The contrast was so stark."

"Don't judge your father too harshly. We don't know what his story is. He might have started out like she did but failed and got discouraged and disillusioned. Fates know we had so many setbacks over the years that it's a miracle my mother never gave up. Not even after Lilen's death."

"That's what I meant by strength of character. Your mother kept fighting no matter what obstacles she faced.

To me, that is even more admirable and awe-inspiring than her innate godly powers."

When they reached the house Alena shared with her mother, Alena regretted not being able to see whether the lights were on inside. For security reasons, all windows in the village had been equipped with motorized shutters that were timed to close at nightfall to prevent lights from betraying their location.

Orion climbed up the steps with her and stopped by the front door. "I don't wish us to part."

Was that a question in his eyes? Was he waiting for her to invite him in?

Her mother wouldn't mind, but Alena hesitated.

She didn't want to treat Orion like one of her casual hookups. It was nice to be courted for a change and get to know a guy before getting intimate with him. On the other hand, she hadn't been with a man for a long while, and Orion was sexy as sin.

"We can sit on the bench for a little bit," she suggested.

"Okay." He took her hand and led her to the wooden bench under the living-room shuttered window.

When they sat down, he hesitantly wrapped his arm around her shoulders, and when she leaned her head on him, he let out a relieved breath.

The guy was over five centuries old, and she'd managed to reduce him to a schoolboy.

Why was she acting so prim and proper with him? Especially given that her primal instincts urged her to throw him on the porch floor and rip his clothes off?

Because she was Annani's eldest daughter, and he knew who she was.

With human partners, she didn't need to act like a lady, she didn't need to act at all unless she wanted to play. She could assume any role—wanton or shy, assertive or submissive, passionate or reserved. It didn't matter what they thought of her because she never saw them again. She was never interested in getting to know them, developing a relationship.

It was easy to just bed a guy and leave. There was no emotional attachment.

With Orion, she didn't know how to act or what to do.

Because with him, she wanted more.

52

ORION

Orion was keenly aware of the goddess's presence on the other side of the wall. The power Annani radiated couldn't be contained by wood, plasterboard, and the best insulation money could buy.

He'd recognized its signature as soon as they neared the house, and now, sitting so close, he could no longer convince himself that it was all in his imagination.

Did the goddess's power dim when she slept?

She was awake now, he was sure of that, waiting for her daughter to return.

What was the protocol for courting a demigoddess?

Should he even be doing this?

He craved Alena as he had never craved a woman, not even the love of his life.

Miriam had been beautiful, soft and gentle, and he had loved her deeply. But even though he'd been a young man back then, the passion he'd felt for her had been a pale echo of the inferno Alena ignited in him.

The desire was primal, demanding, as if his body recognized its equal and was desperate for her—a strong immortal female who he wouldn't have to hold back with, who could keep up with his stamina, who could possibly exhaust him instead of leaving him only partially satisfied.

Damn, he felt so guilty for having those thoughts.

He wasn't in love with Alena like he had been with Miriam. The novelty of an immortal female was probably to blame for his raging desire, and once he bedded Alena and his hunger was satiated, he would be able to think clearly and examine how he really felt about her.

Except, this could not be a one-time thing for either of them, and if they crossed that line, the consequences would be significant. Especially for him.

Kian would murder him if he misled Alena or hurt her feelings.

Unless he was certain that he could offer her his heart, he should stop right now and find an excuse to cancel their date tomorrow.

The thought made his gut clench so painfully that he had to suppress a wince.

For a guy who prided himself on his cool head and decisiveness, the wavering between extremes was unsettling. For the first time in centuries, Orion wasn't sure about anything.

Logically, he was willing to let go of the vow he'd made centuries ago to never love a woman again, but his heart and gut were not in agreement.

Not consistently.

One moment he was convinced that Miriam would have wanted him to love again and that she would be angry at him if he squandered the only opportunity to mate his equal in every way—a demigoddess who would live as long as he did and not die on him within a few miserly decades. But the next moment he saw his long-dead wife looking at him with accusation in her tear-filled eyes, asking him if he'd ever truly loved her and calling him an oath breaker.

"What's wrong?" Alena asked. "You made a sound as if you were in pain."

"It's nothing. I remembered something upsetting."

"Do you want to talk about it?"

"Not really."

Alena looked offended. "I should get inside," she said quietly, but didn't make a move to get up.

"I didn't want to tell you about the thing that upset me because I didn't want to spoil the mood. I had a wonderful time with you today."

"It's okay." She smiled at him. "We barely know each other. You don't need to tell me anything that you're uncomfortable with."

He swallowed. "I'm not used to talking about myself. I've spent my life among humans, hiding who I was."

Her eyes softened. "That must have been so difficult, being all alone."

"I didn't realize how much until I got here, until I met you."

She smiled, and he wanted to kiss her so badly, but would he be able to stop at just a kiss?

And what about the goddess?

Would she rage at him for taking liberties with her daughter?

Rising to his feet, Orion offered Alena a hand up. When she took it, he slowly pulled her against his chest, giving her every opportunity to back away.

She didn't.

Closing the last inch of distance between them, she tilted her face up with a coquettish smile lifting her lush lips. "Am I getting a kiss goodnight?"

He wanted to tell her that she could get much more than that, but instead, he stifled the impulse and took her lips.

53

ALENA

Orion's lips were soft, smooth, his mouth warm, gentle, and as Alena twined her hands around his neck and kissed him back, the world and all of her earthly concerns receded, leaving only the here and now, only Orion.

Letting go of her lips, he leaned away and gazed at her with wonder in his eyes. "Your eyes are glowing," he murmured.

"So are yours."

One side of his lips lifted in a satisfied smirk, forming a dimple in his cheek. "Are they now?"

Immortal, she was with an immortal male, and everything about this kiss was different from any she'd received or given before.

"Your fangs have elongated as well." It was the first time she'd seen a male's fangs up close and imagining what he could do with them shot a blast of desire through her.

Damn, that was hot.

Orion smiled, baring those beauties for her to admire. "I've never smiled while aroused before. It feels like an unleashing."

And then he showed her what he'd meant by that.

His hands, which had been roaming over her sides before, slipped away, not to let go, but to secure a better hold on her. One gripping her waist, the other her hair, he tipped her head back and plunged his tongue into her welcoming mouth.

A soft moan leaving her throat, Alena gave herself over to the kiss, to Orion, and when a moment later he twisted them around and pushed her against the front door, she dropped her hands from his neck and cupped his glorious behind.

She'd been eyeing it hungrily all evening, and it felt just as hard and muscular as she'd imagined.

Encouraged by the move, Orion slid a hand down to her thigh and hoisted it up around his waist. Thankfully, her long loose skirt did not hinder the maneuver, the thin fabric allowing her to feel every delicious grind of his hard length against her core.

They were making a ruckus, and Alena had no doubt that her mother could hear everything, but she didn't care. She'd witnessed Annani seduce men often enough, and her mother had seen her do the same. They'd been careful to never take things beyond casual flirting in front of one another, but with their enhanced hearing, complete privacy had not always been possible.

When he left her mouth, she was about to protest, but then he began exploring her neck, his fangs scraping delicately over the soft skin, and her protests died on her lips.

She dug her fingers into his bottom, which earned her a stinging ear nip, and when she retaliated by digging her fingers deeper into the hard muscle, he seized her mouth again to plunder it.

Fates, how she wanted him to reach under her skirt, tear her panties off, and plunge that long, hard length into her. But they were out in the open, necking like a couple of horny teenagers, not by the front door, but actually leaning against it, and she couldn't allow a random passerby to catch her acting like that in public.

Uttering a frustrated groan, she pushed on his chest. "We have to stop, Orion."

He let go of her immediately. "I'm sorry." He backed away.

"Don't." She put a hand over her racing heart. "I loved every moment of it, but we can't be doing this out here."

His fully elongated fangs protruding over his lower lip, and his eyes glowing blue light, Orion was a gorgeous predator, and Alena wanted him so much that she had to bite her lips to stop herself from inviting him inside.

Annani wouldn't say a word, but it would be highly inappropriate.

"Come to my place." He reached for her hand.

"Not tonight," she heard herself saying. "We shouldn't rush into this."

Nodding, he wiped a hand over his mouth. "You're right. We shouldn't."

He didn't sound convinced at all, but she appreciated that he wasn't trying to pressure her.

"Good night, Orion." She leaned over and kissed him one last time, intending it to be a soft parting kiss, but Orion had other ideas.

His arms locking around her, he took over the kiss, and soon they were exactly where they had been a few moments ago, their lips and tongues and hands roaming, touching.

This time it was Orion who let go first. "I'd better go before I do something stupid and take you right here on this porch." He walked backward down the steps.

She managed a chuckle. "The clan's rumor mill would keep turning for months." She lifted a hand and waved. "Good night, Orion."

"Good night, Alena. Don't forget, tomorrow at noon."

"I'll be ready."

She opened the door and ducked inside.

Thankfully, it was dark, and there was no one in the living room. Down the hallway though, the door to her mother's room was open, and a movie was playing on the television—a comedy, given her mother's laughter.

Alena stopped at Annani's door. "I'm back, Mother. I'm going to sleep. I just wanted to say good night."

Annani tore her gaze away from the screen and gave Alena a bright smile. "Good night, my dear daughter. I wish you sweet dreams."

54

ALENA

Alena stood in front of her closet and looked at her collection of dresses. Why on earth had she donated the clothes Amanda had gotten her for the New York gig?

She knew perfectly well why she'd done it.

It had been too upsetting to see all those fashionable outfits hanging in her closet, remembering the fun she had while pretending to be a supermodel, and knowing that she had nowhere to wear them.

While traveling with her mother, they both tried to look as ordinary as possible so as not to call attention to themselves. Annani shrouded herself, but while it was effortless for her mother, keeping a shroud for a prolonged period of time was tiring for Alena. Besides, dressing plainly did the trick for her. She was pretty, but she wasn't a stunning beauty like her mother or like Amanda.

Except, now she had nothing to wear for her date with Orion.

Perhaps she should call Amanda and go over to her place. They were almost the same height, with Amanda being about an inch taller but slimmer, or she had been before the pregnancy. Before, Amanda had also been less endowed, but the difference had shrunk to about half a cup size, if that.

Hopefully, she hadn't donated all her pre-pregnancy clothes, which knowing her sister was very likely.

Amanda was a fashionista, and she seldom wore the same article of clothing more than a few times before donating it. She probably planned on getting a whole new wardrobe as soon as she regained her pre-pregnancy figure.

"Here you are." Her mother glided in through the open closet door, the glow from her luminescent skin casting light on the row of dresses. "Are you hoping new outfits will materialize if you stare at your closet for long enough?"

"I don't have anything nice to wear for my date with Orion. I love my comfortable, soft dresses, but no one else does. He will not be impressed if I show up in one of these."

Annani chuckled. "Orion will not care what you are wearing, my dear. You can show up wearing a potato sack, and he will still look at you as if you are the most beautiful woman he has ever seen because you are."

"Thanks for the pep talk." Alena leaned down and kissed her mother's cheek. "But for this date, I want to look like a young woman from this generation. I'll call Amanda and ask her if she can lend me one of her outfits."

"That is a very good idea. Your sister loves giving makeovers, and you will make her day by requesting one." Annani took a quick glance at the mirror and flipped the mass of her red hair back. "I will be out most of the day and evening, visiting clan members, so enjoy your time with Orion and do not hurry to come back." She smiled. "In fact, you do not have to come back tonight at all." She winked at Alena and then motioned for her to dip her head so she could kiss her cheek. "Have fun, sweetheart."

"Thank you, Mother. I will."

"Oh, before I forget." Annani turned around. "We need to get decorations for our solstice celebration and put them up, so do not make plans with Orion for tomorrow, unless he wants to come over and help, that is."

"I'll ask him."

"Are you inviting Eva and Bhathian?"

"Would they be offended if I did not?"

Alena shrugged. "You have to draw the line somewhere, or you will have to invite the entire clan."

"Indeed."

When Annani glided out of the closet, Alena pulled out her phone and called Amanda.

"Good morning, Alena." Amanda sounded breathless. "To what do I owe the pleasure of you actually picking up the phone and calling me at eight in the morning on a Sunday?"

"Did I wake you up?"

"No, but I was lounging in bed with a book, and my phone was in the kitchen. Do you know how hard it is to get up and then run with a belly this size?"

Alena cleared her throat.

"Oh, right. You do. My bad. I'm not thinking straight this early."

"So I guess coming over to borrow an outfit for my date with Orion is out of the question?"

"Are you kidding me? I would not miss such a rare opportunity. Be here in ten minutes. I'm getting dressed and having Onidu brew us coffee."

Alena chuckled. "I'm on my way."

55

ORION

Orion walked into the living room wearing a white button-down shirt, gray slacks, and black dress shoes. He thought that he looked quite dashing, but the grimace on Geraldine's face said otherwise.

"Why are you making that face?"

"Is that what you are going to wear?"

He looked down at his slacks, searching for a stain or a crease, but they were clean, and he'd just ironed them. "What's wrong with it?"

"You look like an insurance salesman. A very handsome one, but still. Don't you have a nice pair of jeans and a polo shirt?"

"I don't wear jeans. I detest them. The most casual pair of pants I have is light gray linen, and those are summer pants."

"Let me see." She rose to her feet.

He shook his head. "You're not going into my bedroom. Wait here, and I'll get them."

Her eyes sparkled with interest. "What are you hiding in there?"

"A big mess," he cast over his shoulder.

It wasn't that bad, but he hadn't made the bed, and his clothes were still in the suitcase, which was indeed quite messy.

The pair of linen pants were badly wrinkled, and he debated whether he should show them to his sister.

He enjoyed her being there, advising him on what to wear on his date with Alena even though he didn't need advice.

It just felt nice.

Geraldine had always been a good listener, and he'd shared many things with her before, but the difference was that this time he wouldn't have to make her forget what he'd told her.

It was such a relief to see her happy and healthy and dealing well with her memory issues. He wondered whether having a mate with an eidetic memory was beneficial to her, or did Shai just make her happy.

What a strange and lovely pair they made.

Perhaps those Fates the clan believed in knew what they were doing, and maybe pairing him with a female who had a strong aversion to compellers wasn't their idea of a joke but a way to heal old wounds.

Alena didn't remember anyone compelling her to do something she hadn't wished to do, but if part of the compulsion was to forget the encounter with the compeller, she wouldn't remember it, and there was nothing that could be done to retrieve that memory.

The goddess had been able to override Kalugal's compulsion of Amanda because she'd known precisely what he had compelled Amanda to do. In Alena's case, that couldn't be done. Annani couldn't compel her daughter to remember something she'd forgotten without knowing what it was.

The only thing the goddess could do was to thrall Alena and have a look at her memories, but if the compulsion to forget had been strong, even that probably wouldn't work.

Holding the pair of linen pants in his hand, Orion returned to the living room and sat on the couch next to Geraldine. "How did the goddess retrieve your memories of me? Did she just tell you to remember, and you did?"

Geraldine shook her head. "The Clan Mother asked me to relax, and then she spent a long time sifting through my memories. Why do you ask?"

"Alena is irrationally afraid of compellers. I suspect that she encountered a compeller before, and the experience was traumatic. Perhaps she can't remember it because she was compelled to forget it."

Geraldine's eyes widened. "Do you think Kalugal did that to her? Other than you and the goddess, he's the only one who could have done it. Oh, wait. I was told of one more person who can compel immortals, but I don't think Alena ever met him."

"Who is that?"

"His name is Emmett Haderech, and he used to be a cult leader, but then the clan caught him."

He was about to ask her more about that when a knock sounded on the door.

"That's probably Mason." Orion opened the door to let the Guardian in.

"Hi." Geraldine pushed to her feet. "I should be going."

Geraldine, Cassandra, and their mates were also going out for lunch to meet with Darlene, and the plan was to tell her about her dormancy and offer her immortality.

Orion thought that it was premature, and to do so in a public place was a mistake, but Geraldine had insisted that it was a rare opportunity to talk to her daughter while Leo was not around.

"If I didn't have a date, I would come with you."

"Why?"

"I don't think your plan for Darlene is a good one."

"Oh. We are not meeting her today after all. She called Cassandra and told her that Leo was coming back today."

"Good. It will give us time to come up with a better plan."

Geraldine eyed him from under lowered lashes. "You can't compel Darlene to agree. The decision has to be hers."

Did she really think that he would do that even if Darlene wasn't his niece? The only times he bent people's will to his was when it was either a life and death situation or they were trying to cheat him.

"I would never even try to convince her to consider transition, but I could compel her to keep it a secret, which would allow her more time to think it through. Thralling her to forget what you tell her only a few minutes later is not going to give her enough time. How can you expect her to make a decision like that on the spot?"

She let out a breath. "Yeah, that occurred to me as well. We will talk about this after your date." She lifted on her toes and kissed his cheek. "Have fun with Alena, but don't do anything to upset her."

"Why would I do that?"

Geraldine shrugged. "You're a nice guy, but sometimes people say things that they don't mean or that just come out wrong, and feelings get hurt. Alena is Annani's eldest daughter, and she's loved by her clan. If you do or say something stupid, you will wind up with a lot of enemies."

Smiling, he took her hand and clasped it between his. "I appreciate the sisterly advice, but I'm over five hundred years old, and think I know how to handle myself around a lady."

56

ALENA

Alena brushed nervous fingers through her hair. Amanda had trimmed and styled it the way she'd done for the New York trip, and she had also done Alena's makeup. It was subtle, and the change wasn't huge, but the eye shadow and mascara made her eyes pop.

Her sister hadn't been happy when Alena refused to have foundation on her skin, or blush, or lipstick.

She didn't like the caked-on feeling of cosmetics, and even the eye makeup bothered her. She'd put up with it during the New York mission because she'd been playing a part, but it was not needed for her date with Orion. For that, she wanted to be herself.

What a lie.

Glancing at the mirror by the entry door, Alena grimaced. The slim black pants and loose white blouse were not her usual style, and neither were the three-inch heels, but she craved change, and updating her appearance seemed like a good place to start.

It was easy.

The rest was not.

Leaving the sanctuary, no longer accompanying her

mother on her trips, coming up with adventures of her own…

Was she ready for that?

Was it even happening?

Alena shook her head at her reflection in the mirror. It was only a date. She and Orion had shared one passionate kiss. It wasn't as if they were truelove mates ready to ride off into the sunset.

The moment she felt his presence on the other side of the door, her heart rate accelerated, and when the knock came, she took a long, steadying breath, forced her lips to curve in a smile, and opened up.

Orion looked splendid in a white button-down and a pair of gray slacks, the white accentuating his tanned skin and nearly black hair. He was a magnificent male, and she couldn't wait to peel these nice clothes off him.

As his eyes widened and then blazed with inner light, Alena's smile relaxed.

"Hello," she managed to chirp as she lifted her small purse off the entry table.

"You look different." He offered her his arm.

On the path behind him, Mason grinned like a fiend and gave her the thumbs up.

She threaded her arm through Orion's. "Good different or bad different?"

"Do you need to ask?" He led her down the steps.

"In fact, I do. This is Amanda's work." She waved a hand over herself. "The hair, the clothes, the makeup. I don't feel like me."

"It's still you no matter what costume you don, but I know what you mean." He smiled. "Geraldine said that I looked like an insurance salesman and asked if I had a pair of jeans. She was surprised that I didn't, but I never saw the appeal, and if I had worn a pair, I would have felt like an imposter. I guess it's because I'm old."

Compared to her he was a youngling, but even though he knew that she was over two thousand years old, Orion had never commented on her age, and Alena appreciated it.

"I can't stand jeans either. They are so uncomfortable."

He leaned closer. "I bet they would look good on you, though. You have amazing legs."

A blush creeping up her cheeks, she cast a quick glance over her shoulder at Mason, but the Guardian must have been listening to music on his earpieces because his expression remained neutral.

"You've never seen my legs," she whispered into Orion's ear. "So how do you know that they are amazing?"

A predatory gleam sparkled in his eyes. "I felt one around my waist, and it was perfect, and since it is safe to assume that the other one is its precise twin, they both are." He released her arm only to drape his over her waist. "I hope to see them in their full glory soon."

Alena didn't know whether to applaud his boldness or to be offended by it.

He'd been polite and reserved until their kiss last night. Had it emboldened him?

Pretending innocence, she arched a brow. "Is that an invitation to the beach? It's a little cold this time of year, but we can go to the pool in the training center. It's kept warm."

He chuckled. "Actually, the beach is where we are heading, but not for a swim. To do that, I'd rather take you to Hawaii or the Caribbean, where the water is warm year-round."

That sounded so lovely that Alena stifled a wistful sigh. "I would love that, but it is not in the cards unless you don't mind traveling with my mother and four Odus. Not that I know for sure that Annani would agree for you to come along, but since she likes you, she might."

"Can't you go anywhere without her?"

"I can, but unless it's necessary, I don't like leaving her alone."

"Was it ever necessary?"

"Once." Alena smiled. "I went on a mission to New York with a team of Guardians. It was so much fun."

"Are you allowed to tell me about it? I'm sure it's a fascinating story."

"Frankly, I'm not sure. I'll have to check with Kian."

He arched a brow. "You said that you don't answer to him."

"I don't, but when it's a question of security, and lives are at stake, I'd rather make certain."

Areana's communication with her sister and son was better kept confidential. Although most of the clan was aware of them, so it wasn't such a well-guarded secret.

"Lives at stake sounds ominous."

"It might be a slight exaggeration. By the way, where are we going? Did you choose a restaurant?"

He nodded. "Onegus recommended a place, and I have a feeling you will see some familiar faces when we get there." He turned to smile at Mason. "He didn't say anything, but I doubt one Guardian and one Odu are deemed sufficient protection for Annani's heir apparent."

57

ORION

Alena shook her head. "Annani is going to live forever, so the title is meaningless."

There had to be a reason the goddess was keeping her eldest daughter close, and Orion doubted that it was only because she needed a companion. She must be grooming Alena to become the next Clan Mother.

"What if she decides to step down?"

"She already has. Kian and Sari are running the clan, and our mother gives them almost complete autonomy. She's like the queen of England—a figurehead."

"I think she's much more." Orion smiled as he saw Kian's butler inside the pavilion, waiting for them with his chauffeur hat clutched in his hands. "Our other escort awaits."

"Hello, Okidu," Alena said. "Thank you for driving us today."

The cyborg's smile looked too human, too genuine for a machine. "It is my pleasure, mistress." He bowed his head. "But I do wish you would reconsider the limousine. It is so much more comfortable than Master Kian's SUV."

"I don't wish to draw too much attention, Okidu. The SUV is perfect."

Clearly disappointed, the butler bowed again. "As you wish, mistress."

The cyborg was quite opinionated for a machine. How intelligent was this AI? Or was that just mimicry and the Odu had repeated Kian's opinion?

Orion wished he knew more about technology. With his endless lifespan, he had the time to learn whatever he pleased, but he'd never been drawn to the sciences. He loved art in all its various expressions—drawings, paintings, sculptures, furniture, architecture, literature, poetry —but since he had no talent to create things, he collected them and sold them for profit.

When they reached Kian's SUV, Orion was surprised to see that it was an older model from more than five years ago. Surely Annani's regent could afford a new car every couple of years or so? Was he keeping the older model to avoid attracting attention? Or was the vehicle equipped with specialized technology that was deemed too costly to switch over to a new one often?

As images of the Batmobile flitted through his mind, Orion stifled a chuckle. Perhaps not being technologically savvy had its advantages. He could suspend disbelief more easily and let his imagination soar.

"What are you smiling about?" Alena asked as they settled in the SUV's back seat.

"I was wondering if this automobile could turn into an aircraft or a submarine like in the comics."

Mason, who sat next to Okidu, turned to look at him. "Are you a fan of comics?"

"I'm a collector, and furniture is not the only thing I deal in. A few years back, I found a box of original comics in an estate sale that was worth a fortune. I had some fun with them before selling them. I also watched the Marvel and DC Universe movies." He cast an apologetic glance at Alena. "I hope you don't think less of me for enjoying such trifling entertainment."

She laughed. "You watched *Frozen* three times. I think Marvel and DC are a step up."

He narrowed his eyes at her. "To have an opinion, you must have watched them as well."

"Guilty." She leaned her head against his shoulder. "They are fun to watch and don't leave me sad. There is enough sadness in the real world. When I need an escape, I prefer it to be a fun place."

"I couldn't agree more." He reached for her hand, enveloping it in his.

With Okidu and Mason listening to every word, they talked about many more trivial things on their way to the restaurant. It was located on a hotel rooftop and overlooked the ocean. Onegus had recommended it, and he'd even reserved two tables for them and asked that they would be within sight of each other but not too close.

The table the waiter escorted them to was the best the place had to offer, right against the railing, with the Venice boardwalk below and the ocean no more than fifty feet away.

People usually gawked at Orion, but with Alena at his side, most of the gawking rightfully went to her. She was a rare beauty, soft and feminine, but with an inner core of strength and determination that shone through her eyes.

Orion hadn't met Sari, but out of the three siblings that he had met, Alena was the best choice for Annani's heir. Kian was too focused on security and making money to support the clan and its various humanitarian endeavors. Amanda didn't seem interested in a leadership position. Alena was wise, coolheaded, and empathic, and he guessed that her mother had chosen and groomed her to step into her physically tiny but metaphysically enormous shoes.

Once the goddess decided it was time for her daughter to lead the clan, as a figurehead or more if she chose to, Alena could not only slide into that role with no difficulty, but she would also be accepted by the clan as its Clan Mother with no reservations.

58

ALENA

After their lunch had been served and consumed, Alena excused herself to the bathroom, not just because nature called, but because she wanted to text Kian and ask him if she could share with Orion the story of her New York adventure.

It wasn't that she needed to impress him. For some reason, he seemed overly impressed with her already, but she wanted him to know that she could be more than just the responsible and dedicated daughter everyone saw her as. She could be fun as well.

Kian's return text was short. *Just make sure no one other than Orion can hear you.*

Frankly, she'd expected more opposition and was surprised that he'd agreed so readily. He either trusted Orion or wanted to win him over.

With her mother pressuring Kian to find Toven, he needed Orion's cooperation, and that was probably the reason why he was being so uncharacteristically accommodating.

Her lips quirking in amusement, she texted back. *Aren't*

you afraid that Orion is Navuh's spy and that revealing Areana's secret rebellion might endanger her?

His reply was *Very funny. I'm not that paranoid.*

As she put the phone back in her purse, Alena was suddenly worried that her teasing might have planted the idea of Orion being a spy in Kian's head. Despite his protests, her brother was paranoid enough as it was.

The next item on her agenda was figuring out where and when she could tell Orion her story. The safest place would be back in the village, but she wasn't ready to end their date yet.

She could cast a silence shroud around them, but with so many people on the rooftop terrace of the hotel, that wasn't practical, and a walk on the beach while wearing Amanda's pumps wasn't either. They were slightly too small and pinched her toes.

Perhaps Gerard could squeeze them in for dinner. His place was built to provide privacy for his clients, and he wouldn't dare refuse a request from his grandmother. She knew that he always kept one booth on standby for his star clients, and hopefully it was available.

Leaning against the sink in the ladies' room, she typed up a text and sent it, but she didn't stay to wait for his reply. *By Invitation Only* wasn't open yet, so he probably wasn't busy in the kitchen at the moment, but knowing her grandson, he didn't carry his phone with him. Not that she blamed him. If he wanted a moment's peace, he needed to turn the thing off.

Her phone buzzed as she returned to the table, and as she sat down and pulled it out of her purse, she had to smile at Gerard's answer.

How can I say no? Of course, I'll have a table for you and your date. I heard of Orion's capture, but I was too busy to come to the village and get a look at him. Thank you for bringing Toven's son to see me. Your reservation is for six.

Apparently, Gerard's curiosity was a stronger motivator than his love for his grandmother.

"Good news?" Orion asked.

"Yes." She put the phone away and leaned forward. "Have you heard of an exclusive restaurant called *By Invitation Only?*"

"I think so. Very rich people buy memberships for the privilege to make reservations, and then they have to pay extravagant amounts for the meal itself."

"You've heard right. My grandson is the chef, and he owns it together with Kian. I texted him to ask if he could squeeze us in tonight, and he said of course." She chuckled. "Not out of respect for his grandmother, but out of curiosity. He heard about you and can't wait to meet you."

Orion frowned. "I thought that all local clan members lived in the village."

"The vast majority do. I think Gerard and Brandon are the only exceptions."

"Which one is the chef?"

"Gerard is the owner of the restaurant. Even though he's much younger than Brandon, he's my daughter's son, and we are quite close. Brandon is my many times great-grandson, so to him, I'm more like a distant aunt."

Leaning forward, he said quietly, "Tell me about your children. Who are they, and what do they do?"

"Why do you want to know?"

"Because I want to know everything about you, and your children are no doubt a big part of your life."

"They are." She leaned back. "First came three girls—Sorcha, Morag, and Alisa. After that, two boys—Tavish and Malcolm. Then five girls—Blair, Una, Alison, Innis, and Lyell. Next, two more boys—Caelan and Arran. And last but not least, my youngest, Gavina."

"Nine girls and four boys," Orion said.

She nodded. "How about you? Did you ever have children?"

59

ORION

The question hit Orion hard.

He'd given up on having children centuries ago, and when he'd learned that he wasn't infertile, he hadn't internalized that until Alena had voiced her question.

He could one day be a father.

Could he, though?

What if he turned out to be a jerk like the god who'd sired him?

And who would he have his children with? Alena?

It had been on the tip of his tongue to ask her whether she wanted to have more children, but he swallowed the words. If she could have more, he had no doubt that she would.

For the clan.

"I never had children," he said instead. "I thought that I was infertile."

Her eyes turning sad, Alena nodded. "Perhaps you were lucky not to have fathered children. I can't imagine how terrible it is to outlive your offspring." She pushed a strand of hair behind her ear. "After Lilen was killed, I cried myself to sleep for years. During the days, I had to be strong for my mother, who just fell apart and was like a walking ghost, but at night I allowed the tears to flow." She let out a shuddering sigh. "Some nights, I wished not to wake up the next morning and face the gaping hole in my heart again, but I knew it was selfish of me to wish for death as a way out of my misery. My mother needed me, my people needed me, and quitting was not an option."

He reached for her hand and brought it to his lips for a soft kiss. "I wish I could have been there for you."

She smiled. "It happened before you were born. I'm ancient, Orion."

"You're like a superb wine, aged to perfection."

She chuckled. "That was smooth." Then the merriment faded from her lovely face, and she lifted their conjoined hands to her cheek. "Neither of us is a stranger to loss."

Someone must have told Alena about his wife, probably Geraldine, but it wasn't a secret, and eventually he would have told her about Miriam, but their first official date was not the right time for it. Then again, Alena had told him about her own devastating loss, so maybe he should share his as well.

"Did Geraldine tell you about Miriam? The woman I was married to a long time ago?"

Alena nodded. "Geraldine didn't mention her name, but she told me that you loved her very much and never truly recovered from her loss."

"Never is a strong word," he admitted. "It no longer feels like a gaping hole in my soul, but I still think about her often."

"Tell me about her."

He arched a brow. "Are you sure? Former loves are not what a couple on their first date should be talking about."

"Miriam helped shape the kind of man you are today. To know you, I need to know the kind of woman she was.

But if it still hurts too much to talk about her, and you don't want to, I'll understand."

"It doesn't hurt." He let go of her hand, leaned back, and lifted the wine glass that the waiter had refilled for them while Alena had been in the ladies' room. "In fact, I need to talk about her so I won't forget. After nearly five centuries, my memories of her are starting to fade."

"You were very young when you married her."

"I was twenty-one."

Alena smiled. "The young love the most fiercely."

"We did, very much so."

"How did you hide your fangs from her?"

"I didn't. Miriam knew I was different and loved me anyway." He ran his fingers through his hair. "At first, I hid it from her, thralled her after each time we made love, but she was smart, and she figured it out. I was afraid she would think I was a monster, which was what I thought I was, but she said that I was pure goodness, and that having fangs might make me strange, but it didn't change who I was on the inside."

"She was a remarkable woman." Alena reached for her wine glass. "Especially given the time she lived in, with all the superstitious nonsense humans used to believe in."

"She was, and she was taken from me too soon. Miriam was twenty when I married her. She died at fifty-three."

"That was a good lifespan for that time. Back then, most humans didn't live past forty. Your venom probably kept Miriam healthier than most."

"I suspected that. She didn't age as fast as other women, and I hoped that was because she was with me. But I couldn't save her in the end." He lifted his eyes to her. "If I had known of your clan's existence, do you think your doctors could have helped her?"

Alena shook her head. "The knowledge my mother took with her out of Sumer was all about technology. Her uncle, from whom she pilfered the tablet, was an engineer and inventor, not a doctor. Back then, our healers knew no more than the human ones, and the same goes for today. We have no advanced medical knowledge. If we had, we would have shared it with humanity."

In a way, that was a relief. As it was, he'd lived with enough guilt for not being able to save Miriam, always thinking that there was something he could have done, some expert he could have found who would have known what to do. But if even the clan, with all their godly knowledge, wouldn't have been able to save her, then there had been no cure, and perhaps it was time to let go of the guilt.

60

ALENA

Alena had known that the walk down the Venice boardwalk was a stupid idea, and now her poor toes were paying for it dearly.

When Orion had suggested it, she hadn't wanted to admit the pinching shoe situation. Besides, a walk on the beach had sounded romantic, and she hadn't wanted to miss out on it just because of her footwear.

"What's the matter?" he asked when she winced.

"I'm not used to wearing heels," she said, admitting to a partial truth that was not as embarrassing as telling him about the half-size-too-small shoes she'd borrowed from her sister just because she'd wanted to look pretty and sophisticated for their date. "I don't know what possessed me to wear them."

"You thought that we would be sitting most of the time." He looked down at her feet. "Let's head back, and you can take the shoes off. After all, we are on the beach, so it's not a big deal to walk barefoot."

Knowing what went on in Venice at night, she'd rather not.

"That's okay. I'll survive a few more minutes until we get back to the car."

He glanced at his watch. "Can we arrive at that restaurant earlier than six?"

She laughed. "Gerard wouldn't let us in. He only opens the place at six. But we can go for a drive, and I can show you the sights. How familiar are you with the greater Los Angeles area?"

"I've never lived here if that's what you're asking. I have several wealthy clients who I occasionally visit in Beverly Hills and Bel Air, owners of high-end galleries who are interested in particular period pieces I specialize in, and there is Geraldine."

"Let me guess. You are unimpressed with the city."

He smiled apologetically. "Frankly, it's not very interesting. The architecture is blah, most of the stores are inside malls, and there is no real center. I like New York, Manhattan especially, and I like Boston. Other than that, most of my favorite cities are in Europe."

"You said that you travel a lot. Where is your home?"

He shrugged. "I don't think about any of the flats I own as home because I never stay long in one place. I treat them as an investment more than anything else. I have an apartment in Manhattan, a townhome in Paris, a flat in London, and a flat in Milan."

"You are a true international man."

He nodded. "You said that you travel a lot as well."

"I do, but other than that one New York adventure, it's always with my mother. We have our own jet, and our trips are usually short. We only stay a couple of days and then return home to the sanctuary."

"Why do you call it a sanctuary? Are the trafficking victims you rescue brought over there?"

"That would have been impractical. We have a local sanctuary for them. I think my mother started calling it that because it's a place of rest and relaxation. Using some of the gods' technology, the clan built an oasis in the snow for Annani."

"Alaska or some other eternally snowy place?"

Behind them, Mason cleared his throat, reminding her that she should be careful with what she said to Orion.

She ignored him. "It's in Alaska, but as you know, Alaska is vast, and the sanctuary is small. No one other than the Odus knows how to find it. They fly the jets in and out, shuttling clan members back and forth."

"On windowless planes?"

"Our jets use the same technology as the clan cars. The windows turn opaque." Not on Annani's jet, but he didn't need to know that.

Besides, even though she'd looked out the windows plenty of times, Alena still couldn't have found the sanctuary if her life depended on it. It was located in the mountains where there was always snow, and to her, one snowy mountain looked like another. Perhaps if she'd paid better attention, she could have memorized some distinguishing features, but navigation was never her strong suit.

"Is your home called sanctuary because it's the goddess's secret shelter?" Orion asked.

"That's one reason. Beside being my mother's happy place, it also serves as a safe place for expectant mothers. They come to the sanctuary to deliver their babies, where they are safe until they are ready to transition. Not all do, and we didn't have any for the longest time, but it's there for anyone who needs it."

"Is it a happy place for you as well?"

She took a moment to think about it, and then nodded. "When we have babies and children in the sanctuary, it is, but when many years pass without any young ones, it gets boring despite the waterfalls and the tropical greenery under a dome of ice."

"I would love to see the place. Do you think that I would be allowed?"

If he was her truelove mate, then yes, he would.

But was he?

The guy was still mourning the woman he'd loved even though centuries had passed. Had Miriam been his one true love?

He might think so, but a bond was only possible between immortals, or between a Dormant and an immortal, and Miriam couldn't have been a Dormant. She would have transitioned if she were.

When Kian had fallen in love with Lavena, he'd believed that she was his one and only, but falling in love so deeply was often a young heart's folly. Kian had been with Lavena for a little over a year, and if he'd been with her as long as Orion had been with his wife, he might have realized that she wasn't the be-all-end-all he'd believed her to be.

Orion had been married for thirty-three years, and his love for Miriam had time to mature and deepen. It hadn't been just a young man's infatuation—it had been the real thing.

When he'd lost Miriam, Orion had been so devastated that he'd vowed never to love again.

But then, he'd never expected to encounter an immortal female who would live as long as he did. That was a game-changer that Orion was well aware of.

Otherwise, he wouldn't be here with her.

Alena knew that he desired her, and he also seemed to admire her, so perhaps love was possible, but if they were truelove mates who'd been fated for each other, shouldn't they have fallen in love at first sight?

But what she felt for him was not love. It was a strong like with a hefty helping of lust.

As they reached the car, Okidu rushed to open the door

for her, and as soon as she was seated, Alena kicked the damn shoes off and sighed in relief.

"I have an idea." Orion slid next to her. "How about we stop at a shoe store and get you comfortable shoes? I don't want you to suffer, and I also don't want to cut our date short."

She gave him a grateful smile. "That's so sweet and considerate of you." Not to mention sexy.

Imagining Orion kneeling at her feet and putting shoes on them was so damn erotic that she had to bite on her lower lip to stifle a moan.

He grinned. "So I guess it's a yes?"

"It's a yes, please."

Damn, she'd sounded like she was pleading for something that had nothing to do with shoes but everything to do with him kneeling between her legs.

61

ORION

For some reason, Alena seemed disappointed as they left the shoe store, but Orion didn't have the foggiest idea why.

She'd spent over two hours trying on nearly every pair of shoes they had in her size and had ended up buying four pairs. He'd tried to pay for them, but she wouldn't hear of it, had paid for them herself, and walked out in a pair of black pumps that looked as comfortable as they were stylish.

What had she expected from him that he'd failed to deliver?

A silly thought of another princess story flashed through his head, the one with the glass slipper. Had she wanted him to put the shoes on her feet?

He would have done so gladly, but only in the privacy of his bedroom. He would have kissed each toe separately, driving her crazy before dipping between those long legs of hers and kissing a much softer place. But to do so in a shoe store would have been scandalous.

Besides, Mason had been with them, so even the most innocent flirting had been out of the question. The most

Orion was comfortable with in public was having his arm around Alena's shoulders or her waist and a chaste kiss on the cheek.

As Okidu pulled up in front of the valet station, Alena tapped Mason's shoulder. "You can't come in with us. Gerard won't have a table for you."

"I know. I'll stay in the car with Okidu. I've already cleared it with Onegus."

A guy in a blue blazer who didn't look like he was a valet waited until they got out of the car. "Good evening, Ms. Alena, Mr. Orion. I'm Caleb, your host for tonight."

"Good evening, Caleb," Alena said.

As they followed the guy through a lush garden, Orion leaned closer and whispered in her ear. "Are any of Gerard's people like us?"

She shook her head.

Good, so Caleb couldn't hear him. "Did I do something to upset you in the shoe store?"

"No, why do you ask?"

"You seemed disappointed when we left, but you liked the shoes, so I figured it must have been something I did or didn't do."

"It wasn't because of you." She took his hand and gave it a squeeze. "I got tired of us having no privacy and Mason trailing us everywhere." She looked at him and smirked. "That's why I came up with the idea to come here in the first place. I knew he couldn't follow us into the restaurant, so we could finally enjoy each other's company without an audience."

"Beautiful and clever." Orion lifted their conjoined hands and kissed her knuckles. "Am I lucky or what?"

"It depends," she murmured.

"On what?"

She shook her head. "Never mind."

It had been a long time ago, but Orion hadn't forgotten

the lessons he'd learned from his marriage to Miriam. When a woman said never mind, it was a very bad sign, and the worst thing a male could do was to pester her to explain what she meant by it. The best thing to do was to wait until her mood improved and then prod gently, showing her that he hadn't forgotten and that he cared.

Lifting Alena's hand, he kissed her knuckles again. "You'll tell me when you're ready."

The doubtful look she cast him wasn't encouraging, but he was a patient man, and he would eventually get her to tell him what had bothered her.

Inside the restaurant, the host transferred them into the care of a pretty young woman who led them to a secluded corner booth. "Can I get you something to drink while you look over tonight's offerings?"

"Just water for me," Alena said.

"Sparkling?"

"Yes, please."

"Same for me." Orion picked up the wine menu. "I'll let you know our wine choice later."

"Very well." The waitress dipped her head and walked away.

"Gerard has a different menu for every night," Alena said. "He also keeps adding new dishes, which keeps the members coming back."

Orion cast a look around the opulent dining establishment, noting that all the tables were occupied. "He's definitely doing well for himself."

"Gerard will probably show up for a couple of seconds to satisfy his curiosity, and then we will not see him again. He's way too busy in the kitchen lording it over his staff."

"I heard that." A smiling man in a chef's outfit sauntered toward them. "Alena, you look as lovely as ever, my dear cousin." He winked at her before embracing her briefly.

"Thank you." She smiled. "Gerard, meet Orion. Orion, this is Gerard."

The chef offered Orion his hand. "When I heard the news, I couldn't believe it. What an incredible coincidence that your sister and niece both found their way into the family and brought you to us as well."

"Indeed. The Fates must have been involved." Orion hadn't believed in fate or the Fates before he'd been captured by the clan, but he was becoming a convert.

Gerard cast him a knowing look. "My cousin is a very special lady. I hope you know that."

There was a threat implied in that statement.

"I do."

"She is loved and admired by the entire family. If anything were to happen to her, many people would be upset."

"I know that, and I can assure you that she's perfectly safe with me. I'll protect her with my life." He meant every word.

"You'd better." In a flash, Gerard's expression turned from threatening to haughty and condescending. "I must return to the kitchen. Thank you for choosing *By Invitation Only* for your outing tonight, and I hope you enjoy your dinner."

"I'm sure we will," Alena said.

62

ALENA

It was silly to feel disappointed over a fantasy that couldn't have been realized even if Orion could have read her mind. And yet here she was, sitting in a booth in the fanciest restaurant in town, feeling frustrated and antsy.

Perhaps her long hiatus from sexual activity was to blame, or maybe her valiant effort to hide her attraction from Orion had finally collapsed under the onslaught of his male pheromones.

She would have gladly skipped dinner and dragged him to the nearest private place where she could have her way with him.

Except, with Orion it wouldn't be enough, with him she wanted more, but his heart still belonged to a woman who'd died four and a half centuries ago.

Could she win his heart?

Her mother would not have shied away from the challenge. On the contrary, it would have made Orion even more appealing to her because he wouldn't have been blinded by her beauty and might have actually resisted her for a little bit.

Annani would have told her to fight for what she wanted, even if it meant going against a ghost, and not to give up until she won.

Her mother would have been right.

Hiding behind the two-foot-tall menu, Alena pretended to ponder the selection while contemplating her next move.

Tonight, she was going to seduce Orion, and the night after that, and the one after that, until he couldn't imagine himself going to bed without her, until he couldn't be apart from her for more than a few hours without missing her terribly.

The question was how to get rid of Mason.

After driving them back to the village, Okidu wouldn't follow them to Orion's house. He would go back to Kian and Syssi's. Mason would follow his orders, though, and at the end of his shift, he would be replaced by another Guardian.

Did she care that they would know that she spent the night with Orion?

If there were no Guardians assigned to watch him, she might be able to sneak out in the early hours of the morning and get back to her and Annani's place unnoticed.

The problem was that Orion's house was in phase two of the village, while their place was in phase one and right next to the office building. Someone would notice her slinking around for sure.

Except, why hide their relationship?

Kian had brought Syssi over to his place and had seduced her within days of meeting her, if that. Amanda had closely followed their story and had reported the highlights to her and their mother, but several years had passed since then, and Alena didn't remember all the details.

In any case, Kian hadn't courted Syssi for days on end,

and no one had batted an eyelid over it. Why should it be different for her?

Just because she was a female and however many times great-grandmother of most of the clan didn't mean that different rules applied to her. If she wished to do so, she could spend the night with Orion and then bring him over to have breakfast with Annani for all to see that he was hers.

Stake her claim, so to speak, in which case the Guardians had to go for sure.

If she was making it official that she considered Orion a potential mate, Kian needed to stop treating him as a suspect.

Putting the menu down, Alena gave Orion a tight smile. "I need to powder my nose." She pushed to her feet. "I'll be back in a minute."

The perfect gentleman that he was, Orion got to his feet as well. "Have you decided on your selection?"

She hadn't read even one line on the menu. "Everything Gerard makes is delicious, so it's hard to decide. I'll ask the waitress to recommend a course." She gave him another come hither smile. "Or you can choose for me. We can share."

"As you wish." Orion remained standing until she turned the corner, staring at her with his blazing eyes.

Given that glow, he was just as hungry for her as she was for him.

In the ladies' room, Alena pulled out her phone and texted Kian. *I intend to spend the night with Orion, and I don't want Guardians snooping around. I also want you to stop the surveillance feed from the house. I don't want to feel self-conscious.*

The three dots indicating that he was typing kept blinking for a long time, but his answer was short. *Your safety is paramount. The Guardians stay.*

He must have typed several different answers and then erased them, but if he expected her to accept his final version, he didn't know her very well.

Alena typed back, *Did you have Guardians watching you when you and Syssi first got together?*

This time the reply came back quickly. *Syssi was human and harmless. Orion is neither.*

Alena ground her teeth. Kian had no authority over her. In fact, as the eldest, she could pull rank over him.

Theoretically.

She'd never done that before, had never felt the need, but as the saying went, there was a first time for everything. Alena typed, *Get rid of the Guardian, or I will. This is not a request, and the same goes for the feed—kill it.*

His reply was short and to the point. *As you command, sister mine. Just be aware that you're assuming responsibility for the consequences, whatever they might be.*

She answered, *I'm well aware of that. Thank you for not fighting me harder on this.*

Alena didn't expect an answer, but a moment later, another text came in. *Who am I to stand in the way of true love? It would seem that the Fates have spoken, and if not, and you are wrong about him, you can't blame me for not warning you.*

63

ORION

Left alone in the booth, Orion tried to figure out what was bugging Alena. The answer she'd given him might have been true, but he doubted that.

Mason had been trailing them the entire day, but she hadn't been bothered by it until the shoe store.

His only clue was the scent of her arousal that had flared as soon as he'd mentioned buying a new pair of shoes, but he'd dismissed it as a female's footwear obsession.

Not that he'd encountered a woman who'd gotten sexually aroused by shoes before, but he'd read and seen films about men with shoe or feet fetishes. If males had a thing for shoes, why not females?

After all, Alena had ended up buying four pairs, so there was that. But although they were elegant and fashionable, he wouldn't call them sexy.

Practical was a more fitting description of the footwear Alena had selected.

But even if she had gotten stilettos, which Orion had to admit evoked erotic imagery, he wouldn't get excited by seeing them in a store or a box. On her feet, though, especially with nothing else on, that was a different story.

The waitress hovered nearby, waiting for Alena to return from the ladies' room, and as soon as she did the woman pounced with her pitcher of chilled sparkling water and a ready smile.

"Have you made your selections?"

"We did." Orion turned to Alena. "Do you still want me to order for you?"

She waved a hand. "Go ahead. Everything Gerard creates is superb."

"Thank you." The waitress inclined her head. "I'll convey your compliments to the chef."

"No need," Alena said. "He's heard it from me many times. We are cousins."

"Oh." The waitress's eyes widened. "That's nice," she stammered, probably not knowing what else to say.

Feeling sorry for her, Orion saved her from having to comment by placing their order. "I would also like a bottle of the Ovid Napa Valley 2016 red wine." He handed her the menus.

"That's a very good choice, sir." She smiled and scuttled away.

"You know that it will cost you a fortune. Gerard does not give family discounts. In fact, he wouldn't have made a table available for anyone else other than Kian and my mother on such short notice."

"Do I look worried?"

She smiled. "I just don't want you to think that you need to impress me. I'm already impressed."

He arched a brow. "I'm glad to hear that, but I don't know what I have done to earn that. I haven't done anything of note since I got here."

Her hands steepled in front of her mouth, Alena hid a

small smile. "You survived on your own, and when you discovered your sister, you took care of her the best way you knew how."

"You must be easily impressed."

She shrugged. "Not really. I'm the daughter and companion of a goddess. It's not easy to impress me at all."

Alarmed, he glanced at the other tables. "You should lower your voice when you talk about her."

"There is no need to whisper in here." She waved a hand at the booth. "I cast a silencing shroud around us the moment the waitress left."

He hadn't known that was even possible. "Can you teach me how to do that?"

"Just imagine us encased in a bubble and then will it into existence. My shroud only works on humans, but yours might work on immortals as well. You have the power of a god."

"I'm glad that you are no longer afraid of my compulsion ability."

Alena leaned forward and leveled her eyes at him. "I trust you, Orion." She left it at that, but her eyes told him the rest. *Don't make me regret it.*

"I trust you too." He reached for her hand and gave it a gentle squeeze.

She looked confused. "What can I ever do to you?"

"You have enormous power over me, but I know that you won't use it. I trust you."

"Give me an example."

"You can get upset with me and tell your mother and brother that I'm a horrible person and that I shouldn't be allowed anywhere near the clan. You can also capture my heart and then break it."

She arched a brow. "Can I capture it, though? Is it even available?"

That was a poignant question, one he would have answered very differently only a couple of days ago. "It's not available to just anyone, but it could be yours if you want it."

64

ALENA

For a long moment, Alena was speechless. What could she say to that? What could be said?

Orion hadn't told her that he loved her, he only said that he could, but even that was a huge deal for a guy who'd believed that he would never love again.

That he was opening himself up to her was precious.

"It means a lot to me to hear you say that." She reached for her glass of water. "I know it must have been difficult for you to open your heart to me."

He let out a breath. "Miriam wouldn't have wanted me to be alone. The vow I made all those years ago was not to her. In fact, she asked me to live my life, and I did not honor her by vowing not to love again. It was an expression of my grief and despair, the absolute certainty that I never wanted to experience that kind of suffering again."

Reeling from his confession, Alena hadn't noticed the waitress approach their booth until the woman was standing right over her, a bottle of wine in her hand. Quickly dropping the silencing shroud, Alena forced a pleasant smile onto her face.

The woman expertly uncorked the wine, poured it into their glasses, and then waited for them to taste it and make a comment.

"Excellent," Orion said. "Thank you."

She nodded her head, promised that their first course would be arriving shortly, and pivoted on her heel.

As soon as the woman was a few feet away, Alena recast the silencing shroud around them.

"Are we in a bubble again?" Orion asked.

"Yes."

"That's a very useful trick. What else can you do?"

It seemed that Orion had reached his limit of emotional revelations and needed a change of subject.

"I can thrall, but I don't have much use for the skill. Frankly, I don't have much use for shrouding either because my mother takes care of that when we travel together. It's as effortless for her as breathing, while it's work for me."

"What are the rules regarding thralling and compulsion? I'm still not clear on when it's allowed and when not. Clearly, shrouding is permitted, and I wonder what the difference is."

Wow, he was really crawling back into his shell after his confession. Clan law was the last thing Alena wanted to talk about while she had seduction on her mind, but it seemed like Orion needed a palate cleanse, so to speak.

"Both thralling and shrouding affect human minds. Shrouding changes what they see, hear, smell, and even touch, while thralling is more invasive and changes what they remember and what they believe. Thralling can also be used to look into people's recent memories or those that have left a lasting impact on them. Because it is intrusive and has the potential to cause permanent damage, it is only allowed to conceal immortals' existence and when lives are in danger. Shrouding is allowed unless it is used to gain an unfair advantage. Compulsion, curiously, is less dangerous to human minds than thralling. I assume that they work on different areas of the brain and use different brain wavelengths."

"Are there any immortals who can thrall others of their kind?"

She shook her head. "So far, we've only encountered immortals who can compel other immortals, but not thrall. I don't know about shrouding, though. Once you learn to use it, it would be interesting to see whether it works on us the same way as your compulsion. I know that Kalugal's shrouding does, but I don't know to what extent."

"If Kalugal's shrouding can do that, then mine should as well. What about the goddess? What can she do?"

Alena hesitated. "Why do you want to know?"

"I'm just curious."

"The gods can do to immortals everything that immortals can do to humans, but even among the gods, their abilities and power vary. Areana, my mother's half-sister and Kalugal's mother, is a very weak goddess who can't even do what any strong immortal can. Kalugal's father, who is a first-generation immortal like you and me, is much more powerful than her. In fact, he's the most powerful immortal to ever exist."

"So I've been told." Orion crossed his arms over his chest. "How does his power manifest?"

"He has an entire army of immortal warriors under constant compulsion. I can't imagine the energy he needs to pump into that. I wouldn't be surprised if that was one of the reasons he lost his mind."

"And still, his mate loves him."

"She does." Alena leaned back. "Mentioning Areana reminded me of the New York mission that I promised to tell you about. Kian said that it was okay as long as no one overheard me."

Orion grinned. "That calls for another glass of wine." He refilled their glasses.

65

ORION

The arrival of the first course had put a halt to Alena's story, but given how tiny the dish was, the delay had been short.

Putting his fork down, Orion smiled. "This little thing was as pretty as it was delicious, but if the main course is proportionally small, we will have to stop for a hamburger on the way back."

Alena laughed. "Don't worry. By the time all five courses are done, you won't be hungry. You won't be over-stuffed either, and your wallet will be much lighter." She leaned closer. "Besides, when we get back, I can whip something up for you. Geraldine and Cassandra did a good job filling up your fridge and pantry. There is plenty for me to work with."

The hinted message wasn't lost on him, not with the way her eyes blazed, and her intoxicating feminine scent flared. She had plans for tonight that he was a thousand percent on board for.

"Can we skip the rest of the meal?" His words came out a little slurred, not because of the two glasses of wine he'd had but because his fangs had elongated.

His eyes were probably glowing like a pair of torches.

"No, we can't." Her smile was full of promise. "I'm a decent cook, but nothing I make could ever equal Gerard's creations."

Pretending that they were talking about food, Alena was teasing him and enjoying every moment of it. She knew perfectly well what had been on his mind when he'd suggested skipping dinner.

"Are your clan members aware of your evil streak?"

She assumed an innocent expression. "I'm only looking out for your culinary delight. I wouldn't want to deprive you of one of the best gourmet offerings in the world."

He could play along. "I prefer a home-cooked meal."

"So do I, but sometimes, I need something to whet my appetite first."

He let out a breath. "At least distract me with the story of your New York mission."

"With pleasure." She lifted her wine goblet and took a sip.

"It all started with Lokan, whom you haven't met yet, wanting to find his mother and not being scrupulous about the means." Alena went on to tell him about the two Dormants with telepathic powers whom Lokan had tried to kidnap and use to infiltrate the harem and the trap they'd set up for him. The plan had nearly failed, but all had ended well.

It was a fascinating story that provided him with a lot of information about Navuh, the clan's archenemy, and Pleasure Island—his secret base in the Indian Ocean.

No wonder Kalugal had wanted to find out how powerful Orion's compulsion ability was. The people living on that island, humans and immortals alike, were deprived of the most basic rights, and they needed to be liberated. The problem Kalugal and his brother faced, though, was that unless they could take control of the immortal army, removing Navuh from power would do more harm than good, and neither of them was powerful enough to do that. Besides, whoever took the reins would be chained to that island, and it seemed that Kalugal had much loftier goals.

Alena paused her story when the second course arrived —a small salad that was as artfully presented as the appetizer.

Once they were done with that, Alena continued, "When we found Areana, she revealed that she and Navuh had another son who was nearly as powerful a compeller as his father, and who escaped his father's stronghold during World War II. He was presumed dead, but both Areana and Navuh knew the truth because Kalugal shouldn't have been anywhere near the nuclear bombing site. Secretly, Navuh hired human detective firms to look for Kalugal, but they couldn't find him."

Alena lifted the wine glass, and Orion refilled it for her. "But then the clan found Kalugal with your help."

"Nope. I did my part to the best of my ability, but the mission failed nonetheless." Alena took a couple of sips and put the glass down. "After Areana told us about Kalugal, we didn't have the slightest idea where to even start looking for him until Syssi had a vision of him walking into the New York Stock Exchange. We knew from Areana's story that Kalugal loved his mother very much, and that's how the idea of me impersonating her was born. We are about the same height, and we are both blonde, but it took a lot of makeup to make me look like her." Alena smiled wistfully. "It was so much fun pretending to be a supermodel. It was such a different persona from my regular one that I wasn't sure I could pull it off, but I did. My face was plastered over the sides of buses and billboards, it was in fashion magazines and even on the subway. I had a blast, but Kalugal was no longer in New York and saw none of what I'd done. So, it didn't work."

Alena affected a sad face, but her eyes still shone with excitement.

"It must have been hard to return to the quiet life of the sanctuary," Orion prodded gently.

She sighed. "You have no idea. It took me forever to stop feeling restless and confined even though my mother has taken me on many other adventures since."

"But they were not your own. You didn't star in them."

She nodded. "Does it make me selfish not to want to walk in my mother's shadow for a change?"

"Not at all. I think you've been doing that for too long." He leaned forward and took her hand. "How would you like to go on an adventure with me?"

"What kind of adventure?"

"Hunting for Toven and any other children he might have sired." He needed to qualify that. "But I also need to make a living, so some of it will involve hunting for antiques as well."

For a long moment, she looked into his eyes, a hundred different emotions floating through hers. "If you're waiting for me to say that I would love to, the answer is yes, but that doesn't mean that I will. I can fantasize about a new life all I want, but I have responsibilities no one else can assume."

He gave her hand a light squeeze. "We shall see about that. The Fates might surprise you with a new twist you didn't see coming."

She smiled. "I didn't see you coming, so that's an unexpected twist."

"A good one, I hope."

"The best." She squeezed his hand in return.

66

ALENA

As the four of them left the pavilion, Okidu bowed. "Good night, Mistress Alena, Master Orion. I shall see you again tomorrow at the party." He pivoted on his heel and walked into the night.

"What party?" Orion asked.

"The winter solstice party my mother and I are hosting." Alena threaded her arm through his. "Did you forget?"

"I must not have paid attention. I didn't realize it was tomorrow."

He must have been really distracted by her not to have heard Annani invite everyone who was at Kalugal's on Sunday to the celebration.

"If you want, you can come over tomorrow afternoon and help me decorate."

His eyes widened. "I didn't get anyone presents." He looked at the two bags of shoes he was holding. "We should have gone shopping."

"No need." She patted his hand. "We didn't get you any gifts either. We've got presents mainly for the little ones, and just a few for the grownups. Our plan was to arrive in a few weeks, and the presents weren't about the winter solstice either. My mother and I were searching for something the clan can celebrate that isn't tied to any particular religion, and we just came up with the idea of celebrating the solstices when we got here." She smiled. "When Annani heard about your capture, she couldn't wait another minute to meet you. We rushed over as soon as our things were packed, and the jet was ready for takeoff."

"I hope she wasn't disappointed."

"You're kidding, right? You are the spitting image of Toven, and she adored your father. Besides, you are charming, intelligent, and caring. What's there not to like?"

He grinned, that adorable dimple making an appearance. "I'm glad you think so."

Mason cleared his throat. "I will part ways with you here. Good night."

"Good night, Mason." Alena cast him a smile. "Thank you for the escort."

"It was my pleasure." The Guardian bowed his head and then walked away as briskly as he could without actually jogging.

Evidently Kian had been true to his word and had instructed Onegus to remove the Guardians. Hopefully, he had done the same for the surveillance feed.

It was a relief to be spared the unpleasant task of telling Mason that he had to leave, and probably also having to argue the issue with Onegus. She'd been serious when she'd told Kian she would do it herself, but it was good that she didn't have to. Her energy would be much better spent on more pleasant activities.

"How did that happen?" Orion watched Mason disappear behind the curve. "Am I not considered a threat anymore?"

"You're not a threat to me, and I told Kian to get rid of the Guardians." She didn't mention the surveillance since Orion didn't know about it.

He arched a brow. "And he actually agreed?"

"I put my foot down."

"Good for you." He transferred the bags to one hand and wrapped his arm around her waist. "I knew that there was a steel core under that soft appearance."

Not many people realized that, but it was true. She'd been with Annani nearly every step of the way, building up the clan and shoring up her mother when the goddess's resolve had faltered.

Orion saw her, the real her, which made him even more dear to her and strengthened her resolve to pursue this thing between them to wherever it might lead.

Strolling along the village's central path, they arrived at Shai's former house in minutes, but when Orion stopped, Alena tugged on his arm and kept on walking.

Hadn't she made her intentions clear?

When she'd said she would come to his place to cook for him, Orion had seemed to get it, but perhaps he was the kind of guy who didn't like to assume anything and needed things to be spelled out rather than just hinted at.

Her walking past her house must have made it crystal clear that she hadn't been talking about actually whipping up a meal for him, and as the scent of his arousal flared, his hand tightened on her waist.

When she leaned into him, he relaxed his grip and smoothed his hand down her hip and then up again, igniting the banked flames of her passion. It shouldn't have been enough to make her breathless, but it was, turning her knees to jelly.

They walked the rest of the way to his house in silence, the sexual tension sizzling between them so strongly it was a wonder that her hair didn't turn into a frizzy halo.

The door wasn't locked, and as Orion closed it behind them and dropped the bags on the floor, Alena didn't care whether Kian had disconnected the surveillance feed or not.

"Kiss me," she breathed.

She expected him to grab for her, was hoping for it, but when Orion reached for her, his hand was gentle. Pulling her against his chest, he lowered his mouth to hers and kissed her ever so softly.

As Alena slid her arms around his neck, pressing herself against him as she deepened the kiss, Orion's hands roamed along her sides, but he didn't get swept away in her passion.

He was holding back, treating her as if she was made from porcelain and might break if he unleashed even a fraction of himself on her.

She knew the ferocity was there, the wildness hidden, suppressed. No matter how charming and civilized he was on the outside, Orion was a first-generation male immortal, the most dangerous predator on earth. She craved the wild ferocity he was stifling with an intensity that bordered on insanity.

Perhaps he needed a little prodding.

"I'm immortal." She nipped his lower lip. "I'm not a breakable human." When he hissed, she nipped his lip harder. "You don't have to hold back with me."

Panting, he lowered his forehead to hers. "I don't know if I can. I've been holding back my entire life."

"So have I." She took his hand and led him to the bedroom.

67

ORION

With a growl, Orion swept Alena into his arms and crushed his mouth over hers. There was nothing remotely gentle in the way he handled her now, but given the way her scent had intensified, it was precisely what she wanted.

Their mouths still fused, he carried her to the bed, set her down, and kneeled at her feet.

Alena sucked in a breath. "What are you doing?"

He smiled up at her. "I'm going to ravish every part of you, starting with your feet and going up from there." He took off one shoe, tossing it behind him.

Lifting her foot to his lips he kissed one toe at a time, and when she giggled, he tickled her arch with a quick sweep of his tongue.

"Stop it." She tried to pull her foot out of his grasp.

"Why?" He lifted her other foot, took the shoe off, and tossed it aside.

"My feet are not fresh." She tried to pull her foot out of his grip.

"They are perfect." He held on and kissed each toe.

When she leaned back on her forearms, he pulled down

her pants, getting dizzy when the scent of her hit him full force.

"I have to taste you." He moved the gusset of her sensible cotton panties aside and without much preamble, licked into her.

"Fates," she hissed. "Don't stop."

He had no intentions of doing so, but he wanted better access, and her panties had to go, as well as her blouse and her bra. He wanted her fully bared to him, wanted access to every part of her—a full possession with no inch of her untouched by his hands, his lips, his tongue.

Moving with immortal speed, he had her just as he wanted in a matter of seconds, and as he knelt between her legs again, his shoulders spreading her thighs wide, a sense of rightness swept over him.

"You're mine," he growled as he licked between her wet folds, finding her entrance and spearing his tongue into her.

He didn't know what had possessed him to say that to Annani's heir. What right had he to call her his?

Thankfully, Alena seemed too lost in her pleasure to have heard the words that had tumbled out of his mouth. And yet, he couldn't help the disappointment of her not claiming him as hers in return.

"Orion—" she moaned his name as her body convulsed in a violent climax.

He sucked and licked, helping her ride the wave for as long as it lasted, and when she finally stopped shuddering, he kissed her folds one last time and leaned away to look at the goddess sprawled on the bed before him.

"Magnificent," he whispered as he shucked his clothing and rose over her.

As his shaft nudged at her entrance, his mouth found her nipple, but when she lifted her hips to draw more of him inside her, the last of his control snapped, and he had to let go.

He surged all the way home, joining them, and the world around them receded into nothingness. There was only her and him and the bed they were on, and as he began moving, going faster and stronger than he'd ever dared before, she was right up there with him, taking everything he had to give her and demanding more.

Her hips lifting to meet him stroke for stroke, her nails scoring his back, and the heels of her feet digging into his buttocks, she was just as wild as he was, if not more.

It took mere minutes for them both to reach the point of no return, and when she turned her head and exposed her neck to him, it took all the restraint he could muster to lick the spot first to anesthetize it before sinking his fangs into her flesh.

Alena groaned, and as her release barreled through her once more, his own shattered through him in an explosive rush.

He must have passed out, waking up from his stupor long minutes later and realizing that he was crushing Alena under his weight.

Not that she was complaining. A blissed-out expression on her beautiful face, she was out like a light. He hadn't expected her to black out like a human woman, but apparently the venom worked on immortal females the same way.

Rolling to his side, he took her with him and held her close. She was so warm, so soft. He kissed her flushed cheeks, her eyelids, her nose, nuzzled her neck, and yet she didn't open her eyes. He knew she was floating on the cloud of post-venom euphoria, and he wanted her to enjoy every moment of it, but he already missed her, wanted her eyes to open and gaze at him and tell him that he had pleased her.

68

ALENA

Alena was soaring over marvelous landscapes, only dimly aware that they weren't real. She'd never felt so relaxed, so happy, so fulfilled, and she didn't want it to end.

And yet, through the haze, she felt Orion's soft lips peppering her face with kisses, and it was the sweetest thing any male had ever done for her after they'd satisfied their needs.

It was as if he loved her, as if he couldn't wait for her to return to him from her trip over the clouds, and the tugging on her heart was stronger than the blissful pleasure. As lovely as soaring was, the emotion conveyed in those kisses meant more to her. It was real. The surreal landscapes were not.

As she forced her eyelids to lift, her eyes beheld the most handsome face she'd ever seen, and a smile lifted her lips. "Hello," she murmured.

"Hello to you too." He softly kissed her lips. "I'm glad to have you back with me."

"I never left." She cuddled up closer and pressed her nose into the crook of his neck. "I felt your kisses." She kissed that warm spot that smelled heavenly. "But it took me time to decide if I wanted to cut my trip short and come back to you. It was my first venom bite, and it exceeded my wildest expectations."

The smug satisfaction on his beautiful face was precious. "There are plenty more where that one came from."

"There are? From what I hear, immortal males can have multiple orgasms but can only generate enough venom for one bite a night."

"Is that a challenge?"

Alena yawned. "I'm too tired for issuing challenges."

He seemed disappointed. "How many times can immortal females climax in one night?"

"I don't know, but I assume at least as many times as the males." She ran her fingers over his hairless chest. "Or more." She followed her fingers with her lips. "You smell so good." She licked his skin. "And you taste good as well." She slid down his body, kissing his chest and belly on the way to the prize.

He swallowed hard but didn't stop her.

Why would he?

She was about to pleasure him with her mouth. What male wouldn't love that?

His manhood was proudly erect as if he hadn't just climaxed, and as her lips brushed over the tip, it twitched in welcome, and as she rubbed her cheek against the velvety skin, his fingers threaded in her hair.

They both sighed when she took the tip into her mouth, her tongue pillowing him as she gently sucked.

His fingers tightening on her scalp, he tried to keep still, but he was fighting a losing battle with his hips, a fight that she wanted him to lose. One hand holding onto his shaft, the other clasping his muscular buttocks, she took him deeper, circling her tongue around the hard length pressing into her mouth.

Every twitch of his went straight to her sex, and as he watched her pleasuring him, his rugged breaths spurred her to take him even deeper. She wanted him to lose control and thrust into her throat, but he never gave her more than what he thought she could handle.

Forcing her throat to open as wide as it would go, she simply sucked him in deeper and kept him there until he swelled to the point that she was choking around him and had to release him to take a breath.

"Come here." He pulled her up his chest and rolled on top of her. "That was amazing, but I'd rather not finish inside your mouth."

"Why not?" She pouted.

"Because—" He thrust into her and her eyes rolled back. "We both enjoy this more." He retreated and surged back in.

"Yes." She locked her ankles on the small of his back.

This time their lovemaking was less frenzied, and as he dipped his head and kissed her, the kiss was slow and lazy, his tongue thrusting inside her mouth to the rhythm of his manhood doing the same between her lower lips.

The slow and tender didn't last long though, and soon he was thrusting between her legs with the same ferocity as before, and as she sank her tiny fangs into his neck, he roared his climax and shot his seed into her, pulling another orgasm out of her.

69

ORION

For long moments they lay on their sides, chest to chest, tangled in each other's arms, panting from the powerful climaxes that had torn through them, satisfied, but only partially.

Orion could go for rounds three and four if Alena was up to it.

As if she'd read his mind, a ripple from the muscles in her sheath coaxed a twitch from his shaft.

"You're incredible." He kissed a spot on her neck right below her ear.

"So are you." Her hands circled to the back of his neck, massaging for a moment before continuing down to his shoulder blades and then further down his back to cup his buttocks.

He trailed his fingers up the soft underside of her arm, circling the crease at her elbow, and as she shivered, he dipped his head and took her lips in a soft kiss.

As she kissed him back, her hands went back up to caress his side, his ribs, his pectorals. And as their passion flared, he rolled over her and braced his weight on his forearms, still kissing her, still buried deep inside her, but not moving.

He wanted to savor the closeness while his brain was still functioning and not consumed by lust.

She lifted her long, powerful legs and wrapped them around his hips, caging him between them.

The message was clear, and as he retracted and surged back in, her sheath tightened and rippled along his shaft. When she nibbled on his lower lip and then pulled it between her teeth and sucked, he became undone.

Drawing his hips back, he slammed back in, and his thrusting became faster and harder, she met him blow for blow, and then with a strength that he'd never encountered in a female before, she flipped them around and rode him even harder than he had ridden her.

With her long blond hair flying, her heavy breasts bouncing with each lift and descent, her lips red and swollen from their kisses, Alena was a dream vision, a fantasy he never wanted to end.

The force with which she slammed down on his shaft was incredible, and although his hand gripped her hips, she didn't need him to lift her.

Orion had never expected to be taken like that but being possessed by this amazing female didn't diminish his masculinity one bit.

On the contrary, he'd never felt as desired, as wanted as he did lying nearly passively under Alena and letting her take him for the ride of his life.

Her body gripping him wet and tight, her hands gripping his shoulders, she brought him to the cusp of a climax, but he held back, waiting for her to reach her peak and milk his seed out of him.

Going faster and faster, she threw her head back and commanded, "Now, Orion!"

The orgasm exploded out of him with a force he'd

never experienced before, his muscles locking, and her sheath milking him just as he'd imagined, exquisite relief pouring out of him.

Despite the powerful climax though, his hunger wasn't satiated.

Rolling them over, he started thrusting again, and in mere moments, another orgasm ripped out of him with a roar that must have been heard across the village.

He had just enough presence of mind to roll to his side instead of collapsing on top of her.

"Wow," Alena whispered into his chest. "That was one hell of a ride." She chuckled. "You won."

"I didn't realize that it was a competition."

"You are still hard inside of me, which means that you can go for another round, but I am exhausted, so you won."

He brushed a strand of damp hair away from her flushed cheek. "My manhood might entertain the idea, but I don't think the rest of my body is up to the task. It's a draw."

"I'll take it," she murmured sleepily. "I don't even have the energy to get cleaned up."

"I'll take care of you." He feathered a tender kiss on her cheek.

He wasn't sure how he would muster the energy to get up and do that, but not taking care of her wasn't an option.

Alena's answer was a smile and a soft sigh, and then her breathing evened out, becoming deep and slow.

Orion gave himself a few more moments to watch her beautiful face as she slept. After catching his breath, he gently extracted himself from her arms and padded to the bathroom.

70

KIAN

"I apologize for the early hour," Kian addressed the team gathered around his office conference table. "But given the winter solstice celebrations later this evening, I thought you'd rather be done early."

Many were not celebrating the new holiday Annani had decided on. It would take time for the tradition to take root, but he was accommodating those who wished to gather with their closest friends and family tonight and needed time to decorate and prepare a festive meal.

"Thank you," Vrog said. "I promised Wendy and Stella to help them decorate. Richard is busy at the construction site."

"How are you getting along with him?" Mey asked.

"He's not as hostile as he was at the beginning."

"I'm glad." Mey cast him a reassuring smile.

"How do you like the village?" Yamanu asked.

"It's beautiful and peaceful, and everyone is very friendly. I like the feeling of community." He turned to Kian. "I'm impressed with your leadership and what you've achieved here, and I'm not saying that to get on your good side. This place is as close to utopia as it gets."

Kian knew full well that not everything was as perfect as it appeared, and Kalugal was not the only one who schemed and planned in secret. Then there was the gossip, which often grated on Kian's nerves, the lack of privacy, and the right everyone felt to butt into others' business and offer their advice. Their community was a strange hybrid creature of a large family, a society with its own laws, customs, and beliefs, a business organization, and a self-ruled democratic monarchy.

Vrog wasn't going to stay long enough to experience all that, though. Kian needed him back in China to assist Mey in her continued investigation of echoes left over by the Kra-ell.

"Thank you, Vrog. I'm glad to hear that you're enjoying your stay, but it will have to be cut short. You're leaving on Wednesday along with Mey, Yamanu, and a couple of Guardians. I need the investigation to continue as soon as possible."

Vrog was visibly taken aback. "I thought I would have more time. Can you postpone it for another week? I'm just starting to get acquainted with my son and his fiancée." He ran a hand over his dark hair. "I am also looking forward to the Kra-ell virtual adventure William is setting up for me. I filled out the questionnaire on Saturday, and I'm just waiting for William to find me a match."

"If you want, you can come back to the village after Mey is done with her echoes investigation. Your help deciphering the files you promised me would be invaluable."

"You can go on the virtual adventure when we return," Mey said. "Besides, William might find you a match today and schedule it for tomorrow."

Vrog let out a breath. "Why the rush, though?" He looked at Kian. "Last we spoke, I was under the impression that you were not in a big hurry."

"I wasn't, but I am now. Kalugal is leaving for the

Mosuo territory on Wednesday. He suspects that an earlier group of Kra-ell influenced the Mosuo society, and he wants to search for artifacts or any other clues that would confirm his suspicions. I want the two teams to work in tandem and, if needed, assist each other. If Mey finds more clues in the echoes, she can communicate her findings to Kalugal and potentially point him in the right direction and vice versa. What you need to decide is whether you want to return here after the assignment or remain in your school."

Vrog looked conflicted. "Can I come back here for a few weeks? I can't abandon the school completely because it will fall apart without me. I'm the one bringing new students in and keeping the administration accountable to the so-called board of directors." He smiled. "That has only one member. I originally founded the school as a cover, but it has become my life project. I'm proud of what I've created." He sighed. "The clan will not need a school for many years to come, and I'm not the kind of male who could be happy idling. I would be delighted to visit, though, if you allow me."

"How much longer do you think you can pull it off?" Yamanu asked. "You're not aging, and eventually people will start noticing."

Vrog shrugged. "I can pretend for at least another twenty years, and by then, the clan might have enough high school-aged students for me to build a school for them. I'll bring a lot of valuable experience to the table."

"A lot can happen in twenty years," Kian said. "So there is no point in making such long-term plans. After you fulfill your obligation to me by assisting Mey and providing the documents you found, you can come here for a longer visit."

"And after that?" Vrog asked.

"You have my permission to visit the village whenever

you want, but precautions will have to be taken. You will have to coordinate your visits with Onegus, the security chief. He will provide you with itineraries that will bring you here in a roundabout way that is difficult to follow. You will also need formal invitations from Vlad and Wendy because they will be responsible for you during your stays."

Vrog inclined his head. "That's very kind and generous of you. Thank you."

"You're welcome."

"So." Yamanu leaned back and crossed his arms over his chest. "Who is coming with us this time?"

"Jay, Alfie, and of course, Morris. You don't need Arwel and Jin this time, and you definitely don't need Stella and Richard. Vrog can translate for you."

71

ALENA

As Alena's awareness re-emerged from under the hazy clouds of dreams, the strong arms holding her tight were a reminder of where she was and with whom.

The room wasn't dark, which meant...

With a start, her eyes darted to the window, and as she'd suspected, the motorized shutters were up, and the sky was the color of early dawn—the top a deep cerulean blue, the bottoms streaked with bronze, orange, and yellow colors.

"Good morning." Orion's hand started a slow track down her spine. "Did you sleep well?"

"What time is it?"

"A little after six in the morning. Is that a problem?"

"People will see me leaving your place, and the rumor will spread like wildfire through the village."

His hand on her back halted. "You can stay until the afternoon, and when you leave, they will assume that you came to visit me earlier today."

She let out a breath. "With the clothes I chose for our

date, everyone would know that I didn't dress like that for a day in the village. You've seen my regular style."

He continued his up and down track over her back. "If you wish, I can accompany you and compel everyone we encounter on the way to forget that they saw you."

"That won't be necessary." Alena shifted to her back, and Orion followed, leaning on his elbow as he gazed down at her face.

"I've run out of ideas." He dipped his head and kissed her lips. "Well, I do have some, just not for getting you home unnoticed." He put a hand on her stomach. "As far as I'm concerned, we can stay here until the food runs out, but even after that, I'm sure Geraldine would be more than happy to replenish the supplies."

Alena smiled. "It's tempting." She could see herself spending an entire month with Orion, making love and getting to know each other. "I'm expected to be back to help my mother host the winter solstice celebration tonight."

He kissed her again and then lifted his head with a smirk tilting up one corner of his sensuous mouth. "That gives us at least twelve hours. I'll barricade the doors, you'll turn your phone off, and we will spend the entire time in bed."

Alena laughed. "Kian would jump to conclusions and come by with a bulldozer to knock the walls down. He's done that before."

"To you?"

"Not to me. He did that to Amanda." Her bladder sending an urgent message to her brain, Alena winced and pushed on Orion's chest. "I need to use the bathroom."

He scooted a few inches to the side. "Go ahead."

For a brief moment, she considered pulling the sheet off the bed and wrapping it around her nude body, but then discarded it and proudly padded to the bathroom with all her femininity on display.

After all, Orion had already seen, touched, licked, and kissed nearly every inch of her, so what was the point in pretending modesty she didn't feel?

Alena had no issues with her body.

Nevertheless, she closed the bathroom door behind her. If this thing between them lasted, she might one day be comfortable enough with him to leave the door open while she used the toilet, but not just yet. It was too familiar, too intimate.

Then again, he'd cleaned her after their lovemaking, and there was nothing more intimate than that.

No one had ever done that for her, not because her casual lovers had all been selfish men, but because she'd always left while they had still been asleep. It was easier to sneak out after her needs had been met and not face the awkward morning after.

She hadn't felt awkward with Orion, though. It was as if they'd known each other for years, and waking up next to him in bed was the most natural thing in the world.

Damn, if he didn't feel the same about her, she was in deep trouble.

Searching through the vanity drawers, she found a new toothbrush still in its original box. After brushing her teeth and combing her hair with her fingers, she opened the door and sauntered back into bed.

The fresh minty smell coming from Orion revealed that he'd used the other bathroom in the house. "You could have come in." She lay next to him and draped an arm around his middle.

"I assumed you wanted privacy." He pulled her closer to him. "So, what's the plan for the rest of the day?" His hand trailed down her hip and then around to cup her bottom.

She smiled. "You are on the right track."

72

ORION

"I wish I at least had a change of underwear." Alena pulled on her pants.

"You can use one of mine."

She stopped. "I'll take you up on your offer." Pulling her pants back down, she put them on the bed and then walked over to his suitcase that still lay open on the floor.

"Bachelors." She shook her head as she crouched next to it. Pulling out a pair of boxer briefs, she tugged them on over her long, magnificent legs.

The rest of her was still deliciously bare.

Orion found it curious that the order in which Alena dressed was like a male would. Women tended to get dressed from top to bottom while men usually dressed bottoms first.

Not that there was anything unfeminine about her. Alena was femininity personified and gloriously so. She was soft and curvy in all the right places, but she was statuesque and strong. She was also soft-spoken, gentle, and kind, but she didn't shy away from confrontations, and put her foot down on what mattered to her.

Not many would have dared to order Kian around, but

Alena had done it and gotten her way. She was the older sister, that was true, but Orion doubted Kian had obeyed her wishes out of respect for her seniority. He'd probably been so stunned by her demand that he'd capitulated out of shock.

Fishing her blouse out from under the bed, she winced and brushed the dust off with her hand.

"You can use one of my shirts as well," Orion offered.

She glanced at the suitcase, shook her head again, and turned to him. "Why aren't you getting dressed?"

He was in bed, lying on top of the messy sheets and wearing the towel he'd wrapped around his hips after their joint shower. "I enjoy watching you getting dressed in my bedroom too much to miss out on a single moment."

A smile bloomed on her face, accompanied by a slight reddening of her cheeks. "If you want to have breakfast with my mother while wearing a towel, that's fine with me, and I'm sure that she wouldn't mind either."

He was out of bed in one second flat. "You didn't say anything about breakfast. Did she invite me, and I forgot that too?"

Had he been so consumed by Alena that he might have missed the goddess's invitation?

"Annani didn't invite you." She buttoned up the blouse. "I am inviting you. Otherwise, I will spend what's left of the morning getting interrogated about last night." She smiled at him sweetly. "Since you were an active participant, you can answer half of her questions."

Orion swallowed. "If you need me to shield you from your mother, I will, but are you sure it is wise for me to show up for breakfast the morning after?"

"It's very wise." Alena leaned down to fish her shoes from under the bed. "You haven't grown up among immortals, but our attitudes about sex are very different from those of humans. My mother will be overjoyed that we spent the night together and that I found pleasure in your arms." She pushed her feet into her shoes and cast him a seductive smile. "Many times over."

As the towel rose, lifted by the pole that had sprung up between his legs, Alena licked her lips. "Save it for later, lover boy. I've already texted my mother that we are coming over." She waved a hand at him. "Get dressed."

Letting the towel drop, he sauntered toward her and enveloped her in his arms. "Is later a promise?"

Her expression softened. "What do you think?"

"I hope that you will spend tonight with me as well, but I don't want to presume."

She chuckled. "You're allowed to presume."

"I'm a simple male, and I need to be told things in black and white. Is it a yes or a no?"

She lifted her arms and folded them around his neck. "It's a yes. I will spend tonight with you, but this time, I'll bring a change of clothes." She kissed him for a long moment before pushing on his chest. "If you need to take a cold shower before getting dressed, hurry up and do it. Keeping my mother waiting will not endear you to her. She doesn't appreciate tardiness."

He definitely didn't want to upset the goddess today or any other day for that matter.

There was no willing his erection to deflate, which forced him to dress top to bottom to Alena's great amusement.

"If you keep watching me, it will take longer for me to get ready."

"Fine." She tore her eyes away from his erection and turned on her heel. "I'll wait for you in the living room. You have two minutes."

73

ALENA

"Good morning, Mother." Alena walked over to Annani's chair at the dining table, leaned down, and kissed her cheek.

"Good morning, Clan Mother." Orion sketched a deep bow.

"It is almost good afternoon." Annani grinned from ear to ear, "So good afternoon to both of you." She waved a hand. "Please, take a seat and let us dine." She turned to Orion. "My Oridu made Okidu's famous waffles. You are in for a treat, and you do not want to eat them cold."

"Thank you, Clan Mother." He bowed again and then rushed to pull a chair out for Alena.

The poor guy didn't know what to do with himself, but he'd bravely accompanied her without complaint, ready to incur Annani's wrath if the goddess didn't approve of their night of passion. Alena had told him that he had nothing to worry about, but he hadn't been convinced.

Obviously, she'd been right because Annani was beaming with barely contained joy.

As Oridu served them waffles topped with strawberries

and whipped cream, Annani lifted the dainty porcelain cup to her lips and sipped on her tea.

"I cannot wait for us to find your father, Orion. I cannot believe that our children are about to be mated, and I am sure the news will gladden him no matter how jaded he has become."

As usual, her mother went overboard.

Alena put her fork down and cast Annani a suffering glance. "Please, Mother. Don't read too much into us spending the night together. Orion and I are just enjoying each other's company for now, and it is too early to talk about matehood or marriage."

They hadn't bonded overnight, and Alena hadn't expected them to. Well, there had been that small kernel of illogical hope that it would happen to them as fast as it had for Lokan and Carol. But even Kian and Syssi hadn't bonded after their first night together, and they were still deeply in love after over four years of marriage.

She and Orion had just met, and they weren't in love, not yet. They were good together, though, in bed and outside of it, so the prospects of them bonding were also good.

With a sigh, Annani put her teacup down. "The Fates have brought Orion to us for a reason, Alena." She smiled fondly at him. "You are each other's perfect match."

He cast Alena a pleading look. "I hope you are correct, Clan Mother."

"I am never wrong about matters of the heart." As she lifted her empty cup, Oridu rushed over to refill it. "When the Fates brought Amanda and Dalhu together in the most unconventional way, my son was overcome with worry for his sister, but I knew she was safe with Dalhu even though he was still a member of the Brotherhood back then. I knew he would never harm her."

"That was different," Alena said.

"Of course." Annani smiled at her indulgently. "A relationship between Orion and you is easy. There are no obstacles standing in your way. Amanda had a much more difficult time convincing Kian and the rest of the clan to accept a former enemy."

If only that was true.

"Orion and I face different difficulties. Perhaps they are not as extreme as what Amanda and Dalhu had to overcome, but Amanda had no duties to the clan. She could've basically done whatever she pleased."

Her mother arched one perfect red brow. "What challenges stand in your way?"

Alena really did not want to answer that. Why was her mother pushing her to say that she viewed her as an obstacle to her happiness?

Annani took another sip of tea and put the cup down. "I want you to do what is right for you, Alena. Do not concern yourself with me or your duties to the clan. Those are minor considerations compared to finding your truelove mate." She shifted her gaze to Orion. "I hope that mate is you."

74

VROG

After the meeting in Kian's office, Vrog had spent the rest of the day helping Wendy, Stella, and Wendy's mother decorate the house while anxiously awaiting a call from William. Not directly to him since he didn't have a phone, but to Vlad, who would in turn call Wendy, who would let him know whether a match had been found for him.

As the hours ticked off though, he'd started losing hope. Computers were fast, and if there was a match for him, it would have been found in seconds. If William hadn't called, it was because none was found or the female declined to participate for whatever reason.

The match was supposed to be anonymous, so hopefully it wasn't because he was Kra-ell, but then the clan females knew precisely which males could be their potential matches, and there weren't that many unrelated and available males in the village. Another possibility was that a rumor had spread out about him looking for a match, and none of them wanted him.

"Don't look so sad," Wendy said from up on the ladder. "You'll be back here before you know it. Two weeks max, and then you can stay for as long as you want." She cut off a piece of tape and attached a section of the paper garland to the door frame.

"That's not why he's moping around," Stella said. "He was looking forward to the virtual adventure, but it doesn't seem like it's happening today."

Wendy rolled her eyes. "Of course not. Everyone is busy with this new holiday Annani came up with. No one can commit to three hours in the lab today."

"If a match was found, William could have scheduled it for tomorrow," Vrog said. "I leave only on Wednesday."

"True." Wendy came down the ladder. "I bet William is busy with something else and didn't even run your questionnaire through the software yet. He didn't know that you were leaving so soon." She walked over to the kitchen counter and lifted her phone off its charger. "I'll text him that he needs to hurry up."

The polite thing to do would be to stop her from bothering the tech genius while he was no doubt busy decorating and making other preparations for the festivities, but Vrog's curiosity was burning hot for the Kra-ell virtual adventure, or rather the Krall, as Kian's wife had named it.

When Wendy's phone pinged with an incoming text, Vrog held his breath.

"I knew it," Wendy said. "He didn't run it yet. He's super busy. His crew is installing holiday lights all over the village, and he's writing a program to make them twinkle in sync with the music he's going to run through the loudspeakers." She put the phone back on its charger. "I'm so excited. We will have a festive spirit throughout the village."

Vrog sighed in relief, but his disquiet had lessened only a fraction. As he'd told Kian, the village was as close to utopia as he'd ever imagined a community could be, but it was not a good fit for a half Kra-ell male like him.

He was very good at hiding his inner nature, at putting on a civilized façade, but he was an aggressive male who needed an outlet for his baser needs, and he hadn't had one since they'd caught him in China.

"What's wrong?" Stella asked. "You still look upset."

"I'm not upset. I'm just restless. I need to go on a run or lift heavy weights to release stress." Or engage in sexual activity, but he wasn't going to add that.

"Tomorrow, Vlad can take you to the gym," Wendy said. "You can run on a treadmill and lift weights and even spar with the Guardians who train there."

"Sounds good." Vrog wiped his sweaty palms on his borrowed jeans. "I think I'll go for a short run if you don't mind."

"Of course not." Wendy put a hand on his arm. "Just come back in time to shower before dinner."

"Thank you." He looked into her soft brown eyes. "You're very kind."

She smiled. "I'm just paying forward the kindness that was extended to me, and I wish with all my heart for you to find as much happiness as I did."

75

ANNANI

Annani surveyed the hearth Alena and Orion had decorated with candles and pinecones and cloves. The mantel had evergreen garlands draped over it, and beautifully wrapped gift boxes were piled on the floor in front of it.

It was almost time, and she was happy with how everything had turned out.

Orion had left to change into festive clothes, Alena was in her room getting ready, and the four Odus were putting finishing touches on the tables and chairs that had replaced the living room furniture, to accommodate her guests.

It was going to be a joyous celebration, but Annani wished she could have invited more people over.

When Kian's new home was ready, she could host a much larger party there, but that would be next winter solstice. For the summer solstice celebration, the village square would be perfect.

Sari could come with her people, and so could everyone from the sanctuary. There was no reason to leave anyone to guard a place that no one outside the clan knew existed.

She could lock it up for a few days.

Her eyes darting to Alena's room, tears welled in their corners as she thought about a future without her sweet daughter to keep her company, to keep her grounded, to keep the loneliness at bay. But Annani was a mother, and her children's happiness would always come before her own.

She had often wondered who could possibly be worthy of a treasure like Alena. The Fates must have heard her plea and answered by sending the most perfect male for her eldest daughter.

Orion was powerful, honorable, charming, handsome, intelligent, kind, and dedicated to his tiny family. Annani had no doubt that he would extend the same kind of dedication to his new one.

All that remained to be seen was whether they would bond, but Annani's gut told her that they would, and it also told her that she would probably return home alone.

Alena was going to remain in the village with Orion or join him on his search for Toven and possibly more of his siblings.

With a sigh, Annani walked up to the window and looked at the beautiful sanctuary her son had built for their people in the Malibu mountains. Perhaps she should come live at the village as well and bring whoever wanted to leave her northern paradise to Kian's southern one. Alaska could serve as a vacation spot for the clan and a potential escape shelter if the unthinkable happened and Navuh discovered the village.

Could she do it, though?

The three separate clan locations were strategically important. It would be nice to move everyone into the village, but it would not be prudent.

Besides, Annani liked her independence, and she did not like having Kian hovering over her and demanding to know where she was going and why. But those were minor things that could be discussed and agreed upon before any final decisions were made, and no decisions were required at the moment. She could take her time and give living without Alena a try.

As her heart squeezed and another tear found its way down her cheek, Annani put one hand over the aching spot and wiped the tear with the other.

Perhaps it would not be so bad. Perhaps she would ask one of the other sanctuary occupants to be her companion or she could rotate between several.

For now, though, she needed to put on a happy face and celebrate the winter solstice with her family.

"Everything is ready, Clan Mother." Ogidu bowed. "Would you like to inspect the tables?"

She gave them a cursory glance and nodded her approval. "You have done a splendid job. Thank you."

The tables were covered with white tablecloths and decorated with small pinecones. Sage and cloves were scattered among lit candles, and crystal goblets stood in front of every plate.

As the door to Alena's room opened, Annani affected the expression her daughter was used to seeing on her and smiled. "You look lovely."

"Thank you." Alena smoothed a hand over her long skirt. "I need to update my wardrobe, but this will do for tonight."

The makeup was gone, her hair was back in its usual thick braid, and a thin band adorned her head. Alena was effortlessly beautiful, and Annani did not want her to change.

"You need to stay true to yourself, my daughter. Do not change to please anyone other than yourself, not Orion, not Amanda, and not me." Annani waved a hand over her long silk gown. "None of my children approve of my style, but it is mine, and it pleases me."

"You are stunning no matter what you have on, Mother." Alena leaned down and kissed her cheek. "But wearing a bra, at least for today, would have been appreciated."

Annani huffed. "That would have made me terribly uncomfortable the entire evening. Why would my children want me to suffer so?"

"Oh, Mother." Alena rolled her eyes. "We would never want that. But doesn't it bother you that you make your male guests uncomfortable?"

Annani smiled. "Not at all. It is good training for them to focus on a female's eyes and not her chest."

76

KIAN

It didn't escape Kian's notice that things had progressed between Orion and Alena. At the dinner table the two were seated together to Annani's left, while he and Syssi were right across from them to Annani's right, giving him a perfect vantage point to observe his sister and her new love interest smiling at each other and holding hands under the tablecloth, as well as Annani and the expression of smug satisfaction on her face.

Hadn't she realized what a union between Alena and Orion would mean for her?

Could it be that their mother had tired of Alena's company and wished to make a change?

Kian doubted that. More likely, Annani was putting her daughter's needs and happiness before her own, as any mother should.

Leaning toward Syssi, he kissed her cheek and whispered in her ear, "I love you."

Grinning, she kissed him back and lifted her glass. "Happy solstice, my love. I'm looking forward to thousands more."

As he clinked his glass with hers, other couples followed suit, and then Kalugal rose to his feet and turned to Annani. "I would like to propose a toast."

Annani nodded. "Of course."

He smiled. "First of all, many thanks to the Clan Mother and Alena for coming up with this wonderful new tradition for the family to celebrate and for hosting this dinner."

As everyone clapped and then lifted their glasses, Kalugal continued. "To many more joyful family celebrations."

Annani's face beamed with happiness as she lifted her glass higher. "To our ever-growing family." She cast a quick smile at Orion.

The guy didn't look comfortable. In fact, he looked like the cat who'd snuck into the kitchen, had been caught with his nose in the cream bowl, and was still waiting for his punishment to be announced.

Despite being a powerful immortal, Orion was behaving like a human from a different time period, when seducing a lady without asking for her hand was a grave crime that could cost a guy his head.

"I would like to propose another toast," Annani said. "To Alena and Orion, may they find love and joy with each other."

Apparently, their mother had noticed the same thing he had and wanted to put poor Orion at ease, but by doing so, she'd embarrassed Alena.

His sister's cheeks reddening, she cast Annani a withering look. "Thank you, Mother."

Annani ignored the sarcastic tone and smiled sweetly at Orion. "Is there something that you would like to toast?"

The guy cleared his throat, glanced at Alena, and then at Kian. "Yes." He rose to his feet and lifted his glass. "To my newfound family and friends, thank you for welcoming me into your clan. In my wildest dreams, I could have never imagined that such a large and virtuous community of immortals existed, and that it was led by an incredible goddess—a goddess who is just, kind, wise, and cares deeply for her people as well as humanity at large." He turned to Annani and bowed deeply. "Thank you for never losing your spirit and your drive to better everyone's lives, immortals and humans alike." He lifted his glass higher. "To Annani!"

As everyone oohed and aahed and clunked their glasses, the cynic in Kian wondered whether Orion was a superb actor or a great manipulator. With one toast the guy had cemented his place in the clan without having been offered membership.

Naturally, Annani wouldn't have it any other way, especially now that Alena had claimed Orion for herself, but things hadn't been official, not until Orion had gotten up and declared himself a member of the family.

Presumptuous? For sure. Gutsy? Somewhat. Manipulative? You bet.

Except, the non-cynical part of Kian had heard the sincerity in Orion's voice and believed that the guy had meant every word he'd said.

"Oh, Orion." Annani sighed. "Thank you for your lovely toast. I am overjoyed to welcome Toven's son into my clan, and I hope to one day welcome your father and your other siblings as well."

77

ALENA

Alena was glad for the loose dress she'd donned for dinner. She'd eaten too much, not because everything the Odus had prepared had been delicious, although it was, but because she was nervous, and stuffing her face had been a good way to avoid conversation.

Annani had put both her and Orion on the spot with her comment about their relationship, and even though Orion seemed unfazed by it, Alena was still seething.

Her mother's intentions were good, but as usual, her methods could use some refinement. As someone who had lived for five millennia, Annani should have developed more subtlety, but Alena suspected that her mother was just too impatient to bother. The goddess was used to getting what she wanted when she wanted it and how she wanted it, and this time, she wanted a union between her daughter and Toven's son.

Preoccupied with her thoughts, Alena hadn't been paying attention to the conversations going on around the table until Kalugal said, "I haven't heard yet whether any of you have decided to join Jacki and me on the trip to the Mosuo territory."

"Where is that?" Orion asked.

"In China." Kalugal took a sip of his coffee and looked at Kian. "Have you told the newest member of our family about the Kra-ell?"

"I've heard the name mentioned before," Orion said. "But not who they are and their connection to the Mosuo people in China."

"The Kra-ell are a different kind of immortals that we've recently discovered," Kian said.

Wide-eyed, Orion kept looking at Kian, but that was all her brother had to say.

Kalugal picked it up from there. "We know very little about the Kra-ell. So far, we've found only two members of their original community, and we have three of their descendants. The rest of their tribe is presumed dead—ambushed and murdered either by their own rebelling half-breeds or another tribe. We don't know whether there are more of them, but we suspect that small communities like the one those two males belonged to are scattered throughout the globe. The reason we are interested in the Mosuo is that their unique and peculiar social structure closely resembles that of the Kra-ell. Both societies are female dominated, with children belonging to the female's household and raised by her family. The fathers have visitation rights." He shifted toward Jacki and put his arm around her shoulders. "But where the Kra-ell had a good reason for structuring their society that way, the Mosuo didn't, which leads me to believe that they were influenced by contact with the Kra-ell. I have organized an archeological dig in their territory, and since my wife wanted to visit an archeological site, I figured that she would enjoy a lakeshore vacation in Yunnan, China much more than a dusty dig in Egypt."

"What was the reason you were referring to?" Orion asked. "I mean for the structuring of the Kra-ell society."

"Four to five Kra-ell males are born for each female. To prevent endless fighting over females, they organized themselves in family structures that were not couple based. Two or more Kra-ell females share a harem of males, and the children belong to the tribe. One female is the ultimate leader, and the others are her lieutenants. The males are not allowed to even initiate sex. They have to get invited, and then they have to fight the female to prove their worth."

"Their females are nasty," Amanda said. "They enjoy inflicting pain."

As an argument started about the Kra-ell females and whether their nastiness was biologically necessary for the process of natural selection or cultural in nature, Alena tuned it out and imagined a lake-shore vacation—a real lake, not the glorified pond of the Scottish arm of the clan.

When no one won the argument, Orion asked Kalugal, "What are you hoping to find?"

"Clues to a Kra-ell presence that predates the arrival of these latest newcomers." Kalugal shifted his gaze to Kian. "We are also sending a crew to investigate the Kra-ell tribe's former location. Hopefully, we will collect enough information to give us a better picture of who they are, where they came from, and what they are after." He smiled at Kian. "My cousin is worried that they might pose a threat to the clan."

It hadn't escaped Alena's notice that Kalugal had started to talk in terms of 'we.' It seemed that Orion's arrival had solidified the ties between their two groups because Kian had not corrected him even once. Furthermore, her brother hadn't appeared to be even annoyed by that.

"And you're not worried?" Orion asked Kalugal.

"I think that if they haven't bothered us so far, they are not going to, but I'm a curious fellow, and I'm a passionate part-time archeologist. I'm assisting Kian's investigation for purely selfish motives."

"What else is new?" Kian muttered under his breath.

78

ORION

After another round of coffee and tea had been served, Kalugal's wife said, "Lokan and Carol are joining us."

Kian's sharp inhale made everyone's eyes turn to him. "Isn't that incredibly dangerous?" he asked.

Kalugal shrugged. "Lokan and Carol are isolated, and they miss hanging out with people they don't need to pretend around. Naturally, they will take precautions." He leaned back and took his wife's hand. "We all use Turner's evasive protocol. I'm not saying that it's infallible, but I believe it's good enough. Besides, they will have me there, and I can compel immortals, so I think my brother and his mate will be safe."

"We will have a wonderful vacation on a lakeshore," Kalugal's wife said. "I've seen pictures and YouTube videos of the area, and it's breathtaking."

Alena sighed. "I would love to join you, but I can't."

"Why not?" the goddess asked.

"Because it's not safe for you to go, and I can't go without you."

"Nonsense." Annani waved a dismissive hand. "I am not

a child who needs to be looked after. I am in the village, with plenty of things to do, people to visit, and you, my dear, need a vacation. I can survive a couple of weeks without you." The goddess turned to Orion. "Do you have anything important that you need to do over the upcoming weeks, or can you accompany Alena to China?"

Next to him, Orion felt Alena tense.

This was precisely what she craved—an adventure that didn't involve her mother—and he'd be dammed if he didn't help her get what she wanted.

"I can combine business with pleasure." He squeezed Alena's hand under the tablecloth. "I deal in antiques, and since Kalugal is running an archeological dig there, he might find artifacts that he's willing to part with. I have several clients who I can interest in artifacts from China."

"Then it is settled," Annani said. "Alena and Orion will join Jacki and Kalugal."

Kian lifted his hand. "Not so fast. I'm not going to allow Alena to head into danger without a heavy Guardian escort, and Kalugal's jet has limited seats."

Kalugal snorted. "I'm taking three men with me. Besides, if I thought that the Mosuo territory was dangerous, do you think I would take my pregnant wife there?"

Kian pinned his cousin with a hard stare. "When I sent the team to investigate the Kra-ell former compound, no one expected to encounter any trouble. Nevertheless, I had an uneasy feeling despite sending two head Guardians and two additional ones to safeguard the ladies. You know how that story ended. Need I say more?"

"What happened?" Orion asked.

"One of the teammates was attacked."

Kalugal shook his head. "By her former lover who would have never hurt her."

"First of all, we don't know that." Kian crossed his arms over his chest. "And secondly, that's beside the point. The point is that the team was taken by surprise, and that they weren't prepared. I don't want to repeat the same mistake with anyone, and especially my sister."

Kalugal cast a quick glance at Orion before going back to his verbal ping-pong with Kian. "Alena will have three strong compellers with her. Orion, me, and Lokan. Do you really think that anyone would be able to get to her?"

Kian's hard expression didn't soften. "You'll be busy with other things, and you need to sleep sometimes. I want Alena to have Guardians whose only job is keeping her safe."

"We are short on Guardians," Alena said. "Besides, Mother and I travel with just our Odus, who don't need to sleep, and who can handle any threat to us. I can take Ovidu with me. Together with Kalugal's men, that should suffice."

This time some of the hardness left Kian's face. "Ovidu is a good idea, but I want one more warrior in addition to Kalugal's men watching your back."

Like everyone else at the table, Orion read between the lines. Kian wanted his sister to be protected by someone he trusted, and he apparently didn't trust Kalugal or his men, and he didn't trust Orion either.

Orion put a hand over his heart. "I vow to protect Alena with my life."

Kian didn't look impressed. "When was the last time you fought anyone, Orion?"

"It has been several centuries," he admitted.

"The only weapon that you know how to use is your compulsion ability, which I don't discount, but you have no training to speak of. You are a civilian."

Meaning, not good enough to protect his sister.

"That might be true, but I have a vested interest in keeping Alena safe." He draped his arm over her shoulders.

"She's precious to me. Wouldn't you tear out the throat of anyone threatening your mate?"

Kian's eyes blazed, and as he opened his mouth to speak, his fangs were elongated. "I certainly would, but I'm trained. You're not."

His brother-in-law cleared his throat. "When was the last time you visited the training center?"

"It's been a while," Kian admitted. "But I can still kick your ass."

"I have no doubt." Andrew chuckled. "But what I'm trying to say is that Alena will be safe with three compellers, three warriors, and one Odu. And let's not forget Carol. She is a force to be reckoned with as well."

79

ALENA

Excitement rushed through Alena, electrifying her like a live wire. She was going on another adventure, only this time it would be even better than New York because she wouldn't be sleeping alone at night. Orion was coming with her.

She knew that he'd agreed to accompany her only because she'd told him that she craved adventure, and he wanted her to have it.

Alena could fall in love with him just for that.

Wow, she needed to put the brakes on that.

They'd met just three days ago, for Fates' sake, and Orion had vowed never to love again. But that was focusing on the half-empty portion of the glass instead of the half-full, and that had never been Alena's style. She shouldn't fear the hope surging in her heart. She should allow it to take flight and electrify her like it was doing now. She should focus on the positives.

Kian and Syssi had fallen for each other in a matter of days, and Orion had admitted that his wife hadn't wanted him to be alone. He was ready to open his heart to her.

"What about finding Toven?" Cassandra asked. "Doesn't

he take priority over the Kra-ell? If Orion is going to China, who is going to lead the investigation?"

And just like that, the hope winked out.

Kian had no say in what Alena did, but he could prevent Orion from going to China with her, and there was no point in her going without him.

Their mother waved a hand in dismissal. "Orion can do that once he returns."

Orion shook his head. "There isn't much I can do. I've exhausted everything from the journal I took from Toven. I was hoping that the clan has resources I did not and can access more information."

"Where is that journal?" Kian asked.

Orion hesitated for a split second before replying, "I have it with me."

Kian eyed him with renewed appreciation. "Thank you for trusting us with that. Will you allow us to make a copy?"

"Of course. But it's written in Aramaic. Can you read it? It's not one of the languages Google can translate."

Kian chuckled. "I would be very surprised if it could, but maybe someone should come up with artificial intelligence translations for dead languages." He shifted his gaze to Kalugal. "It could prove very useful to you. Imagine how much time it would save you deciphering those tablets."

"Not likely," Kalugal said. "The problem with the tablets is that they are missing pieces, and I doubt AI can tackle that. Not yet."

Kian shrugged. "It was just an idea." He turned back to Orion. "I can't read Aramaic, but Edna can. I'll ask her to translate the journal, and we will take it from there. It will probably take her the entire two weeks you are gone, if you're planning to stay that long, that is. Perhaps you and Alena will choose to return earlier."

Orion seemed conflicted. "After the trip to China, I will

have to make a few stops in Europe for auctions I've already committed to. I won't be able to return here until a month from now."

Alena's heart sank. He was going to leave her for two whole weeks. How was she going to survive without him?

Damn, she shouldn't let herself fall down the rabbit hole like that. They hadn't bonded yet, thank the merciful Fates. She'd survived alone for over two millennia, she could survive two weeks.

But what if they bonded while vacationing at Lake Lugu?

Orion's hand tightened around hers. "I hope that you will accompany me on those trips. I know that we've only met, but I can't imagine being without you."

Across the table, Syssi sighed.

Alena's heart did a happy flip, but then she looked at her mother. "I would love to if it's okay with you."

"What about me?" Amanda asked before Annani had a chance to respond. "My baby will arrive in less than a month. I want you here with me. You promised."

It was so much like the spoiled princess to think only of herself, but given how terrified she was of losing another child, Alena forgave her. "We will be back before your due date. If Orion's obligations prevent it, I'll come alone."

Kian cleared his throat. "Aren't you going to ask if I approve of your travel plans?"

Alena's knee-jerk response was to say no, but Kian had been more accommodating than usual with her and Orion, and she didn't want to repay him with rude dismissiveness.

"If you want to suggest safety precautions, I'm willing to take them under consideration. Just please, don't overdo it."

He gave her a smile. "I wouldn't dream of it. If the Chinese part of the trip goes without incident, a couple of Odus will suffice for the European part." He turned to Annani. "I'm sure you will have no problem with contributing one of your Odus to Alena's entourage and programming him accordingly."

Annani pretended to consider it for a moment and then laughed, the sound so beautiful it lightened the mood in the room. "It would be my pleasure." She pushed to her feet. "Who wants to help me give out the gifts?"

"Me!" Phoenix rushed to her many times great-great-grandmother.

Reluctantly, Alena pulled her hand out of Orion's. "I should help."

"I'll come with you." He followed her up.

Kian leaned back and folded his arms over his chest. "Bring the journal to my office tomorrow morning. Shai will copy it with the utmost care and return it to you before your trip."

Orion swallowed. "Will it be okay if I copied it for you?" He glanced at Shai. "No offense, it's just that this journal is priceless to me for many reasons."

"No offense taken," Shai said. "I understand."

Alena understood as well, and her heart swelled in appreciation. Orion was doing it for her, bargaining his most treasured possession to Kian for the privilege of spending time with her.

She wanted to tell him that he didn't need to do it, that her time belonged to her and that she decided how she wanted to pass it, but that would have taken away from what he considered a sacrifice, and she didn't want to diminish it in any way.

Besides, letting Kian have a copy of the journal would help find Toven and possibly Orion and Geraldine's other siblings.

Alena hoped that they would find many. If they were good people like the two they had found so far, then all of their lives would benefit from Toven's children joining their clan.

What about Toven himself, though?

Could Annani find happiness with him despite her vow to never love again?

Perhaps Annani could learn from Orion's story of love lost and then found again centuries later. If Khiann had loved her as much as Orion's human wife had loved him, then he wouldn't have wanted her to spend her eternal life alone either.

It wasn't Alena's place to suggest that to her mother, though. All she could do was to tell Annani Orion's story and let her decide whether it applied to her or not.

Alena had taken care of others her entire life, never thinking of her own needs and desires. She'd earned the right to her own happily ever after, and for now, she should focus just on that.

COMING UP NEXT

The Children of the Gods Book 57

Dark Hunter's Prey

To read the first 3 chapters JOIN the VIP club at ITLUCAS.COM

Dear reader,

Thank you for reading the ***Children of the Gods***.

As an independent author, I rely on your support to spread the word. So if you enjoyed the story, please share your experience with others, and if it isn't too much trouble, I would greatly appreciate a brief review on Amazon.

Love & happy reading,

Isabell

To find out what's included in your free membership, flip to the last page.

If you're already a subscriber, you'll receive a download link for my next book's preview chapters in the new release announcement email. If you are not getting my emails, your provider is sending them to your junk folder, and you are missing out on **important updates, side characters' portraits, additional content, and other goodies.** To fix that, add isabell@itlucas.com to your email contacts or your email VIP list.

Also by I. T. Lucas

THE CHILDREN OF THE GODS ORIGINS

1: Goddess's Choice

2: Goddess's Hope

THE CHILDREN OF THE GODS

Dark Stranger

1: Dark Stranger The Dream

2: Dark Stranger Revealed

3: Dark Stranger Immortal

Dark Enemy

4: Dark Enemy Taken

5: Dark Enemy Captive

6: Dark Enemy Redeemed

Kri & Michael's Story

6.5: My Dark Amazon

Dark Warrior

7: Dark Warrior Mine

8: Dark Warrior's Promise

9: Dark Warrior's Destiny

10: Dark Warrior's Legacy

Dark Guardian

11: Dark Guardian Found

12: Dark Guardian Craved

13: Dark Guardian's Mate

Dark Angel

14: Dark Angel's Obsession

15: Dark Angel's Seduction

16: Dark Angel's Surrender

Dark Operative

17: Dark Operative: A Shadow of Death

18: Dark Operative: A Glimmer of Hope

19: Dark Operative: The Dawn of Love

Dark Survivor

20: Dark Survivor Awakened
21: Dark Survivor Echoes of Love
22: Dark Survivor Reunited

Dark Widow

23: Dark Widow's Secret
24: Dark Widow's Curse
25: Dark Widow's Blessing

Dark Dream

26: Dark Dream's Temptation
27: Dark Dream's Unraveling
28: Dark Dream's Trap

Dark Prince

29: Dark Prince's Enigma
30: Dark Prince's Dilemma
31: Dark Prince's Agenda

Dark Queen

32: Dark Queen's Quest
33: Dark Queen's Knight
34: Dark Queen's Army

Dark Spy

35: Dark Spy Conscripted
36: Dark Spy's Mission
37: Dark Spy's Resolution

Dark Overlord

38: Dark Overlord New Horizon
39: Dark Overlord's Wife
40: Dark Overlord's Clan

Dark Choices

41: Dark Choices The Quandary
42: Dark Choices Paradigm Shift
43: Dark Choices The Accord

Dark Secrets

44: Dark Secrets Resurgence
45: Dark Secrets Unveiled
46: Dark Secrets Absolved

ALSO BY I. T. LUCAS

DARK HAVEN

47: DARK HAVEN ILLUSION

48: DARK HAVEN UNMASKED

49: DARK HAVEN FOUND

DARK POWER

50: DARK POWER UNTAMED

51: DARK POWER UNLEASHED

52: DARK POWER CONVERGENCE

DARKMEMORIES

53: DARK MEMORIES SUBMERGED

54: DARK MEMORIES EMERGE

55: DARK MEMORIES RESTORED

DARK HUNTER

56: DARK HUNTER'S QUERY

57: DARK HUNTER'S PREY

PERFECT MATCH

PERFECT MATCH 1: VAMPIRE'S CONSORT

PERFECT MATCH 2: KING'S CHOSEN

PERFECT MATCH 3: CAPTAIN'S CONQUEST

THE CHILDREN OF THE GODS SERIES SETS

BOOKS 1-3: DARK STRANGER TRILOGY—INCLUDES A BONUS SHORT STORY: **THE FATES TAKE A VACATION**

BOOKS 4-6: DARK ENEMY TRILOGY —INCLUDES A BONUS SHORT STORY—**THE FATES' POST-WEDDING CELEBRATION**

BOOKS 7-10: DARK WARRIOR TETRALOGY

BOOKS 11-13: DARK GUARDIAN TRILOGY

BOOKS 14-16: DARK ANGEL TRILOGY

BOOKS 17-19: DARK OPERATIVE TRILOGY

MEGA SETS

INCLUDE CHARACTER LISTS

FOR EXCLUSIVE PEEKS AT UPCOMING RELEASES & A FREE COMPANION BOOK

JOIN MY *VIP CLUB* AND GAIN ACCESS TO THE VIP PORTAL AT ITLUCAS.COM

(http://eepurl.com/blMTpD)

INCLUDED IN YOUR FREE MEMBERSHIP:

- FREE CHILDREN OF THE GODS COMPANION BOOK 1
- FREE NARRATION OF GODDESS'S CHOICE—BOOK 1 IN THE CHILDREN OF THE GODS ORIGINS SERIES.
- PREVIEW CHAPTERS OF UPCOMING RELEASES.
- AND OTHER EXCLUSIVE CONTENT OFFERED ONLY TO MY VIPS.

If you're already a subscriber, you'll receive a download link for my next book's preview chapters in the new release announcement email. If you are not getting my emails, your provider is sending them to your junk folder, and you are missing out on **important updates, side characters' portraits, additional content, and other goodies.** To fix that, add isabell@itlucas.com to your email contacts or your email VIP list.

Made in United States
North Haven, CT
23 June 2022